# MURDER ON THE S.S. CLEOPATRA

# MURDER ON THE S.S. CLEOPATRA

RETAILER EDITION

LADY TRAVELER IN EGYPT
BOOK TWO

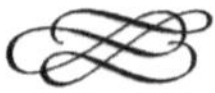

SARA ROSETT

Murder on the S.S. *Cleopatra*
Book Two in the *1920s Lady Traveler in Egypt* series

Copyright © 2025 by Sara Rosett

Hardcover Special Edition:
ISBN: 978-1-950054-92-3

Trade Paperback Special Edition:
ISBN: 978-1-950054-94-7

Audiobook:
ISBN: 978-1-950054-95-4

Retailer Trade Paperback Edition:
ISBN: 978-1-950054-96-1

Large Print Edition:
ISBN: 978-1-950054-97-8



This is a work of fiction, and names, characters, incidents, and places are products of the author's imagination or used fictitiously. Any resemblance to persons, living or dead, incidents, and places is coincidental.

❈ Formatted with Vellum

# CHAPTER 1

Passengers on the S.S. *Cleopatra*'s latest Nile cruise include the charming Miss Honeyworth and her traveling companion, Miss Windway. They plan to depart this week and are bound for Luxor.

*—Arrivals and Departures, The Nile*

"Welcome to the S.S. *Cleopatra*, Miss Windway." The steward opened the door to my cabin and stepped back. I'd expected everything on the Nile steamer to be tucked away, with recessed cupboards and portholes, but except for its diminutive size, my cabin with its brass bed and full-size wardrobe looked much like the room at Shepheard's Hotel, where I'd just checked out. There was even a desk under a large casement window. Linen curtains framed a view across the Nile to the fringe of greenery on the far bank. The whole room—walls and ceiling—was paneled in mahogany with a high gloss that gleamed nearly as much as the brass wall sconces.

Hildy passed the open door, her aqua dress a flash of color, as she followed another steward to her cabin, one of the suites, which was located closer to the bow at the front of the steamer.

Her delighted tones floated through the air. "Oh, but this is lovely! So luxurious . . ." Her voice faded into the din of the passengers arriving, a cacophony of footfalls on the deck, shouts of the laborers on the dock, and a sharp whistle from a steamer docked nearby. It was rather difficult to believe it was only a few weeks ago that I'd met Hildy while crossing the English Channel.

In that short time, she had become very dear to me. My original travel plans had fallen through when the ferry docked at Calais, and Hildy had invited me to join her as her traveling companion. As we traveled from Paris to Alexandria and then on to Cairo, we discovered we rubbed along quite well together. She was several decades my senior and had an income that dwarfed my tiny bank balance, but because of what we'd experienced in Cairo—a shocking murder that the British officials had been reluctant to investigate—she was now a friend.

The steward's white robe swished as he crossed the cabin and placed my single suitcase at the foot of the bed. "I apologize for the narrowness of the room."

I approved of the gentle way he treated my luggage, which contained my lecture lantern and glass slides. "It does feel rather like one is in a dollhouse, but it's delightful, Hassan."

"Excellent." The tassel on his red tarboosh swung forward as he dipped his head. Like most of the crew, he was a native of Egypt and spoke English with a slight French accent. "The Blue Lotus Steamer Line will be happy you are pleased. This is the upper deck, and the saloon and promenade are located toward the bow. The dining room is on the main deck, which is below this one. You can reach that deck by using the staircases. Would you care for any refreshments? A drink or perhaps a sandwich before we depart?"

"No, thank you. I don't need anything else. I'll unpack now."

As he bowed and turned to the door, a female voice screeched, "Boy!"

The shrill call was repeated, and Hassan's shoulders tightened. He quickened his step, moving silently in his ornate slippers from the cabin's thick rug to the wooden planks of the deck. He paused on the threshold. "Please ring if you need anything. Would you like the door closed?"

"Open is fine." I was sure Hildy would be along in a moment. I put down my handbag and valise, then worked off my gloves. The strident female voice carried over the hubbub of boarding. "Ah, there you are at last. These dresses were not put away properly. That must be corrected immediately, or they'll wrinkle terribly."

"I apologize, Miss Fairweather. I'll see to everything." Hassan's muted, soothing tones contrasted with the woman's strident voice.

How could she call a middle-aged man *boy*? The wrinkles around Hassan's eyes and the lines on either side of his mouth indicated he probably had children of his own. I made a mental note to increase the amount of my tip for him at the end of the journey.

The woman's imperious tones carried through the open door. "I should hope so. For the amount we're paying, the service should be flawless. Now, about the ventilation. I require at least—"

I changed my mind and closed the door to silence the annoying Miss Fairweather, a stout aristocratic matron who had boarded the steamer with an attitude more reminiscent of an admiral taking charge of a battleship than of a passenger departing on a holiday. Her instructions on how her luggage should be carried up the gangway had delayed our boarding by a quarter hour.

I tossed my gloves on the bed as I crossed to the desk, then pushed the linen curtain completely back. I unlatched the window, taking in the bustle around the steamer and the distant view of the pyramids of Giza. The constant slap of waves against the hull of the steamer at the waterline was a quiet, rhythmic counterpoint to the frenzy of activity on the deck and the dock.

The whistle sounded again, this time from our steamer. It was the warning that we'd be underway soon, and Hildy and I had agreed to meet at the railing after seeing our cabins.

I closed the window, then paused to pick up an envelope from the floor. Odd that it hadn't been put away when the cabin was cleaned before our arrival. Everything else was spotless. I intended to put it in the desk with the other stationery, but once I picked it up, I could tell from the weight that it wasn't empty. Had a prior passenger forgotten to address and post their letter?

It wasn't sealed, so I pushed back the flap and took out a single folded sheet of paper, which was the steamer's letter-head. A handwritten note in blocky letters filled the page.

*Liar!*
*Yes, that's right. I know you're a fraud.*
*Not much longer, and your secret will be out.*
*Everyone will know.*

HILDY LOOKED up from her unpacking, spotted the envelope, and took it from me. "Oh, is that for me? Thank you, dear." Her bed was covered with an explosion of color—fabrics and feathers in every shade of the rainbow were mixed with tissue, scarves, and handbags. The desk and bedside table were clear except for the expected lamps and ashtrays.

It wasn't unreasonable for her to assume it was for her. Hildy was a prolific letter writer. How she kept up with her mountains of correspondence, I couldn't imagine. She chattered on, her mood effervescent. "The poor stewards are probably run off their feet. It's not surprising they'd mix up our rooms on the first day and deliver this to you instead of me."

I'd returned the note to the envelope and gone along to Hildy's cabin, not quite sure what to do with it. I had no secrets to conceal—my name had already been dragged through the gossip sheets years ago when I was dubbed "the Jilter"—so it couldn't be for me. I'd considered throwing it in the rubbish, but the malicious tone had made me think that I should hand it off to Hassan when I next encountered him. He could pass it along to the head steward. I hadn't intended to show it to Hildy, but she'd plucked it out of my hand before I could say anything.

She flipped it over, and a faint wrinkle appeared between her brows as she glanced at the blank envelope.

"Hildy, the note is rather vile," I said as she drew out the paper, but she didn't seem to hear me. Her gaze was fixed on the page she'd just unfolded.

Hassan tapped on the door. "A reminder that we will arrive at the first stop in Badrashin in a few hours."

I thanked him and turned back to Hildy. "The note—"

Hildy was back at her trunk, unfolding tissue from around a dress. "A bit of trash, I think. A previous passenger must have left it behind." The envelope was gone. She must have put it in her pocket or shoved it into the pile of dresses.

She shook out a magenta evening gown and swept to the wardrobe in a whirl of spangles, disappearing behind one of the cabinet's open doors. Above the clatter of the hangers, she said, "Do you still want to take a turn about the deck as we depart? It will be our last view of Cairo and the pyramids for several weeks."

"Ah—yes, of course."

Hildy bustled back to the bed and took up a peach day dress. "I'll meet you on the deck in a few moments, then."

I considered pressing her about the note, but she had an air of determined busyness about her, so I only said, "You know the steward will put away your clothes for you."

"Oh, but why would I let someone else have the fun of handling all these lovely dresses? After years of wearing scratchy, ill-fitting, mended clothing, hanging each one up and admiring the beautiful tailoring is one of my little joys in life. It won't take me long."

I doubted she'd be done in a few moments, so I returned to my cabin and set about my own unpacking. I didn't expect the steward to put away my clothing. I wasn't that class of passenger, not like Hildy. My cabin was tiny, and I wouldn't be fawned over by the crew, but I'd paid for the passage myself, a fact that gave me extreme satisfaction.

As I unpacked, I tried to shake off the uneasy feeling that

had settled over me. Why hadn't Hildy had some sort of reaction to the note? After reading it, I'd been baffled, repulsed, and curious in equal parts. Who would write such a thing? And who was it intended for? Hildy hadn't shown any reaction at all, except to get on with her packing, which was odd. Could the note have actually been intended for her? No, absolutely not. Of course not.

It didn't take me long to hang up my dresses, then I closed the wardrobe and stood motionless for a moment. The thought that someone as vivacious and open as Hildy could be a liar or a fraud was absurd.

I closed my suitcase and returned to tap on Hildy's door. When there was no answer after a moment, I continued along the steamer to the promenade deck at the bow. The sun's rays reflected off the polished wood, and I put up a hand to shield my eyes.

I spotted Hildy at the far end of the deck, her back to me. As I approached, she leaned over the railing, and a cascade of tiny pieces of torn paper fluttered from her hand. The fragments floated on the surface of the Nile as the water soaked into them.

S.S. Cleopatra
Deck Plan

Miss
Fairweather
Miss
E.
Hildy
Mr.
Listergraff
Blix


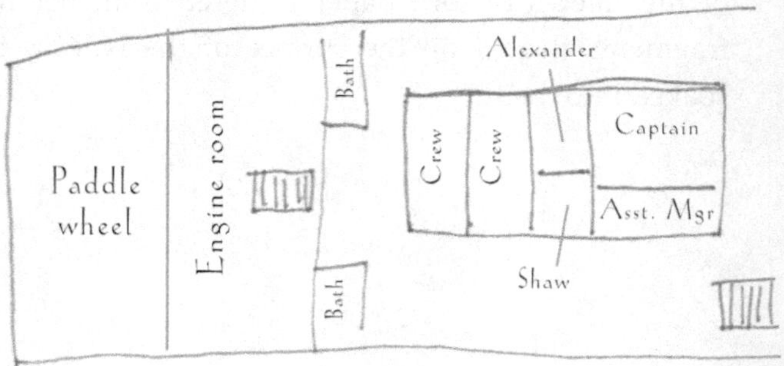

Alexander
Bath
Captain
Paddle
wheel
Engine room
Crew
Crew
Asst. Mgr
Bath
Shaw

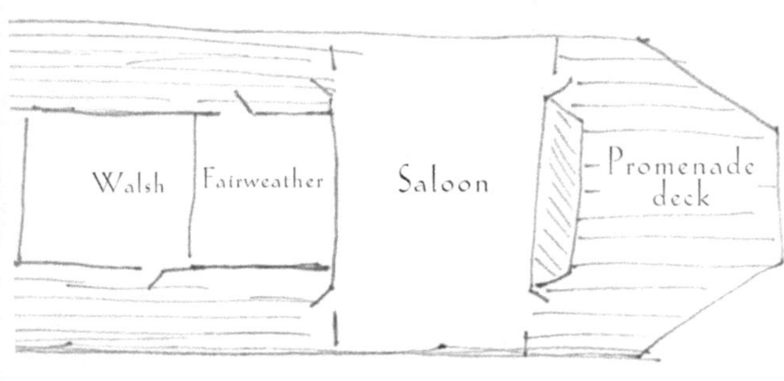


Upper Deck

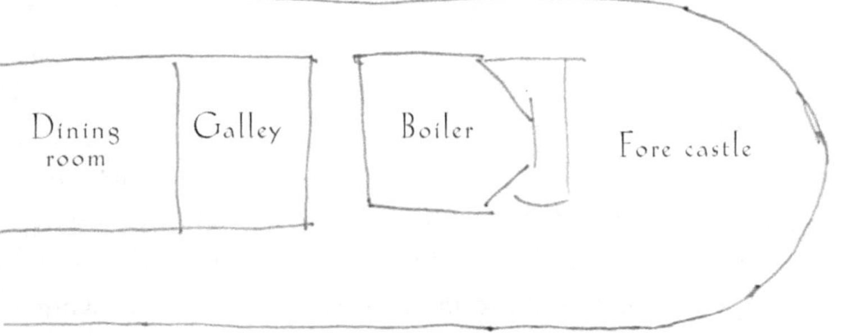


Main Deck

# CHAPTER 2

The Ministry of Public Works reports a deep crack has appeared in the neck of the Sphinx. Repairs are to commence with all haste to prevent further damage to this ancient marvel.

—*The Nile*

*I* paused several feet away from Hildy as she folded the now empty envelope and stuffed it deep into a pocket while watching the bits of paper submerge. I was hesitant to intrude. She clearly didn't want to talk about the note since she'd just torn it to bits and thrown it in the Nile. After a second, she pushed away from the railing, turned, and immediately ran into an older gentleman, an acquaintance of ours from Cairo, Mr. Listergraff. The collision set her hat askew and caused him to drop the book he was holding.

"Hello! Well met, Miss Honeyworth!" Henry Listergraff

was in his late sixties and had a substantial gray mustache, the build of a bulldog, and a good-natured disposition. His faint German accent carried to where I stood. "My apologies for bumping into you." The last time I'd seen Mr. Listergraff, he'd been in the desert outside of Cairo, and he'd been wearing knee-high boots, rough trousers, and a scruffy blazer with elbow patches. Today he was turned out in a tan three-piece suit and pith helmet. He looked as if he were ready to pose for a photo for the *Arrivals and Departures* column of *The Nile,* the newspaper of the British community in Cairo.

He retrieved his book while Hildy righted her hat. "No need for an apology, Mr. Listergraff. It was I who cannoned into you."

"In any case, I'm delighted you're traveling on the S.S. *Cleopatra.*"

"Likewise, Mr. Listergraff." Was it the heat of the day that made Hildy's cheeks a touch pink, or was it Mr. Listergraff who brought a blush to her face?

The deck shifted, and I realized we were moving away from the bank.

Hildy noticed too. "Oh, we're off. How exciting!"

"Shall we?" Mr. Listergraff asked, motioning to the port side of the steamer where passengers were gathered, waving to people who had come to see the steamer off.

I set off to catch up with them. The deck was quite full, and I was weaving around the other passengers who were also moving to the railing, when a familiar face caught my eye, and my steps slowed. Surely I'd been mistaken? I slowly approached a crew member, who stood away from the railing, his back against the outer wall of the cabins.

He wore the navy uniform of the Blue Lotus Line, a double-breasted suit jacket with a row of gold braid on each sleeve and matching trousers. His head was bent over a clip-board, the brim of his peaked hat hiding his face as he wrote. I dipped down to get a good look at the man's face, then straightened, barely able to believe what I'd seen. "Mr. Briarcliff?"

The pencil continued scratching across the paper.

He looked up as he pushed a pair of thick, black-rimmed round glasses higher on his nose. He had a short beard and a narrow mustache, but it was unmistakably Mr. Briarcliff. "It is you! What are you doing in that uniform?"

I'd also met Rafe Briarcliff in Cairo, where I'd made the faux pas of thinking that he might be a murderer. We hadn't exactly gotten off on the right foot, but once I discovered he worked for Mr. Martin, a man who owned most of the major hotels in Egypt, he moved down my suspect list and we eventually formed . . . well, not exactly a friendship—he was far too standoffish for that. I suppose you'd call it an alliance, and an uneasy one at that.

"You're mistaken, miss. I'm Assistant Manager Cordial."

A laugh burst out of me. "Mr. *Cordial*? You?"

He scanned the passengers around us, who'd taken no notice of us, then he snapped the pencil down to the clip-board and motioned with it toward the stern of the ship. He raised his voice as he put his hand on my arm above the elbow. "Yes, there are some points of interest on the star-board side. Allow me to show you." He propelled me along the deck to the stern of the steamer, then around to the oppo-site, deserted side of the craft.

"Is this a new line of work, Mr. Briarcliff? Are you no longer a free agent?" He turned to face me, and I took a step back. "You're furious." I was astounded at the heat of his gaze, and despite the beard, I could see his mouth was in a flat line, as if he were clenching his jaw.

"What do you think you're doing?"

"I *thought* I was greeting an acquaintance," I said tartly, twitching my arm.

His hand fell away. "I apologize." He looked away, his view focused on the cloudless sky. The buttons on his jacket moved as he drew in a deep breath. He swiveled, his gaze locking on mine as he closed the distance between us, his broad-shouldered form blocking out the bank of the Nile. I held my ground, even though I had to tilt my chin up to see his face. His voice was low as he said, "It's imperative that no one else knows I'm on the steamer—*especially* Hildy. It's hush-hush."

Irritation fired through me. "You are an insufferable and annoying man. Surely you know by now that I'm not a gossip."

"Yes, that's true." He said the words as if he didn't want to admit the fact. "You do keep your own counsel, but you're traveling with Hildy. Please don't tell her. I'm here in the role of the assistant manager, and my task is to assess the crew's performance and make sure everything's running smoothly. The best way for me to do that is to be incognito, as far as the passengers are concerned. Normally, an assistant manager wouldn't have friends among the passengers, and if Hildy greets me as you did, then it could give the game away to the crew."

"You mean they might figure out you're spying on them."

"Job assessment is what it's called. This is one way the Blue Lotus Line maintains its high standards."

I tipped my head to one side. "So, you're asking me for a favor. You *are* asking for a favor?"

His gaze darted to a passing couple, and he lowered his voice even more. "Yes."

"I see. And you chose *Cordial* as your surname?"

He let out a huff and twisted his chin as if his collar were too tight. "One of Mr. Martin's employees—the one who arranged my passage and my cover identity—has a rather broad sense of humor."

"Quite." Rafe Briarcliff's disposition was the opposite of cordial. *Prickly* would have been a better choice for his assumed last name.

"So this is part of the work you do for Mr. Martin? I thought he owned hotels."

"Occasionally, yes. Mr. Martin's holdings include the steamers of the Blue Lotus Line and a few other venues that are key parts of the tourist trade."

"Goodness, I had no idea his business was so vast. That's interesting, but I'm far more curious about something else— your first name. Is it still Rafe?"

"No, the joker wasn't content with changing only my surname. I'll certainly make the stipulation that I keep my first name if I ever do this in the future. However, that's neither here nor there. I'm simply Assistant Manager Cordial."

The deck shifted and water churned as the steamer, now that we were away from the dock, altered course. I crossed my arms and leaned against the railing. "The price of my silence—especially with Hildy—is your temporary first name." Since he didn't want to tell me, it must be a doozy.

# CHAPTER 3

Lord and Lady Ashbourne have arrived at Shepheard's
Hotel for their annual winter sojourn. After a fortnight, they
plan to journey up the Nile aboard the steamer *Osiris* next
month.

—*Arrivals and Departures, The Nile*

He looked out at the spiky palm trees on the far
bank of the Nile as the steamer picked up
speed. "Fine. For this journey, I must endure the moniker of
. . . Cosmo."

I pressed my lips together to keep in another laugh that
threatened to bubble up. "Cosmo? Cosmo Cordial?" His
mustache wrenched into a grimace as I added, "Very
urbane."

"Isn't it?" He closed his eyes briefly and shook his head,
his shoulders relaxing. "I have to admit that I can see the
humor in it." One corner of his mouth turned up, which was

the closest Mr. Briarcliff ever came to a smile. "Cosmo Cordial is more appropriate for an English tourist who lounges about the casinos."

"Extremely memorable too."

"Which is exactly what I don't want to be." He straightened his suit jacket. "How did you recognize me?"

I waved a hand from his head to his feet. "It's you. Despite the spectacles and the beard, it's obviously you. I'm sure Hildy will recognize you in an instant as well."

His fingers beat a quick rhythm on the railing. "It's odd. I've run across a few acquaintances from Cairo, and no one has recognized or noticed me." He cut his gaze toward me. "Except for you."

"I'm a noticing sort of person."

"Yes, you are." His tone indicated it wasn't a good thing. "It must come from you being a photographer. You see things that other people miss."

"Well, I won't reveal your identity, *Cosmo*. I'll keep your secret. The question is, can *you* keep your secret?"

"What do you mean by that?"

I ran my hand along the railing as I surveyed him again. "You don't have a deferential air about you." I angled my chin toward the cabins. "Every passenger on this steamer is your superior. They'll expect you to carry out their wishes, answer their queries, solve their problems. You'll have to let go of that self-assured, commanding manner of yours." I felt my brows draw together. "*Have* you done this masquerade successfully before?"

"Of course. Subterfuge is my specialty."

I gave him a long look. He broke eye contact first.

I saw a splash of color among the people strolling along the starboard deck. "That plume of aqua feathers can only be

Hildy's hat. I believe she and Mr. Listergraff have just rounded the stern and are heading toward us."

Mr. Briarcliff—I couldn't think of him as Mr. Cordial—adjusted his glasses and dipped his head over his clipboard.

Mr. Listergraff nodded a greeting at me as he came even with us, then gave Mr. Briarcliff a wink, which Hildy didn't see. She said to me, "Blix, dear, I missed you at the railing. It was quite a crowd. Don't forget to change for the donkey ride to Saqqara this afternoon." She inclined her head in a polite way to Mr. Briarcliff, then continued on her promenade with Mr. Listergraff.

I waited until they were out of earshot, then said, "I can't believe it. Hildy didn't even look twice, but Mr. Listergraff obviously knows you're incognito."

"I had to let him in on the secret. He's an old friend, and his cabin is next to mine. I knew our paths would cross frequently. At least Hildy didn't recognize me."

"Curious, that." I gazed after her. Hildy was usually so astute. She was savvier than me when it came to assessing people and appearances. I was surprised that she hadn't seen through Mr. Briarcliff's disguise at once. "She'll figure it out, though. And when she does, I'll tell her all her anger should be directed at you, not me."

"I'll handle it, should the occasion arise. Hopefully, she'll depart the steamer in Luxor never knowing I was on the S.S. *Cleopatra*."

The rustle of fabric drew my attention to the woman who was approaching, Miss Fairweather. The scent of hyacinths filled the air as she joined us. Her mahogany hair was piled on top of her head, which emphasized her slightly jowly cheeks. She had delicate little hands and big brown eyes, which were open wide in a way that brought to mind the cows on the home farm at Burywood Hall. While most of the passengers were dressed in linen or cotton, she looked as if she were on her way to the Savoy. She wore a lavender silk day dress with rope-length pearls and a wide-brimmed hat with a swath of lavender tulle tied around the crown.

She held a lacy handkerchief in her left hand, and it fluttered as she shook it at Mr. Briarcliff. "I have a small question, Mr. . . .?"

"Cordial," he supplied in a clipped tone. "What is it?"

I caught Mr. Briarcliff's eye—I couldn't think of him as Mr. Cordial, even when he announced it—and gave a small shake of my head. I sent him a look many a governess had sent my way when I'd misbehaved.

His brows lowered as he watched me for a second, but then he tucked his clipboard under his arm and turned fully toward Miss Fairweather and spoke in a milder tone. "I'm happy to help you with whatever questions you have." He pressed a hand to his chest, covering the buttons on his double-breasted jacket. "That's why I'm here." He seemed to have to push out the words, but they did emerge.

The full force of Mr. Briarcliff's attention seemed to disconcert her. The lace handkerchief danced. "Oh my—um. What was I saying? Oh yes. I'd like to confirm—I'm sure you'll think it's silly of me—but the schedule says our departure this afternoon is at two o'clock for Saqqara, but another passenger told me it was at four. I would so hate to miss it. Can you enlighten me?"

Mr. Briarcliff didn't need to look at his clipboard. "The outing is indeed at two. And you've no need to worry. There's no way you'll miss it. The whistle will sound when we arrive."

The handkerchief flitted as Miss Fairweather daubed at her temple under the brim of her hat. "Oh, thank you so much. I must say that it is so good to have a man confirm these things. You know, we ladies get mixed up so often. I wouldn't want to miss our first outing."

"No need for you to worry, Miss Fairweather, isn't it?"

The lace twitched double-time as she shook it at him. "Yes, but how did you know?"

"Simply doing my job, madam." He paused, removed his own handkerchief, turned away, and wiped his nose. As he put his handkerchief away, he apologized and said, "My hay fever sometimes flares up. Now, where were we? Oh yes, there will be plenty of warning to give you time to go to ashore. You should go along to your cabin now." Mr. Briarcliff shot a quick glance at me out of the corner of his eye, then said, "What I mean is, the heat of the sun will be quite intense this afternoon, and you'll want to be well rested. Let me introduce you to a fellow passenger, Miss Blix Windway. Miss Windway, Miss Millicent Fairweather."

Miss Fairweather shook my hand with the barest touch of two fingers, then turned back to Mr. Briarcliff. "Thank you, Mr. Cordial, for your guidance. I do so appreciate it." She departed without glancing my way or saying goodbye.

Another man stepped up to speak to Mr. Briarcliff. The new arrival had sandy hair gone gray at his temples and the beginnings of a paunch under his linen vest. His fair complexion was tinged pink from the heat. A pipe filled one pocket, and a black notebook stuck out of the other one, spoiling the line of his white linen suit jacket. He ran a folded handkerchief across his forehead. "About the excursion this afternoon, my wife is fatigued. Is it possible for her to stay behind on the steamer?"

"Of course, Dr. Walsh. Our guests are always welcome to stay aboard the steamer when we dock. In fact, tea will be . . ."

I stepped back and went in search of Hildy, thinking that

Mr. Briarcliff might not have realized what he was signing up for when he agreed to work as the assistant manager on the steamer.

A FEW HOURS later I looped my camera strap around my neck and went to tap on Hildy's door. "Did you have a good rest?" I asked. We'd retreated to our cabins after lunch to rest before the excursion. Hildy sat at her dressing table, adjusting her pith helmet. She'd changed into a long linen skirt with a matching suit jacket.

"Couldn't sleep at all. I find all of this too exciting to nap. Will you do the step pyramid or the tombs? Apparently, we'll only have time for one or the other."

I sat down on the edge of her bed. "The tombs, I think. The mural reliefs are supposed to be exquisite."

"I agree." Hildy suddenly swiveled toward me, spinning completely around on the little stool. "Who was that dashing man, the crew member you were speaking to when we departed Cairo? I forgot to ask you at luncheon."

My conscience pricked at me. I swallowed and looked down, smoothing the fabric of my riding breeches. I'd agreed to keep Mr. Briarcliff's secret, but I couldn't look Hildy in the eye and lie to her. "That was the assistant manager, Mr. Cordial."

"Perhaps you'll see more of him . . ."

I looked up. Hildy's eyebrows were raised to the brim of her pith helmet, a speculative expression on her face.

"Perhaps. Although I suppose interactions of the type you're insinuating between passengers and crew would be frowned upon."

"Nonsense. You should always judge a person by their inherent characteristics, not their social position."

"I agree, but you know society takes a completely different view. In fact, my mother would faint dead away if she thought I was even *considering* speaking to a member of the crew in any way except to give an order."

"Well, we shall see. There's another young man on the steamer." She picked up the printed card with the passenger list. "Howard Alexander."

"Fair-haired, a bit shabby, with weathered cuffs and worn shoes? I did see him, but I didn't meet him at luncheon."

"Yes, that's Mr. Alexander. I spoke to him briefly earlier. An archaeology scholar. That explains the scruffiness—you know how scholars are. They can work the most complicated maths in the world but won't notice if their shirt is wrinkled, their spectacles are smudged, or their tie is spotted with egg yolk. They don't give two figs for looking fashionable. The young man is on his way to a dig in Luxor."

Hildy tapped the name at the top of the list. "I didn't meet Mr. and Mrs. Ambrose Fairweather. I'm surprised they weren't at luncheon. Rather ill-mannered not to attend the first meal. He's quite well-known. I saw a mention of them in *Arrivals and Departures*. A captain of industry was all it said in the column."

I'd only glanced at the passenger list that had been placed in my cabin. "Fairweather, did you say? I met a Miss Millicent Fairweather earlier today. She looked to be in her late forties or early fifties and was fluttery and accommodating when speaking to the assistant manager, but she behaved quite differently to her cabin steward."

"Badly, you mean?"

"Yes."

Hildy made a tsking noise. "I can't understand why

people treat staff poorly. At a very minimum, one doesn't want to get on the bad side of the person who brings one's food, runs one's bath, and takes care of one's clothes." Hildy tapped the edge of the card. "Yes, Miss Fairweather is listed separately. She must be related to the couple." She tilted her head to the side as she murmured, "Ambrose Fairweather. Why does that name ring a bell?"

"Do you think he's *the* Mr. Fairweather? Of Fairweather Rubber? The company that manufactures hot water bottles and sink plugs? If he is, then he's the man who married the much-younger stunt-girl reporter."

Hildy pointed the card at me. "Yes, I think you're right. What was her name? Louisa something. She wrote such interesting articles years ago. There was that truly horrifying series about factory girls and their working conditions. The description of her time with the flying circus was much easier reading—although frightening in its own way. Imagine being a wing walker!" Hildy had been speaking more to herself than to me, her unfocused gaze directed out the window. She snapped her fingers. "Louisa Lancaster. That was it!"

"She sounds like a fascinating person. I haven't read any of her articles."

"They were in the American papers. My brother was stingy as Scrooge, except when it came to subscribing to newspapers and periodicals. I might not have had money to buy a nice roast, but one thing we did have was a surplus of reading material."

I'd heard very little about Hildy's brother, for whom she'd kept house before his death, and I would have asked her more about her background, except I realized where I'd encountered the Fairweather name. "Oh, I know why the name is familiar. I gave a lecture at the Fairweather estate,

Nobilis Domus." Lectures were how I made ends meet, and they tended to blend together in my memory. Drafty meeting rooms in town halls were very alike, meaning echo-y and usually supplied with creaky chairs, but the meeting at Nobilis Domus stood out in my memory. "It was several months ago, and the village WI coordinated everything, so I only met Mrs. Fairweather briefly. The estate was enormous and had miles of gorgeous gardens as well as an orangery."

A whistle sounded, and Hildy popped up from the stool. "Let's see if Mr. and Mrs. Fairweather join us for Saqqara."

# CHAPTER 4

At last week's Heliopolis races, Have a Go proved to be a good bet, but those with money to burn flocked to back Golden Whisper, despite the horse's lackluster history. One wonders if the sudden interest has more to do with the owner's famous charm than the stallion's speed.

—*About Town, The Nile*

*H*ildy and I were at the railing, waiting our turn to disembark, when Mr. Fairweather emerged from his cabin. He was short and had a squat build, but he wore his status like a mantle. He cut through the crowd, which fell back as if he were royalty. He didn't look left or right, but headed straight for the gangplank, which had been set up moments earlier. A cream-colored Monte Carlo hat shaded his bulbous nose and prominent brow, which hung over deep-set dark eyes that turned downward at the outer corners. Below a thick, grizzled mustache, a cigar poked out of the corner of his mouth. He wore a cream flannel suit with a pale blue bow tie that matched his pocket square.

He reached the top of the gangplank and jerked his cigar out of his mouth. "We're a quarter hour behind schedule."

The crew member stationed at the top of the gangplank was a young man with a slender build who looked as if he hadn't quite grown into the navy suit jacket he wore. "Apologies, sir. We can't let down the gangplank until the captain gives the order."

"We better have an extra quarter hour at the site."

Our tall dragoman, Tabia, who had introduced himself at luncheon, stepped forward with a swish of his robe. He towered over Mr. Fairweather and announced in a booming voice, "All will be well, I assure you, Mr. Fairweather. You will have ample time and won't be rushed."

Mr. Fairweather made a huffing sound that conveyed extreme disbelief, then turned and shuffled down the gangplank, a waft of cigar smoke trailing after him.

Mr. Fairweather had cut in front of Mr. Alexander, the scruffy Egyptology scholar, who hesitated a few beats before following Mr. Fairweather down the gangplank. Hildy and I were at the back of the group disembarking, and as we waited, Mr. Fairweather's wife emerged from their cabin. She moved through the crowd, nodding and speaking to a few of the passengers.

Mrs. Fairweather was dressed in riding breeches with a vest over a long-sleeved white shirt. A copper-colored neck scarf that matched her wiry hair was tied in a square knot at her throat and rippled at her shoulders. Her face was wide with a blocky jawline. Freckles sprinkled across her large nose and under her close-set eyes, and her build was sturdy with generous curves. I heard someone say, "She's not much to look at, is she? One wonders how she caught Fairweather." She was probably at least a decade younger than her husband, who I thought was probably near fifty.

Mrs. Fairweather paused by Hildy and me, the scent of her Chanel No. 5 wafting around us. "Hello, Miss Windway. Perhaps you remember me? We met when you gave a lecture at Nobilis Domus."

"Yes, I do. It's lovely to see you again." I'd only spoken to her briefly at the time and was impressed that she remembered me.

She shook my hand enthusiastically, then reached for Hildy's hand after I introduced her. "Charming to meet you, Miss Honeyworth." Mrs. Fairweather bounced on the balls of her feet, looking over the heads of the passengers ahead of us. "Isn't this wonderful? A pyramid and tombs!"

"Indeed," I said. "It's an excellent way to start our trip up the Nile." She seemed a robust, plucky, have-a-go type person, and I wondered what she had in common with her husband, who appeared to be a rather self-important and surly individual.

A male voiced shouted, "Louisa!"

Mrs. Fairweather looked toward the riverbank. "Oh, that's Ambrose. He always charges ahead." Her tone was a mixture of fondness and exasperation. Mr. Fairweather stood near the donkeys, poised at the front of the line, motioning for her to join him. Tabia had disembarked and held the reins of two donkeys. "My husband does hate to be kept waiting. Since I'm anxious to see the sights, I'll indulge him this time. I'm looking forward to hearing your impressions of Cairo, Miss Windway, and also getting to know you, Miss Honeyworth, during our journey."

The passengers stepped back, but she refused to cut in front of them. When her turn came, she strode down the gangplank, and Hildy said in an undertone, "Well, *she* seems lovely."

Hildy and I claimed a donkey. I was surprised to see a wan, petite woman accompanying Dr. Walsh among the passengers going ashore. She was as slender and pale as a lily and had the fragile air of someone recently recovered from a serious illness. His face was still flushed, and his suit jacket looked even more droopy than it had earlier. He stood beside the woman as she mounted a donkey. "Seffie, you should stay on the steamer. You'll tire yourself—"

"Oh, poppycock. I've recuperated and recovered." Her voice was surprisingly strong and at odds with her frail appearance. "You said I was fit as could be not a fortnight ago. I'm not missing this excursion—or any other. I've promised I'll do the tomb, not the pyramid. If I become fatigued, I'll sit and rest." She touched her heels to the donkey, and it ambled forward. I'd taken a look at the passenger list before we left Hildy's cabin, and I felt confident I'd identified Mrs. Walsh.

Our traveling companions also included a teacher, Miss Entwhistle, and Mr. Fairweather's secretary, Julius Shaw. There was no sign of Millicent, the third member of the Fairweather party. Miss Fairweather must have decided to skip the excursion and remain on the steamer. After seeing Mr. Fairweather, I was quite sure he was Miss Fairweather's brother. They looked to be near the same age. They had the same build, and there was a resemblance in their faces.

Our group set off, clomping through the lush green cultivated strip of land that bordered the Nile. The fronds of tall palms rattled overhead while acacia, sycamore, and willow trees provided ample shade. I found my donkey was a nice steady fellow—I was even able to get some photographs of the vegetation as well as of our group while riding—but Hildy's donkey kept dropping behind.

We came out of the greenery abruptly, and miles of pale sand scattered with rocky debris surrounded us. In the distance, pyramids rose, some merely rounded heaps of stone, others in the recognizable triangular shape. Hildy and I paused so I could take photographs of the unusual step pyramid, which Tabia said was the oldest of the pyramids.

Our group split up. Mr. Listergraff and Mr. Shaw, who had a beaten-down air and moved with his head tipped forward and his shoulders rounded, stayed to tour the step pyramid.

The rest of us set off again, this time with the sun scorching down with a blast of heat that reminded me of the intense temperature one felt if one wandered too near the blaze on Bonfire Night. Mr. Fairweather put his heels to his donkey and left the rest of us in a gritty cloud of dust. When we arrived at the tombs, Hildy unwound the fine veil of cotton lawn she'd wrapped around her face and pith helmet. "I must say, I don't find donkey rides nearly as comfortable as camel rides. When the camel stands up, it's a bit frightening, but once that's over, they have a nice steady gait, not nearly as bouncy."

I had to agree with her. "Yes, I feel rather like an American cocktail. Let's go at a slower pace when we return."

We left our donkeys with a group of boys who Tabia directed us to. After snapping some photos, I was glad to follow the steps down into the shady coolness of the private tomb, the Mastaba of Ti, a wealthy landowner and official of the Fifth Dynasty. It had originally been built above ground, but the sand had covered it. Tabia directed us into a vestibule with pillars and murals on the walls, some of them preserved and beautiful, but others had been destroyed, perhaps removed by tomb robbers, either ancient or modern.

We gathered around in a half circle, and the dragoman's sonorous tones filled the small space as he pointed out Ti's image and the reliefs depicting village women carrying items for the tomb. I took a step back to create some space between myself and the young archaeologist, Mr. Alexander, who had been standing rather closer to me than I felt comfortable with. Tabia described the layout of the tomb and what we could expect to see in each room, then released us to explore on our own, saying he'd be on hand to answer any questions.

The group dispersed, with Mr. Alexander and Mr. Fairweather going immediately to the rocky staircase in the next room, the great court where offerings had been made. They descended to the empty underground tomb chamber.

I took some photos, then strolled around the pillars in the great court and stopped beside Hildy, whose head was angled to the side as she studied the image of Ti. "He obviously had quite a good opinion of himself. Look at how much larger he is compared to everyone else."

We shared a quiet laugh, then she wandered off to the other side of the room, and I moved through the narrow corridor and into a smaller room, studying the mural reliefs, amazed at the level of detail and rich color that remained even after thousands of years. I moved into the final chamber and was immersed in studying reliefs, snapshots of everyday life from ancient times that depicted an array of animals, including oxen, gazelle, antelope, geese, cranes, fish, and birds, along with men and women going about tasks such as making pottery, fishing, fattening birds, farming, and shipbuilding.

One panel showed the bounty from the sea, and I was

caught up in the detail of a fish when the odd prickling sensation of being watched came over me. I glanced around the chamber.

Dr. Walsh, pipe clenched in his mouth, had taken out his black notebook and pencil and was making notes. Hildy and Mrs. Walsh were absorbed in pointing out different plants in a large mural of a boat among papyrus reeds. It was beautifully done, with cranes, lotus flowers, a hippopotamus, and a crocodile. Mr. Alexander, absently smoothing his wrinkled tie, stood in the corner opposite me.

As soon as I looked toward him, he dipped his head and opened his guidebook. An uneasy feeling rippled through me. I moved around the room, head tilted back to look at the upper panels. Mr. Alexander matched my pace, staying at the same distance from me. The uncomfortable sensation of being watched intensified, yet each time I glanced at him, he quickly looked away. I went back into the corridor, and a few seconds later, the rumpled young man appeared in the hallway behind me.

I considered slipping away, maybe waiting outside, but I'd be in company with Mr. Alexander quite a bit. I didn't want to be uncomfortable during the whole trip. I drew in a breath and adjusted the strap of the camera on my neck. I wasn't going to let his actions ruin my time in the tomb. I marched up to him. "Are you enjoying the murals, Mr. Alexander?"

He took half a step back. "Yes, of course."

"Which one is your favorite? I'm curious to hear your opinion since you're an archaeologist. I'm partial to the one depicting the boat in the papyrus. The level of detail is superb."

"Oh yes. That one is—um—as you say, superb." His

Adam's apple bobbed as he surveyed the hallway. "In fact, they're all quite nice. I couldn't pick one over the other."

"Have you seen them before?"

"No, this is my first trip to Egypt."

Miss Entwhistle, the American teacher I'd met at luncheon, entered the corridor. She was tall and thin with an elongated face and lovely dark eyes, like a Modigliani painting that had caused a sensation a few years ago. Hands behind her back, her pointy elbows jutting out, she inched along, her gaze fixed on the reliefs.

I turned my attention back to a row of men carrying bundles—offerings, I assumed. Mr. Alexander did likewise, but I could sense he was watching me out of the corner of his eye.

Miss Entwhistle tapped him on the shoulder, and he started as if he'd gotten an electrical shock. "Mr. Alexander, as you're an archaeologist, perhaps you could answer a question I have about this image." Her accent reminded me of the people I'd met during my travels across the United States, and I wondered if she was from the Midwest. She certainly didn't have a southern accent or the nasal intonations of some northern Americans that I'd heard.

"Oh—well, of course. Except, I believe it's time to return to the steamer. We'd best make our way—"

"It will only take a moment. Look at this line of figures . . ."

I took the opportunity to leave and headed back to the great court, but I stopped short at the doorway. Mr. and Mrs. Fairweather stood on the opposite side of the square chamber, their backs to me. At a glance, it seemed they were looking at the damaged carving of Ti being carried on a bier or litter, but Mrs. Fairweather's posture was tense with her shoulders squared. Her scarf fluttered at her neck as she jerked to face her husband, a crumpled piece of paper in her hand. "Why didn't you tell me about this? If it hadn't fallen out of your pocket—" She stopped and drew a breath, then continued in a calmer tone. "Let's contact the authorities. It's absurd to deal with this on our own."

Mr. Fairweather's squat figure remained facing the mural. He took his cigar out of his mouth in a leisurely movement. "You're mistaken, my dear. It's not *our* concern. It's mine."

I was caught in an awkward spot. I could back up, but I had no desire to rejoin Mr. Alexander and Miss Entwhistle, who was now pointing to something and saying, "This inscription near the ox, is it saying, 'Take the sharpened knife,' or is it 'Take the knife which I have sharpened'? The difference is quite subtle, isn't it?"

On the other hand, I couldn't leave without going through the great court, where the Fairweathers were arguing.

Mrs. Fairweather flexed her free hand, fingers going wide, then curling into a fist. Her voice was lower when she spoke again, vibrating with anger. "You're absolutely insufferable at times, so sure you're perfectly right. This is not something you should try to take care of on your own. If you don't want to go to the police, I have contacts—"

She broke off as he made a sharp motion, his cigar cutting through the air near her sleeve. "I said I'll handle it." He jerked the paper out of her hand and stuffed it in his pocket.

I took a step back, intending to move out of sight and cough loudly before entering the chamber, but Mrs. Fairweather heard my footfall and whirled around.

I dipped my head. "So sorry. I didn't mean to intrude."

She lifted her chin. "No need to apologize. We shouldn't

be discussing matters such as this in public." She cut her gaze toward her husband and then strode out of the chamber, her figure flattening into a silhouette as she moved into the doorway's brilliant rectangle of sunlight.

Mr. Fairweather didn't acknowledge my presence. He stuffed his cigar back in his mouth, made a little impatient motion, twisting his chin and straightening the lapels of his jacket, then waddled after her, navigating around the opening in the ground at the center of the room—the staircase to the subterranean tomb chamber.

Well, what a spot of bother! I didn't want to follow Mr. Fairweather's squat figure too quickly. I went over to the staircase, but the hiss of whispered words floated up.

A woman's voice said, ". . . known he was a passenger, we could have taken another steamer."

The deeper register of a man's voice replied, "Can't change anything now. We'll have to make the best of it."

"How can we make the best of it? He's a vile and vicious person. I don't see how I'll be able to be civil."

"Mr. Fairweather is a powerful person, my dear. We must put on a social mask."

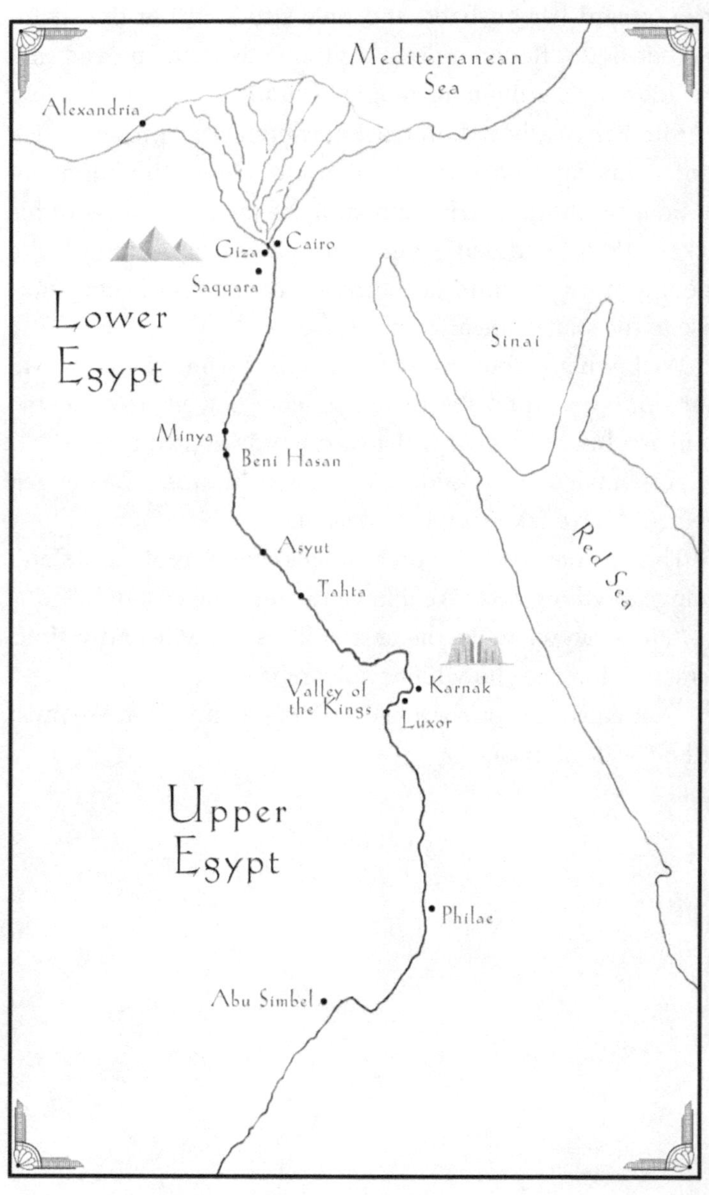

Mediterranean
Sea
Alexandria
Giza
Cairo
Saqqara
Sinai
Lower
Egypt
Minya
Beni Hasan
Red Sea
Asyut
Tahta
Valley of
the Kings
Karnak
Luxor
Upper
Egypt
Philae
Abu Simbel

# CHAPTER 5

Dear Aunt Amelia,

My mother-in-law insists on rearranging my furniture every time she visits. How do I stop this without causing a rift?

Dear Vexed,

Ah, the age-old dance of in-law diplomacy! Next time greet her with, "I'm so glad you're here—I've been experimenting with furniture placement and would love your opinion." This way, you acknowledge her input while maintaining control. If all else fails, develop a sudden passion for impossibly heavy antiques.

*—Ask Amelia, The Illustrated Dispatch*

*I* returned to the steamer with an uneasy feeling. It seemed we were in for an awkward, if not downright uncomfortable, journey, but to my surprise, we settled into a pleasant routine. The next day was spent completely on the Nile, and I was fascinated by the variety of the land-scape. I'd expected a wide river lined with palms, but on that first day, the river narrowed, and we passed mountains with limestone cliffs that dropped straight down to the water. Later I spotted brick chimneys poking up above the palms. Dr. Walsh, who was keen on documenting our trip in his notebook, was jotting down the landmarks we passed and the distance we'd progressed from Cairo. He removed his pipe and informed me, "We just passed seventy miles on the river. What you're seeing are sugar cane factories."

I spent a good portion of that day in the saloon, which was located on the upper deck and had a good view. It was furnished with comfortable chairs along with square tables covered with pristine white tablecloths, which were an ideal place for a card game or letter-writing. Chinese rugs covered the wooden deck, and pot plants dotted the area, some of them tall ferns that provided a bit of a screen if one wanted a measure of privacy. Two small bookshelves were placed back-to-back in the center of the space and contained the well-thumbed volumes of the steamer's library. I divided my time between the saloon and the promenade at the very front of the upper deck, where there was a delightful breeze.

We settled into a shipboard routine, a restful time tinged with a hint of ennui. The steamer was one of the smaller vessels, and after one had admired the sunrise, taken in the birds and palms, and studied the occasional islands and passing steamers and barges, there wasn't much to do except read, write letters, and chat with fellow passengers until it was time to admire the sunset, dine, and play card games.

After breakfast the next day, our third day on the Nile, I was standing at the railing near the saloon looking through the viewfinder of my camera, snapping photos of the Coptic convent perched above limestone cliffs on the east bank of the Nile. Hildy was in the saloon reading a book, but she had also brought along her portable writing desk so she could work on her correspondence. The American teacher, Miss Entwhistle, was sketching, and Mrs. Walsh was having a cup of tea. Except for her rather washed-out coloring, she didn't seem to become tired easily, which made me wonder why her husband insisted she needed to rest in their cabin in the afternoon.

Hildy and I had chatted with Mrs. Walsh and Mrs. Fairweather yesterday, and Mrs. Fairweather had suggested we use our given names, saying, "I feel as if you're all my friends, now that we've discussed books and shared gardening tips. Please call me Louisa."

"And you must call me Seffie," Mrs. Walsh had said. "No one calls me Persephone except my great-aunt, who is frightening and fearsome."

The sound of a chair being dragged across the floor drew my attention. Seffie was gripping a heavy deck chair, her thin arms straining as she maneuvered it. I crossed the room. "Here, let me. Where do you want it?"

"Oh, thank you, my dear. There, in the patch of sunlight. So kind of you. Won't you join me?"

I took the chair she indicated as she picked up her teacup, then leaned back and closed her eyes as she turned her face up to the sun. "We're always told to protect ourselves from the sun, but I find a bit of sunlight each day rejuvenating. It's something I learned in the sanatorium in Cairo—not to fear the sun, but to embrace its warmth."

"You were in a sanatorium?" That would explain Dr. Walsh's hovering, worried attitude toward his wife.

Seffie opened her eyes and took a sip of her tea before nodding. "Yes, several months. Tuberculosis."

"I'm sorry to hear that."

"Thank you, but I'm fully recovered now, thank goodness. If only I could convince Edmund of it. He is such a fussbudget." She sounded exasperated, but in a mild way, and I could tell from her tone that there was quite a bit of fondness mixed into her irritation. She grinned. "What do you think of that word?"

"Fussbudget? I haven't heard it before."

"Neither had I. It's an Americanism. I heard it from Miss Entwhistle. She said it means someone who's fussy about trivial things. She's quite fond of words. Of course, since she's a teacher, that makes sense."

We both glanced over our shoulders at Miss Entwhistle, who'd just let out a gusty sigh. During the excursion at Saqqara, she'd been in riding breeches, but today she wore pale yellow wide-legged trousers and a matching short-sleeved shirt with white polka dots and a Peter Pan collar edged with lace. At breakfast, I'd noticed Miss Fairweather look with disapproval at Miss Entwistle's trousers, but I thought the teacher looked smashing.

Seffie raised her voice. "Is our chatter disturbing you, Miss Entwhistle?"

She put down her sketchbook and leaned back in her chair. "Not at all. I'm frustrated with myself. I just can't quite capture the view."

Miss Entwhistle's bobbed light brown hair was tucked behind her ears, but a long thick fringe covered her forehead down to her eyebrows. She wore a pair of smoked spectacles with dark lenses. Earlier, she had a palm frond propped up on the table and had been working on a sketch of it, but she'd turned to a new page in her sketchbook. I recognized the view from the steamer—the rough outline of the cliff with the monastery on top. It seemed to be a good likeness to me.

Miss Entwhistle motioned to my camera. "I envy your camera and the ability to capture the view quickly and exactly."

The constantly changing panorama scrolling by would be difficult to capture in the detailed sketches that Miss Entwhistle seemed to favor. Seffie finished her tea, then settled back again and closed her eyes, her face to the sun. I moved closer to Miss Entwhistle and noticed that underneath her partial drawing she'd scrawled a few words. "Convent of the Pulley?" I asked. "Is that its real name?"

"It's what European tourists call it," she said in her flat American accent. Except for a few interactions, like when she spoke to Mr. Alexander about the reliefs in the tomb, she'd kept mostly to herself. She wasn't a chatty person, and I didn't expect her to continue, but she removed her glasses with the shaded lenses. "Apparently, it has several names," she continued. "Another of them is Deir Gebel et-Teir. That limestone hill is called *bird mountain* or *mountain of the birds. Deir* means convent or monastery, so Convent of Bird Mountain."

I pulled out the chair across the table and sat down, careful to avoid setting my camera on the palm frond she'd spent the morning sketching. We'd met briefly, but I hadn't spoken to Miss Entwhistle in any depth. She appeared to be perfectly content to keep her own company. At dinner, she'd been seated with Miss Fairweather, and when she'd been informed of her dinner partner, I'd heard Miss Entwhistle murmur, "Seating the two spinsters together, are we?" However, she seemed to be completely different from Miss Fairweather, who had a distinctly Victorian attitude, always turning the conversation to her brother or relaying his opinions and preferences in relation to any topic that was introduced.

Miss Entwhistle's artist box was open beside her. She picked up her pencil and sketched in some shadows, giving the rugged cliff face some texture as she spoke. "The nickname about the pulley came about because in the past they hauled tourists up the cliff face with a rope attached to a pulley. In the heyday of the dahabeeyah, the convent was one of the stops during a tour of the Nile."

"Ah, I see. Pity we don't have that option now. What a ride."

"Just seeing it is enough for me. Besides, if we stopped, it would throw us off our schedule, and Mr. Fairweather wouldn't be happy." Mr. Fairweather was a stickler for punctuality. Anytime something didn't happen as scheduled, he was extremely vocal about his displeasure.

"Yes, he'd be in high dudgeon."

We shared a smile as Miss Entwhistle drew the outline of a knife in the lower corner of the page. Her manner was absentminded, as if it were a doodle, but it was a rather odd thing to draw. I must have looked puzzled, because when she noticed my face, she chuckled and put down her pencil. "I read once that the origin of *dudgeon* comes from a word for the handle of a dagger."

"How . . . interesting."

"Etymology is a hobby of mine."

She erased the dagger and brushed the debris away from the page, then tapped the tip of the pencil on the sketch of the cliffs with the rough outline of the monastery above. "This frustrates me. I'm not good at quick sketches. We're moving too fast for me to get the level of detail I like." She flipped back to the previous page. The sketch of the palm frond was incredibly elaborate and could be included in a textbook of botanical illustrations.

"Would you like a copy of one of my photographs? You could work from that."

"Oh, that would be wonderful. Thank you."

"We'll be in Luxor a few days, and I'll get the film developed there." My hand rested on my camera. "Would you like me to take a photograph of you? I'm photographing all the passengers, if they'd like me to."

It had begun with Miss Fairweather, who'd asked me if I'd take a picture of her and her brother. It hadn't escaped my notice that she'd picked a moment when her sister-in-law, Louisa, was absent. I wondered if that had been intentional, because there seemed to be a tension between the two women. After I'd taken the photo of Miss Fairweather next to her brother, Seffie had asked if I'd take a photo of her and Dr. Walsh, and it had gone on from there. Mr. Alexander and Miss Entwhistle, who had been absent from the saloon at that time, were the only passengers I hadn't photographed.

"How nice of you. Yes, that would be wonderful. I'm so rarely in my travel photos." She gripped the seat of her chair. "Should I move to the railing?"

I picked up the camera and stepped back. "No, stay where you are. I like to get photographs of people doing their normal activities. Perhaps you could work on your illustration of the palm frond."

"All right."

"Do you travel frequently?" I'd learned that if I chatted with people, they lost their stiff, posed manner.

"As often as I can. I take trips during school breaks."

I snapped several photos of her with her head down, concentrating on her drawing. "Where have you been?"

"Canada, South America, and Europe. This is my first time seeing Africa."

"Goodness! You're a woman after my own heart."

She lifted a shoulder. "Besides gardening, it's my only hobby. I'd like to visit each continent. My travel stories help me keep my students' attention."

"What do you teach?"

"Science, math, and art."

"Do you enjoy teaching?" I asked, to keep our chitchat going.

"Much more than nursing. I worked in a hospital for a short time during the war. I'm better suited to the classroom than the sick ward."

An abrupt intake of breath across the saloon drew my attention. It was Hildy. She sat, her back rigid, her brow wrinkled, her gaze fixed on a letter. She'd been working so quietly on her correspondence that I'd forgotten she was in the saloon. Several letters and envelopes rested on the sloped surface of her rosewood writing desk. Her letter opener, a gift I'd picked up for her in Cairo, with a turquoise scarab on the handle, had fallen to the carpet. "Bad news?" I asked.

Hildy blinked and looked at me as if she'd forgotten there was anyone else in the saloon. After a beat of silence, she smiled and said in a chipper voice, "No, nothing to worry about. Just a bit of news that caught me off guard." As she picked up the letter opener, she refolded the paper and shoved it into her pocket. She straightened her shoulders and picked up her pen, then positioned a fresh sheet of paper on the writing surface of the small desk.

I took a few more photos of Miss Entwhistle as I watched Hildy out of the corner of my eye. A waiter slipped into the room and quietly cleared away the tea things from the table at Seffie's side, then motioned to Hildy's empty coffee cup, and she said, "Yes, I'm finished." She pulled the folded paper from her pocket and handed it to him. "Take this as well. It's rubbish."

He added it to his tray, straightened a chair, and picked up a few brown leaves that had fallen off the potted plants before leaving.

"I'll let you know when I have the photos developed," I said to Miss Entwhistle. "I'll leave you to your sketching." Hildy's head was bent over her letter, her pen scratching across the paper. She didn't look up as I followed the waiter.

I caught up with him on the stairs that led down to the main deck. "Wait a moment, please. Miss Honeyworth made a mistake about that paper."

# CHAPTER 6

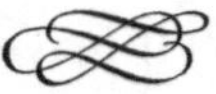

Last night's fancy-dress ball at the Continental-Savoy was a roaring success, with over seven hundred diners assembling in the flower-bedecked restaurant before the dance.

*—The Nile*

"Apologies," the waiter said as I plucked the paper Hildy had discarded from the tray. He looked uncertain, then angled the corner of the tray with the empty cups toward me. "Does she want anything else?"

I let out a little laugh. "No. Just the paper. It's not to be thrown out."

There was a trace of a grin on his face as he bowed and went on his way down the stairs.

I unfolded the paper.

*Fraud!*

*Ticktock, time is running out.*

*Your deception won't stay hidden much longer.*

Like the note I'd found in my cabin on the day we departed, this one was written on the steamer's letterhead. The handwriting was the same as the other note, precise and blocky, obviously a style intended to camouflage the sender.

I resolved to speak to Hildy. Respecting privacy was one thing, but these were threats. I just had to work out how to approach her about it.

I folded the note, put it in my pocket, and turned to trot up the stairs, but I crashed into the solidness of Mr. Briarcliff. We both wobbled on the stairs. He gripped my wrist at the same moment I grasped a handful of his suit coat.

We steadied ourselves. "You surprised me, Mr. Briar—" What pseudonym he was using? Despite the beard and glasses, I still thought of him as Mr. Briarcliff. What *was* the alias he was using? Convivial? Genial? No, neither of those. And not jovial either. "Mr. Cordial!" I said, hitting on it at last. I realized I was still gripping the fabric of his coat and released it. "Oh, I've wrinkled it. I'm sorry." I smoothed the fabric. "I didn't expect you to be right behind me." He jumped back, and I reached out an arm to steady him in case he lost his balance, but he was surefooted as he moved up a step.

"I didn't expect you to be on the stairs going down to the kitchen. You do make a habit of turning up in unexpected places, Miss Windway."

"Is that the sort of thing that Mr. Cordial would know about me?"

He removed his black-framed spectacles and rubbed the bridge of his nose. I thought he was irritated, but then he sighed. "I wasn't cut out to be an actor. I'm rubbish at staying in character." He replaced his glasses, then looked over my shoulder. "Fortunately, there's no one around to see it."

We were alone on the stairs. The waiter hadn't noticed our collision and had left.

Mr. Briarcliff extended his hand to the top of the stairs. "Allow me to accompany you to the upper deck. The dining room is closed at the moment, and I'm sure you don't have business in the galley."

To distract him from asking what I'd been doing on the stairs, I said, "I haven't seen much of you," as we climbed the stairs.

"The duties of a manager are quite heavy. I spend most of my time either working with the staff or monitoring various bits of paperwork. It's a living hell."

I had to stifle a grin at his gloomy expression. "It doesn't seem as if that would be to your taste."

"Thank goodness it's only for a short time."

"You won't do this again?" I waved my hand, indicating the steamer. "Isn't monitoring Mr. Martin's holdings part of your regular rotation of duties?"

"I'm on the schedule to take on the same role on the return trip to Cairo with another of the Blue Lotus's steamers. After that, I'll convince Mr. Martin to have someone else take over."

Louisa's figure appeared at the top of the stairs. Today she wore a linen suit, and the scarf around her neck was a deep sapphire blue. "There you are, Blix."

"Hello, Louisa," I said.

Louisa took a few steps down, and the faint aroma of her Chanel No. 5 filled the air as she moved toward Mr. Briarcliff and me. "I'm organizing a game of charades. I've wrested my husband and his secretary, Mr. Shaw, away from their ledgers and letters. Will you play, Blix?"

"Of course." I was always happy to join shipboard activities, but I was surprised Mr. Fairweather was participating. So far, he'd spent a good deal of time in his cabin with the subdued Mr. Shaw, attending to business matters. Each evening after dinner they'd been largely absent from the saloon, where most of the passengers gathered. Mr. Fairweather usually arrived several hours after dinner and had a cup of coffee with Louisa before they retired for the night. I'd seen even less of the self-effacing Mr. Shaw. I wondered if Mr. Shaw preferred to spend his free time alone rather than in the group with his employer. He kept to himself, and when I'd seen him on the steamer, he always had his head bent forward either reading papers or, if his hands were empty, he kept his gaze focused on the floor and rarely looked up to meet anyone's eyes.

"Brilliant," Louisa said. "What about you, Mr. Cordial?"

"I regretfully decline. Paperwork must be done."

"Perhaps next time." Mr. Briarcliff gave a small nod before departing.

I entered the saloon with Louisa and found Hildy had put away her writing desk and was seated across the table from Mr. Listergraff. "He's challenged me to a game of chess, and I must trounce him soundly to get revenge for my loss at his hand last evening."

Louisa had rounded up most of the remaining passengers. She bustled back and forth, directing the men to rearrange the furniture. The breeze ruffled her wiry copper hair, but she didn't seem to mind that it was disarranged. She untied the blue scarf she wore around her neck and wrapped it around her head in the style of a bandeau to keep her hair out of her face.

Mr. Fairweather arrived and plopped down into a chair as Louisa divided us into two teams. "Titles of books and plays," she called out to Mr. Alexander, who was seated at one of the tables, his head of fair, unruly hair bent over as he wrote on slips of paper and deposited them in a bowl. "Well-known ones, please," she added, then turned to her sister-in-law, Miss Fairweather, who had just entered the saloon and was heading for the chair beside her brother. "Hello, Millicent. Oh no, not there. You're on the other team."

The black fabric of her skirt flared as Miss Fairweather ignored her sister-in-law and settled into the seat beside Mr. Fairweather. Everyone else was in light-colored clothing. In her dark dress, Miss Fairweather looked like a crow among doves. Even with her heavily powdered face and dangling jet earrings, the family resemblance between Mr. Fairweather and his sister was clear in their jowly cheeks and high-handed manner. "But I'd rather be on the team with Ambrose," Miss Fairweather said to Louisa. "I get so muddled at times, and he's so knowledgeable."

Mr. Alexander straightened his saggy tie and smoothed down his blond hair before he came across the room and handed the bowl with the titles to Louisa. His face was flushed, and I wondered if he'd been taking a turn around the deck when Louisa had invited him to the game.

She mixed the strips of paper with her fingers. "Then the teams will be uneven, Millicent."

Miss Fairweather's mouth thinned into a sulky line. "Then I'll be the timekeeper."

"Mr. Alexander has already kindly volunteered." Miss Fairweather drew a breath, but Louisa flapped her hand as if she were waving away a fly. "Go on, Millicent."

Miss Fairweather's head snapped toward her brother, but he was absorbed in lighting a cigar. She exhaled loudly through her nose. "Very well." She stalked across the saloon and took a seat beside Dr. Walsh. I must say that I hadn't felt much sympathy for Miss Fairweather until that moment. I still found her tedious, but it couldn't have been easy for her when her brother married later in life and Louisa took over the role of lady of the manor. Hildy had heard from Seffie that Miss Fairweather had run the household at Nobilis Domus for twenty years before her brother married.

Louisa took the seat her sister-in-law had vacated. "Let's say four minutes per turn. Ready, Mr. Alexander?"

He'd taken off his wristwatch and positioned it the table. "All set," he said as he fanned himself with the scorecard and pulled at his collar, causing his tie to droop again.

"Wonderful. I'll go first, shall I?" At Mr. Alexander's signal, Louisa plucked a paper from the bowl, thought a moment, then jumped to her feet. She tucked her arms close to her sides and began to hop.

Besides her husband, her team was made up of Mr. Shaw and Seffie. Mr. Shaw shouted out *Peter Rabbit*, which surprised me. He was generally so quiet that I hadn't expected him to participate, but it seemed he had a competitive streak.

Mr. Shaw turned out to be the best player, guessing *A Tale of Two Cities* when Seffie, looking refreshed from her nap in the sunshine, held up two fingers and then sketched elaborate outlines of what were supposed to be tall buildings, her shawl flying with her energetic movements.

Our team managed to stay in the game by guessing *The Adventures of Sherlock Holmes* after Miss Entwhistle walked around hunched over, peering at the carpet through her invisible magnifying glass. Dr. Walsh caught on immediately when I gave the signal for *first word* of a two-word title and pretended to put a crown on my head. He called out *King*

*Lear,* and Louisa said he deserved the "fastest guesser" award.

Even Mr. Fairweather, who was silent most of the game, got into the spirit of things when his turn came. He stayed seated in his chair and made rowing motions for the first word of his title. Mr. Shaw muttered, "Row, row," under his breath, then bounced in his chair as he said, "Of course. *Romeo and Juliet!*"

Everyone seemed to be having a wonderful time except for Louisa, who didn't make any guesses, and Mr. Alexander. Between calling out the time remaining for each turn, his gaze kept going to Hildy and Mr. Listergraff. They were focused on the chessboard and didn't seem to notice. I was glad to have Mr. Alexander's attention off of me, but I found it disturbing when he turned his gaze on Hildy and Mr. Listergraff. Since the excursion to the tomb, I'd noticed him watching me and Louisa occasionally, but I hadn't spoken with him again.

The game broke up when Dr. Walsh nodded at the shore. "I believe we're approaching Minya." He took out his small notebook and pencil to record our arrival, which I'd seen him do every time we passed a landmark or arrived at a stopover point.

I went to my cabin to get my hat, but I paused outside Hildy's door. Mr. Listergraff had won the chess game shortly before charades ended, and I'd seen her go into her cabin. I still had the note I'd retrieved from the tray. Clearly, it had bothered her, and I was concerned that someone had sent her a second nasty note.

One vicious letter could be written off, but two poison-pen letters? That was the beginning of a pattern. I raised my hand to knock. But she'd been so dismissive the first time I'd asked her about it. I flexed my fingers tighter for a moment.

When did one push forward and insist on candor, and when did one retreat? I only occasionally felt discontented with my solitary childhood—I was usually quite happy with my own company—but it was at times like these that I wished I'd had the opportunity to form more friendships. It would be so helpful to know how to get on with people. As lovely as my *good* governesses had been—as opposed to the bad ones, who were vicious—none of the pleasant and caring governesses had been a close friend.

I dithered for a moment more, then tapped the wood with my knuckles. I'd make one more attempt.

Hildy called out for me to come in. She was pacing back and forth. "Is everything all right?" I asked. "You seemed upset earlier in the saloon when you opened that letter."

She sat down abruptly at the dressing table and fiddled with her hairpins that were already perfectly placed. "Everything is fine. Why wouldn't it be?"

I perched on the bed behind her and caught her eye in the mirror. "Hildy, you do know if something's bothering you, you can confide in me, don't you?"

"Yes, and I appreciate your concern." She held my gaze for a moment and smiled, her eyes kind. Then she picked up her powder puff, and her voice became brisk. "I was a bit irritated at one of my correspondents, but it's nothing important. I'm sorry I worried you. Are you looking forward to the rock-cut tombs tomorrow?"

I'd been leaning forward, but at her change in tone I sat back. The subject was closed. "I am. I'll be glad to stretch my legs and do some walking, although it sounds as if the tombs are close by, so we won't have a trek or a donkey ride."

"Thank goodness for that," Hildy said in what was

almost, but not quite, her usual jovial manner. I left her and went to my cabin to get my hat.

The excursion to Minya was short, just an hour or so, and that gave us the opportunity "to bazaar," as Tabia called it. We'd have a longer excursion the next morning to visit the rock-cut tombs. For our first short visit, we went ashore at the good-sized village and browsed gold, silver, brightly colored fabric, and all sorts of items essential for the traveler, including ebony-handled fly-swatters, trinket boxes, and veils in bright colors.

When we returned to the steamer, I went to put my purchases away in my cabin, but I stopped short on the threshold, shocked to see the desk drawers hanging open. Then I spotted a trouser leg visible in the space between the bed and the desk.

"What on earth?" I hurried across the room.

Even though I was looking at a man's back, and his face was turned away from me, his weedy build, messy blond hair, and the worn heel of his shoe meant it had to be Mr. Alexander. A stack of blank pages of the steamer stationery, which must have come from the empty desk drawer, were on the floor next to his immobile hand.

Mr. Alexander had said he wasn't interested in the bazaar and had stayed behind on the steamer, and I'd thought it was probably because he was stony. His wardrobe indicated that he probably didn't have the money to spare for trinkets and souvenirs.

Had he started in on the evening cocktails early and had a few too many? Irritation mixed with wariness surged through me. His cabin wasn't even on this deck. What was he doing here, passed out on the floor in my cabin?

I gave the sole of his shoe a shove with my foot. "Mr. Alexander! Wake up!"

He didn't move, and I kicked his shoe again, a bit more sharply, but other than a little ripple of movement running through his leg at the contact, he didn't move. Worry cut through my annoyance. "Mr. Alexander? Are you all right?"

I stepped into the narrow space and shook his shoulder. His body, which had been resting at an angle, rolled back heavily into my toes. I was surprised at the weight of his skinny frame. I shifted backward, bumping into the desk. For a second, I was back in a Cairo courtyard, a dead body at my feet. Blood thundered in my ears, and a jolt of adrenaline coursed through me, as if I'd touched an electric flex. Then I saw the rise and fall of his tie and noticed his skin looked clammy, but his cheeks were flushed.

I drew in a breath to steady myself. Not a dead body, then. Just a man who was ill. I inched forward and pressed my hand to his forehead. It was hot against my palm. Mr. Alexander's eyelids flickered, and he muttered something I couldn't distinguish. The weave of the rug was imprinted on his cheek, and his hair stuck to his sweaty temple.

I went to ring for Hassan but pulled my hand back. I didn't want any gossip. Whispers about a man—even a sick one—in my room could make things awkward.

I slipped out of my cabin, closing the door behind me. The deck was empty, but then I spotted Mr. Briarcliff's broad-shouldered figure leaving the saloon. He was headed away from me, toward the promenade deck at the front of the steamer. I shot down the deck and caught up to him in the bright sunlight on the open deck of the promenade, which was deserted. Apparently, everyone had retreated to their cabins after the trip to the bazaar—everyone but Mr. Alexander.

I caught his arm. "Mr. Briarcliff." He whirled around, his gaze darting around the deck, but I didn't give him time to speak. "Oh, don't give me that ferocious look. There's no one here, and I can't be bothered to remember your absurd assumed name. Mr. Alexander is in my cabin."

His bicep flexed under my hand as he drew his arm out of my grip. "That's not a problem the steamer's crew handles."

"I believe it is when the man in question is lying on the floor, unconscious and ill."

His face became serious. "I'll get Dr. Walsh."

"Wait! Please, can we"—Miss Entwhistle had rounded the corner and was strolling along the deck toward us; I lowered my voice to a whisper—"move him out of my cabin before anyone realizes? I have no idea what he's doing there. I found him just now. He must have gone in while we were at the bazaar."

"It's best not to move him until he's examined."

"But people will talk. You know they will."

He regarded me for a moment, but since he didn't reply, I assumed he recognized the truth of what I said. His tone was resigned as he said, "Miss Windway, you are fast becoming my least favorite passenger."

"Becoming? Oh, excellent. I was sure I was *already* your least favorite passenger."

# CHAPTER 7

Eyebrows were raised when Miss Cordelia Worthington
arrived at the Continental-Savoy's ball this week on the arm
of not one but two eligible bachelors. The season's most
sought-after debutante is certainly keeping her options open!

*—About Town, The Nile*

"*A*nd by '*can we* move him,' you obviously meant
can *I* move him," Mr. Briarcliff said as we huffed
down the stairs to the main deck, with Mr. Alexander braced
between us.

"I *am* helping."

"Yes, but you're tiny."

"Only when compared to a giant like you."

When we'd returned to my cabin, Mr. Alexander was
weakly flailing about, rather like a sleepy turtle on its back.
Mr. Briarcliff had looked at his eyes, checked his pulse, and
helped him ease into a sitting position. I'd resigned myself to

becoming the target of gossip—how did that always happen to me?—when Mr. Briarcliff said, "Take a look out the door. Tell me when there's no one about." At my signal, he'd helped Mr. Alexander to his feet, then looped his arm over his shoulders, and I'd hurried to take Mr. Alexander's other side.

By some miracle, we navigated the short distance to the stairs without anyone seeing us. Getting to the bottom without breaking our necks with a groggy man between us was a second wonder.

Mr. Briarcliff nodded his head at a cabin door. "That one, there. It should be open."

The handle wouldn't turn. "It's not."

"What? No one locks their doors on these journeys."

"Apparently, Mr. Alexander does." Mr. Alexander's head was tipped forward. Mr. Briarcliff awkwardly patted his rumpled suit jacket pockets. As he extracted a key, an envelope fell to the floor. Mr. Briarcliff handed me the key. I opened the door, then retrieved the envelope while Mr. Briarcliff shuffled across the threshold and dropped Mr. Alexander onto the bed.

His cabin was much smaller than mine, clearly the budget option. No polished wood or Oriental rugs here.

I put the envelope on the desk beside Mr. Alexander's portable typewriter, next to another letter. I half turned away, then turned back to look at the letter again, puzzled because it was addressed to a female. A quick look around Mr. Alexander's cabin showed that there was no woman staying there. Shaving things were scattered around the basin on the dressing table, and the wardrobe's open doors revealed only one other suit, the material shiny from lots of wear.

I inched the letter around so that I could read it more

easily. The scrawled handwriting was hard to make out, but it looked like the letter was addressed to *Amanda*. I couldn't make out the last name because the pen strokes had bled together into a dark clump. Had Mr. Alexander perhaps picked up someone else's mail and was delivering it to a friend in Luxor?

Mr. Briarcliff spoke, and I turned away from the desk as he said, "You think I'm a giant, do you?" Mr. Briarcliff was struggling to work Mr. Alexander's arm out of his suit jacket.

One of Mr. Alexander's legs had slipped off the edge of the narrow bed. I grasped the trouser hem and replaced it. "Well, with your height and your broad shoulders—"

One corner of Mr. Briarcliff's mouth had edged up while he battled to free Mr. Alexander's arm. I pulled off one of Mr. Alexander's shoes and set it at the foot of the bed. "Fishing for compliments, Mr. Briarcliff? Now there's something I never thought I'd see."

His lightning smile flashed across his face and then was gone. He gave the sleeve another tug. Mr. Alexander's arm popped free, his hand smacking Mr. Briarcliff's face, knocking his glasses askew, and tracing over his beard.

Mr. Briarcliff rubbed his nose and resettled his glasses. "Just noting an observation."

I moved to the head of the bed and said, "You lift his shoulders, and I'll move his jacket." I tugged it free, then shook it out and put it over the back of the desk chair. "I'll fetch Dr. Walsh."

Mr. Briarcliff loosened Mr. Alexander's collar, then stood over him, hands on his hips. "Yes, that's best. If he were drunk, I'd leave him to sleep it off, but he has a fever."

I went out into the corridor, then returned and stuck my head in the door. "Thank you."

Mr. Briarcliff looked up from throwing a blanket over Mr. Alexander. "For what?"

"For moving him out of my room."

"Consider it part of the kind and courteous service you receive on the S.S. *Cleopatra*." He placed the shoes in the wardrobe and closed the door. "It was my pleasure."

"You sound rather sincere, almost as if you've acclimated to your role as assistant manager."

"Truly, it was my pleasure. You know a secret about me, and I now know a secret about you."

"There's nothing—"

He waved off my heated protest. "I know. There's nothing between you and Mr. Alexander. However, it's always good to have an ace up one's sleeve, isn't it? Now we're even in the secrets department."

I drew in a deep breath. "Exasperating. You're not only annoying. You're also exasperating." I shut the door before he could reply, but I thought I heard a chuckle as I walked away. That couldn't be right. Mr. Briarcliff wasn't the chuckling sort.

Louisa handed me a coffee cup. "Have you heard? Mr. Alexander is under the weather."

"Indeed?" I felt Hildy's gaze on me and realized my tone must have sounded odd.

The sun had set, and the canvas panels had been rolled down, enclosing the saloon, which kept it warm in the evening and also cut down on the bugs. With the soft glow of oil lamps, we might have been in a cozy drawing room instead of on the Nile. The steamer was at a standstill.

Shifting sandbanks made navigating at night too treacherous.

In Cairo, I'd become accustomed to the cool desert nights, but I felt the temperature change even more on the water. After dinner, I'd put on my thick tweed jacket. Hildy and Seffie had draped shawls over their evening dresses, while Louisa wore a blond mink shoulder wrap.

After dinner, Hildy had joined Mr. Listergraff in a game of chess. I'd played a game of patience. Miss Entwhistle had stopped by the table and said, "Oh, you're playing solitaire," calling it by the American name.

"Yes, but I'm ready for a break." I'd handed her the cards, and she'd taken my seat while I'd moved to join the group of ladies with Hildy, whose chess game had ended.

I accepted the cup from Louisa and avoided Hildy's gaze, focusing on turning the handle of my cup so that I could pick it up for a sip. The black coffee was the strongest I'd ever tasted and scalded my tongue. "I suppose Dr. Walsh is keeping an eye on him?"

"Yes," Seffie said. "Edmund wanted to look in on him after dinner. Mr. Alexander was quite done in."

I put down my coffee. "It came on suddenly, didn't it? He seemed to be fine during the game of charades."

Seffie rearranged her shawl, pulling it closer around her thin neck. The wrap covered nearly all of her elfin frame. "Although I noticed he did look a tad flushed. I put it down to the heat of the afternoon. Of course, some illnesses come on quickly." She looked across the saloon, her gaze unfocused, and I wondered if she was thinking of her time in the tuberculosis sanatorium in Cairo.

Louisa said, "I'm thankful we have a doctor on the steamer. Although I'm sorry that your husband has to work during his holiday, Seffie."

"He doesn't mind. In fact, he's restless if he doesn't have something to do. It's why he's keeping that travel journal with the detailed list of stops. That man can't slow down. He's up before dawn. Insists he should get up to watch the sunrise."

I sipped my coffee to hide my smile. Dr. Walsh might rise early, but that didn't mean he was awake when the sun came up. For the last two days, I'd come to the saloon early and found Dr. Walsh in a chair facing east, but with his head tipped forward, chin on chest, occasionally emitting a snore.

Louise angled herself toward Seffie. "Now you must tell me more about your garden. I understand you have quite a few fruit trees as well?"

"We do. Oranges, lemons, limes, and a few others. We do enjoy the citrus. It's so refreshing and revitalizing."

"We only have orange trees, which I adore, but I'm adding some other fruit trees. I've had the most trouble keeping our peach trees healthy. Do you have any of those?"

"Oh yes. Several, in fact." I had a difficult time picturing Seffie with her delicate build as a gardener, which I knew was quite hard work because one of my governesses, Miss Halford, had been an enthusiastic gardener. We'd spent a good portion of the spring and summer digging and weeding in the flower, herb, and vegetable gardens.

Hildy said, "When I lived with my brother, we had a nice little enclosed glass house, but I never had much luck with fruit trees, except for a peach tree. It was over a decade old and well established."

The discussion turned to espalier patterns and pruning. I had little to say on the subject of fruit trees, and when Mr. Fairweather appeared in the doorway, I saw my opportunity to slip away for a stroll around the deck.

Mr. Fairweather took the empty seat on the other side of

Louisa. Mr. Shaw, who had followed his employer into the saloon, lifted his ducked head just enough to spot an empty chair. He began to pull over a chair, but I put my coffee cup down. "Please have my seat, Mr. Shaw." He protested, but I added, "I'd like to spend a little time on the promenade deck." He nodded and took my seat, giving everyone in the group a general greeting, then subsiding into the chair and settling into his normal posture with his head tipped forward and shoulders rounded.

The saloon was designed with doors on either side of the room. I went out the one on the starboard side and onto the promenade deck, buttoning my tweed jacket as the chilly air washed over me.

Mr. Listergraff stood at the railing wreathed in pipe smoke. "Evening."

I returned his greeting and joined him. A few solitary lights twinkled on the shore. Gentle waves slapped at the side of the steamer.

He said, "If you've come out for stargazing, looks like we'll be disappointed. I noticed some high clouds earlier, and they haven't moved on."

"That's disappointing." The night sky with its masses of stars was unlike anything I'd ever seen.

"I'm sure tomorrow will be clear. Rather unusual to have cloud cover on the Nile."

"Even if we can't see the stars, it's still very pleasant tonight." The moment the words were out of my mouth, a high-pitched buzz sounded by my ear, and I waved away the bug.

"Except for the mosquitos. They don't seem to enjoy pipe smoke, though. Perhaps that will keep some of them away."

A thump sounded from the saloon, then a confusion of voices.

# CHAPTER 8

Dear Amelia,
My parents are pressuring me to join the family law firm, but my heart lies in the kitchen. Breads and pastries are my passion. How can I follow my dreams without disappointing them?

Dear Muffin Man,
The age-old battle between expectation and aspiration. Remember, life's too short for half-baked dreams. Invite your parents to tea, serve them your finest creations, and show them that your true talents lie in tortes, not torts. Who knows? They might just eat their words—along with your delicious pastries.

*—Ask Amelia, The Illustrated Dispatch*

*M*r. Listergraff and I exchanged a startled look as the uproar in the saloon continued. We turned and crossed the promenade deck, then Mr. Listergraff held the saloon door for me. A huddle of people was gathered near the chair I'd been sitting in earlier.

Miss Entwhistle had abandoned her game of patience, and some of the cards had fallen to the floor. A pot plant had been knocked over, spilling dirt across the rug.

Mr. Shaw was backing away from the group, a stunned look on his face. His steps were erratic, and he bumped into a table. Mr. Listergraff put a hand on his arm and led him to a chair. "Easy there. Why don't you have a seat?"

Mr. Shaw dropped down heavily. "I can't believe it. We were working only a few moments ago. He was writing a letter and checking the invoices."

"Has something happened to Mr. Fairweather?" The swarm of hunched-over passengers blocked my view, but clearly someone was hurt and lying on the floor.

Mr. Shaw loosened his tie. "Miss Entwhistle says he's dead, but that's—that's—just not possible. I realize she has some nursing experience, but she's not a doctor."

"Mr. Fairweather?" Surely I'd misunderstood. "He's died?"

Mr. Shaw looked around the room. "Where's Dr. Walsh? We need him."

Mr. Listergraff said, "I'll find him." He looked at me over Mr. Shaw's head and said quietly, "I'll find Rafe after I let the doctor know he's needed. Rafe will tell the captain."

"Rafe?" I asked as he headed for the door. Mr. Listergraff mouthed, *Briarcliff,* over his shoulder, and I nodded. I'd forgotten Mr. Briarcliff's given name. My brain was having problems processing the simplest of information.

I moved to Hildy's side. Mr. Fairweather was indeed stretched out on the floor, his face flushed, and his eyes blankly open. Louisa was on her knees beside him, gripping his lapels, shaking him. Her voice trembled as she said, "Wake up, Ambrose. Wake up, you silly man. Charades are over. Stop playing about."

Hildy was patting her on the back. On the other side of Mr. Fairweather's motionless body, Miss Entwistle sat with her knees folded under her and hands in her lap. "I'm so sorry, Mrs. Fairweather. But there's nothing to be done now." She twisted around, spotted Seffie, and said, "Your husband and the captain need to be informed."

Louisa bent over and rested her head on her husband's chest, her shoulders shaking.

I said quietly, "Mr. Listergraff has gone to get Dr. Walsh and Mr.—um—the assistant manager. He'll inform the captain."

Miss Entwhistle stood and looked down on Mr. Fairweather a moment, then said dispassionately, "And then someone must tell Miss Fairweather. She retired directly after dinner."

"Oh, that's right. She was his sister. Poor dear," Seffie said. "It will come as a horrible and terrible shock, I'm sure."

Hildy caught my eye and gave a little jerk of her head, indicating I should move to the other side of Louisa. Hildy crouched down beside Louisa and brushed back the hair from her face as one would do with a child. "Come with me, my dear." Her tone was kind, but a firmness underlined the words. "You must let Dr. Walsh see to him."

Louisa sat up slowly, released her grip on the suit coat, then smoothed the fabric. Her face was tear-streaked. The way she ran her hands over the coat and straightened the lapels struck me as so tender, which surprised me. I realized I'd accepted the general thought that she didn't have much affection for her husband, but her actions contradicted that idea.

I helped Hildy get Louisa to her feet. With her arm around Louisa's shoulders, Hildy drew her away. I made a move to follow them, but Miss Entwhistle took Louisa's other arm. I fell back because she had medical experience and could help more than I could.

After they left, I noticed Mr. Shaw bent forward in a chair. I went to him as Dr. Walsh arrived, carrying his medical bag. He went to Mr. Fairweather and checked for a pulse. After a few seconds, he looked at his watch and closed Fairweather's eyes.

Elbows braced on his knees, Mr. Shaw had dropped his head into his hands. I hovered beside him. "Are you all right, Mr. Shaw?"

He didn't answer, only shook his head. A heavy tread thundered a quick beat as someone ran along the deck, then Mr. Briarcliff burst into the saloon. "What happened?"

Dr. Walsh picked up his bag. "Looks like it was his heart. Nothing to be done for him now. How do you handle a death aboard?"

Mr. Briarcliff rubbed a hand across his mouth, then down over his beard. "I suppose the captain will want to press on to Beni Hasan tomorrow and let the authorities there take over. For now, we could put his body in the cold storage area."

I stepped forward and said quietly, "Dr. Walsh, I believe Mr. Shaw might need some medical attention."

Dr. Walsh picked up his bag and bent down beside Mr. Shaw, which left Mr. Briarcliff and me standing over Mr. Fairweather. "What a shocking turn of events."

"What?" Mr. Briarcliff blinked and seemed to give himself a little mental shake.

"I said it's rather shocking. One doesn't expect something like this to happen."

Mr. Briarcliff's attention returned to Mr. Fairweather's body. He said something under his breath, which sounded like, "It's actually not surprising at all."

"What?"

His gaze snapped from Mr. Fairweather to my face. "Death never surprises me now."

MR. BRIARCLIFF WENT to make arrangements to move Mr. Fairweather's body, and I let him know Hildy and Miss Entwhistle had taken Louisa away. "To her cabin, I assume. Miss Entwhistle pointed out that Mr. Fairweather's sister will need to be told as well."

Mr. Briarcliff looked as if a weight had landed on his shoulders. "I'll make sure Dr. Walsh looks in on Miss Fairweather tonight."

I went back to my cabin and sat on the edge of my bed, not quite sure what to do with myself. One moment Mr. Fairweather had been among us, smoking his cigar and keeping a punctual schedule, and the next he was lifeless on the saloon floor.

I stood up. I should check on Hildy. After all, she'd seen Mr. Fairweather die. If I felt this discombobulated from seeing the aftermath of Mr. Fairweather's death, what must she be feeling?

Her cabin door was open a crack. I tapped on it and poked my head in. She was crouched over beside the desk. "Hildy, are you—?"

She shot up and whirled toward me, one hand to her heart. "Oh, it's you, Blix."

I stepped inside and came around the end of the bed. "I came to see how you were faring—" Letters and envelopes were scattered across the floor under the desk. "Oh my! What happened? Oh, your little portable writing desk is on the floor! Did you drop it?" It was empty, the top open but crooked, the hinges broken.

Hildy gazed at the mess at her feet. "I came in just a moment ago and found it like this. I was so shocked I didn't even close my door properly."

I picked up her portable writing desk. Fresh scars marred the wood around the brass lock where someone had forced it open. "Goodness, someone broke the lock! We must notify Mr.—um"—I dredged my memory and managed to remember Mr. Briarcliff's pseudonym—"Mr. Cordial."

"No, don't do that."

"Is anything else damaged or missing? You should look around."

"I don't need to check anything else. I know the letters were all the person wanted," she said as she crossed the room to close the door. "Take a look, and you'll understand."

I scanned the jumble of envelopes and letters. The handwriting on the correspondence varied, but one name was repeated on the envelopes and the salutations, *Amelia Wise.*

I lowered myself onto the stool at the dressing table. "*You're* Amelia Wise? The agony aunt?"

Hildy sat on the edge of the bed across from me. "Yes, I'm Amelia."

"Then all your correspondence? They're letters from readers asking advice?"

"I apologize for keeping it from you. I do hope you're not angry with me."

"Angry? I'm delighted! I adore the Amelia Wise column, and I was so happy to see *The Nile* syndicated it so I could keep reading it on my travels. You're witty and funny and give excellent advice. Oh, this is brilliant! Oh my, I'm waffling on like a schoolgirl who's met a famous film star, but then again, Amelia Wise *is* a star. I'll try to rein myself in. Why would I be angry?"

Hildy gave me a little smile, then her gaze dropped to her hands, which were clasped in her lap. "Well, I feel we've become quite good friends on our travels. I would have liked to have told you in Cairo, but I'm not allowed to. It's in my contract, you see. I was afraid that if you ever found out, you'd be hurt I kept it from you."

I reached out and covered her hand with mine. "I don't feel like that at all. It's perfectly understandable that you couldn't mention it. I'm just delighted that I know *now*. How long have you been Amelia?"

"Years and years. You know that I chaperoned young ladies for a while, but that was often challenging. Then my brother's health worsened, and I needed to be with him instead of in London. So I started writing as Amelia in 1909 to bring in a little extra for the housekeeping budget. Of course, I couldn't tell my brother. He would have had an apoplexy if he knew I'd done something as scandalous as take a job. When I think now about how—how I scrimped and saved and he had more than enough money to run our household—oh, it makes my blood boil." She blew out a deep breath and relaxed her shoulders. "But I didn't do it only for the money. I truly enjoy it, and I like to think that over the years I've helped a person or two along the way."

"You have. I know you have." I gave her hand a squeeze and released it. "I've been reading *Ask Amelia* since I was—

oh, I don't know—probably fourteen or fifteen years old. And I must say, your advice and can-do attitude was invaluable to a girl who only saw her parents a few times a year, if that."

Hildy looked at the ceiling as she blinked. "I'm happy to hear that." She touched the inside corner of her eye and heaved a sigh. "You don't know how wonderful it is to talk to someone about this. Until today, only my editor at the newspaper knew."

I inched forward on the chair. "But you think someone suspected you were Amelia, someone on this steamer? I did see that first note, you know."

"Yes, I was sure you had, but I didn't want to worry you. I thought it would come to nothing. There have been a few times in the past when someone was determined to discover the identity of Amelia Wise. My editor said they've had people watching the newspaper office in hopes of sighting me. One person even went so far as to take a job as a typist in an effort to discover who I was. Of course, it's impossible to find out that way because I never go into the office. My editor sends me a package of letters once a quarter. I write up my replies and send them back."

"And your brother never noticed the letters arriving from the newspaper?"

"He never bothered with the mail. I made sure I handled any packages."

"Is all the subterfuge necessary? Why keep it a secret?"

"Because Amelia Wise makes the newspaper money. If I decide to retire, they can bring on someone else to fill Amelia's shoes and write the answers. If I'm exposed, then I'm not sure what will happen."

She looked over to the letters and broken writing desk.

"But now someone else—someone other than you—does know my identity."

"And I think I know who it is."

# CHAPTER 9

The opening of the Khartoum Medical School marks "an important step in higher education in the Sudan," according to the Governor-General's speech at last week's ceremony.

*—The Standard*

"What? You know who did this?" Hildy gestured to the papers tossed on the floor.

"Was it like this when you came in to change for dinner?"

Hildy looked down at the narrow space between the desk and the bed, a frown on her face. "I don't know. It may have been. I was in such a rush that I didn't even come around the bed. I'd selected my evening gown earlier. It was hanging on the wardrobe door." She nodded to the other side of the room. "Mr. Listergraff invited me to play a game of chess when we returned from the bazaar, and that took all afternoon. I was cutting it rather fine when I came in to change for dinner. I changed and snatched up my shawl. I didn't even sit down at the dressing table, just used my compact to powder my nose on my way down to the main deck."

"Then I do have an idea about who might have done this, but it's a bit of a story," I said, then halted. In my excitement to share my news with Hildy, I'd completely forgotten that if I told her who I thought had taken the letters, I'd have to reveal the embarrassing events of earlier in the afternoon.

Hildy leaned forward. "Yes?"

I hesitated but then gave myself a mental shake and told myself not to be a goose. Hildy was kindhearted, not a vicious gossip.

I cleared my throat. "When we returned to the steamer this afternoon—this sounds awful—Mr. Alexander was passed out in my cabin."

"How horrible! What did you do?"

"I thought he was blotto, but then I realized he was clammy with fever. I didn't want to set any tongues wagging by calling for a steward. Fortunately, Mr. Cordial was nearby. He and I were able to get Mr. Alexander down to his own cabin before summoning Dr. Walsh."

The corners of Hildy's mouth turned down. "Normally, I'd feel sorry for someone who is ill, but I don't have much compassion for Mr. Alexander right now. Why was he in your cabin? He had no business being there."

"I agree, but the interesting thing is that a letter fell out of his pocket. The handwriting was atrocious, but I noticed it was addressed to someone whose first name started with an *A*. At the time, I thought it looked like the name was Amanda." I patted the untidy stack of letters and envelopes on the desk. "But after seeing these, I think I was mistaken, and it was addressed to Amelia. Oh, and the contents of the desk in my cabin had been rifled through as well."

"So, Mr. Alexander broke open my portable writing desk, took at least one letter, and then went to your cabin and looked through your correspondence as well? How very caddish of him." A deep wrinkle appeared between Hildy's eyebrows. "But why would he leave such a mess in both cabins? It would be obvious someone had been in here."

"Perhaps he thought it would be blamed on the crew." I swiveled from side to side on the stool as I said slowly, "Perhaps he thought we were working together—that we were both Amelia Wise?"

"I suppose that's possible. I've heard rumors that *Go Ask Phyllis* is written by two sisters. There are times when the amount of letters seems like an avalanche, and I'd welcome a partner. But why is Mr. Alexander so interested? He's an archaeologist, for goodness' sake. He should be engrossed in ancient history, not letters from people who are pouring out their troubles."

I snapped my fingers. "That may be exactly it. Perhaps he —or someone he knows—wrote a letter to Amelia, and he wants it back."

A pensive look came over Hildy's face. "I am often shocked at the intimate details people confide in Amelia."

I was surprised that she spoke in the third person, as if she thought of Amelia as a separate entity from herself. But I couldn't let myself get sidetracked and didn't interrupt her as she continued, "But searching through another person's belongings? That's *such* unsavory behavior."

"Perhaps that's not the reason. That theory doesn't quite fit with the note that was left in my cabin on the day we departed from Cairo. The tone of it was accusatory. The writer threatened to reveal your true identity but didn't say anything about wanting a letter returned."

Hildy stood and gathered up the letters and envelopes,

sorting them into stacks. "Perhaps he's someone who wrote me, and the advice I gave didn't work out well. Or perhaps that situation happened with one of his family members. I do often worry if I've given the best answer." She tapped the pages of the letters against the desk to align them. "All I know is that I'm going to have a very frank conversation with Mr. Alexander tomorrow."

"I think you should involve the officials from the steamer."

"I suppose I could send for the assistant manager after breakfast," Hildy said in a considering tone.

"Oh. Or perhaps—" I scrambled, trying to think of another person I could suggest she speak to besides Mr. Briarcliff. He'd done an excellent job of keeping his distance from Hildy. I didn't think his guise as Mr. Cordial would last very long if he and Hildy had a one-on-one conversation.

Hildy lifted one hand, palm up. "No, I don't think I will. This is something I should handle myself. The fewer people who know about it, the better."

"I don't know if that's a good idea."

"Oh, pish. Mr. Alexander may have written a vitriolic note or two, but he's a frail fellow in real life. It's amazing how brave people are when they can hide behind the written word. However, when they're face-to-face, they crumple."

I felt a bit sorry for Mr. Alexander, because there was a steadiness, a determination, in Hildy's gaze. Her movements were sharp as she cleared up the last envelopes from the floor. I moved to help her. I had no doubt that if it came to an altercation between her and the weedy Mr. Alexander, Hildy could hold her own, but I said, "I'll go with you."

"All right. I'll seek him out immediately after breakfast. I'm rather done in tonight."

"So tragic, what happened with Mr. Fairweather," I said as I handed her the envelopes. "How is Louisa?"

"Devastated and shaken. She said Mr. Fairweather had a weak heart, but his doctor said he was strong enough for travel and an Egyptian holiday would do him good. Of course, one never knows how long one has left. Miss Entwhistle insisted that Louisa go along and sleep in her cabin tonight. She had her steward bring a cot for herself and told Louisa to take her bed."

"And how are you?"

"Quite fatigued, honestly. It's been a rather trying day."

"Then I'll wish you good night," I said and promised to meet her at breakfast.

I closed her door, but I didn't return to my cabin. Instead, I went to the saloon to get a book. I was far too wound up to sleep. I paused as I stepped into the saloon, surprised to find it still in a state of disarray.

The lamps were still on, and the room had the look of a stage set abandoned in the middle of a play. The spray of dirt next to the overturned plant hadn't been cleaned, used cups and saucers were still out, and the furniture was disarranged. All the ship's attendants would be busy at this time, drawing baths and turning down bedding for the passengers, but I was sure they'd be back later to clean up. The saloon would be spotless in the morning.

I'd thought the room was empty, but a scuffing, scratching sound made me pause.

Mice? I certainly hoped it wasn't mice. I drew back a step and peered around carefully. Then I located the source of the noise—a man crawling around on the floor near the grouping of chairs where Mr. Fairweather had died. He shifted, ducking his head as he reached under a chair. After a moment, he continued along on his hands and knees, reaching under the next chair. Even though he was scrabbling along the floor with his back to me, I recognized the thinning sandy hair and saggy pockets of the suit jacket along with the faint woodsy scent of pipe smoke. Dr. Walsh let out a grunt of satisfaction, took a handkerchief from his pocket, and shook it out.

I leaned down to see what he was doing. He placed the handkerchief over a coffee cup that had fallen and rolled under one of the chairs. He carefully picked it up, keeping his hands on the handkerchief, not the handle of the cup. He added it to a small tray where several other coffee cups were lined up. Then he braced a hand on the arm of a chair and used it to press himself up to his feet. His back was turned to me, and instead of greeting him, I stayed silent. He picked up the tray and left the room through the door on the opposite side of the room from me, never once turning around.

# CHAPTER 10

Miss Penelope Fairfax, the noted botanist, has taken up residence at the Semiramis for a fortnight. She aims to study the flora of the Nile Delta during her stay.

*—Arrivals and Departures, The Nile*

Several hours later I adjusted my pillow behind my neck and flipped another page in an old issue of *The Saturday Evening Post*. After Dr. Walsh left the saloon, I'd known I'd never be able to concentrate on a novel that evening. I'd picked up a few magazines at random and returned to my cabin, lost in thought. Why was Dr. Walsh collecting the coffee cups? And why was he being so careful not to touch them? Really, there could only be one answer to that, couldn't there? He was being careful of fingerprints. But why would he do that? Did he have some suspicions about Mr. Fairweather's death? He must.

The sounds of people moving about the steamer gradually died away as I turned the pages. I skimmed over ads for the Moon motor car and Lysol disinfectant as my mind replayed the day's events. I reached the end of the magazine and picked up another magazine. I blinked at the title of the story on the cover, *The Agony Column* by Earl Derr Biggers.

I let out a laugh. "How appropriate," I murmured and snuggled down in the bed, propping the magazine up with a pillow. The story of a chance meeting between a man and woman and their communication through newspaper personal ads caught my attention. It was only when I reached the end that I realized it was a story told in installments. My arm flopped down on the bed. "Rats!"

Now I'd have to dig through all the magazines discarded by passengers and hope to find the continuation of the story, because I did want to find out what happened. Having run out of reading material, I snapped off the light despite not feeling the least bit sleepy.

After an hour of turning from one side to the other, flipping my pillow to the cool side, then plumping it and turning it again, I snapped on the light and reached for my dressing gown and slippers. Perhaps the clouds had dispersed, and I could do some stargazing since I couldn't sleep.

Cool night air whispered around my ankles as I gently closed my cabin door. A breeze stirred the fabric of my dressing gown. Maybe it was because of the brisk wind that no bugs zoomed past.

I was on the side of the steamer that looked across to the bank on the far side of the river from the village where we'd stopped for the night. A thin line of light showed along the lower edge of my cabin window, but everyone must have turned in, because the steamer was still and dark.

I moved away from the tiny thread of light into full darkness. After the brightness of the lamp in my cabin, my eyes weren't adjusted to the darkness, and I couldn't make out many details. I reached out blindly until my hand connected with the railing. Then I drew in a deep breath of crisp air, absorbing the stillness of the night as I leaned my forearms on the railing. The clouds still obscured the stars, cloaking the Nile in darkness. The only noises were the faint creaks of the steamer and the lap of the waves.

After a few seconds, a prickly sensation came over me, and I slowly turned to my right. The doors of the cabins had small, illuminated lights over the name cards that listed the passenger staying in the cabin, but I was far enough away from the faint pinpoints of light that there was no ambient light. I might as well have been wearing a blindfold. I couldn't distinguish any trace of a change in the curtain of darkness around me, but I felt as if another person were near me. "Is someone there?"

A deep voice answered, "It's Mr. Briarcliff."

I actually jumped and gripped the railing. He was so close, only a foot or so away. "How long have you been there?"

"Since before you came out. I didn't want to frighten you when you first stepped out of your cabin, and then I didn't want to disturb you." His voice shifted, becoming more muted, and I realized he'd turned away. "No stars tonight, but most passengers don't think the night sky is as spectacular as the sunsets."

"I disagree. One isn't better than the other. They're both stunning. I don't think I've ever seen so many stars as I have the last few nights. It's dazzling. I truly understand now why it's called the Milky Way." The previous evening, the stars had seemed to be poured out like a spill of milk, but now the night sky was empty. It was as if a chalkboard had been erased. "Mr. Listergraff said the clouds probably won't linger. Why was the sky so clear the other night?"

"Something to do with the dryness of the air, I think. We'll probably have a clear night tomorrow."

We stood in silence for a few moments, and I was surprised to find that I didn't mind Mr. Briarcliff's presence.

I had my head cranked back and was concentrating on a section of the sky, trying to decide if one area was a bit lighter than the rest, and if there was possibly a thinning in the clouds, when Mr. Briarcliff said, "Why have you never been to Egypt, Miss Windway? Your father's in the diplomatic service, isn't he?"

"He and my mother traveled. They left me at home." I realized my words were sharp, so I added in as breezy a tone as I could manage, "I have always wanted to see the pyramids and the tombs. That's why I took the job as a travel companion."

Fabric rustled. "Care for a cigarette?"

I leaned my elbows on the railing again. "No, thank you. I don't smoke, but you go ahead."

"Neither do I." I thought there was a small sigh in his words. "Except on days like today."

"I understand."

His lighter flared, illuminating his face and flashing off his glasses. He'd removed his jacket, and the white sleeve of his shirt glowed brightly for a moment, then he snapped the lighter closed, and we were in darkness again. "It's not a good habit to cultivate. I'm sure you're much better off not smoking. I admire your self-discipline."

"You admire something about me? Shocking," I said with a little laugh. "But it's nothing as noble as willpower. Cigarettes are a frivolous expense that I can't afford. A working girl must watch her funds."

I could tell from the faint glow of his cigarette as it moved through the air that his posture mirrored mine, with his forearms braced on the railing. "Your parents don't support you?" He sounded genuinely taken aback.

"No." To move away from the subject of my parents, I asked, "And your family? Are they in business here? Or perhaps the military?"

"My parents died in the Spanish flu."

"Oh." I swallowed and straightened, running my hand along the smooth wood of the railing. "I'm sorry."

"Thank you. It was only a few years ago, but it seems much longer. I have a sister, who lives in England. She's older and quite bossy."

I looked out across the blackness, where I knew the waves of the Nile were undulating. "There was a time when I was young that I thought it would be nice to have a sister— or any sibling at all, really." What was wrong with me? Why was I telling Mr. Briarcliff things I'd never uttered aloud before? It must have been the enclosing darkness that was bringing out these statements. Before I let any other tidbits about myself escape, I turned in his direction. "What brought you to Egypt, Mr. Briarcliff?"

"Does one need a reason to visit Egypt?"

"No, but you don't fit into the usual categories."

"Categories?"

"Yes, since arriving here, I've realized that there are only a few reasons the British come to Egypt. Some people are interested in antiquities and want to see the sites. Others— mostly women, but some young men as well—are here for the *fishing fleet.* They hope to catch a spouse without going all the way to India. Still others are in Egypt for the social life. And finally, another group is here because their company or the military moved them here. You don't fall into any of those brackets."

"Keen insights. I agree with your assessment about the types of travelers, by the way. But you need to add another category—the rambler. I was knocking around the world after the war. I'd seen most of Europe, so I bought a ticket for Alexandria. It's as simple as that."

"But you don't seem to be rambling now. Will you stay in Egypt indefinitely?"

"No, I don't think so. I suppose one would call this a lull in my wanderings. Once I was here, I met Mr. Martin and offered to solve some problems for him."

"I see. So you created a job and pitched yourself as a candidate for it?"

"A man has to eat, after all, even while rambling. But as I told you when we first met, I'm a free agent. I rarely do the expected thing."

"Neither do I, much to my parents' chagrin."

"Is that the source of the rift between you?"

"That and about twenty years of absence. In the case of a parent and child, absence does not make the heart grow fonder." We were drifting to personal subjects that were as tender as a toothache, so I added, "But I don't know that a single person warrants a whole category."

"Aren't you a rambler too, Miss Windway?"

The sound of a muffled thud floated through the air. Mr. Briarcliff said, "Was that you? Are you all right?"

"It wasn't me."

"I haven't moved either."

Another clatter rang out, louder this time. The noise came from the larger cabins near the bow of the steamer. A beam of light traced across the window of one of the cabins, briefly illuminating the gap between the half-drawn curtains. In the blackness, it glared for a second, like a light-house beacon.

The red tip of the cigarette arced through the air into the water. "That's the Fairweather cabin."

"But Hildy said Louisa is staying in Miss Entwhistle's cabin tonight."

The air stirred as Mr. Briarcliff moved past me.

I wasn't about to be left alone in the darkness with strange sounds ringing out. I followed him, letting one hand trace along the railing and extending the other in front of me to make sure I didn't run into Mr. Briarcliff's back. I followed the sound of his footsteps, which turned and went along the passage that divided the first- and second-class cabins.

Once we were on the port side, where a few lights from the village still glowed, I could distinguish a broad swath of white, Mr. Briarcliff's shirt. I tracked the shifting white square, passing first Hildy's cabin, then the Walshes' cabin, which were both in darkness.

As we approached the Fairweather cabin, a bar of light glowed in the narrow gap between the door and the threshold, sliding back and forth as the torch moved. Mr. Briarcliff rapped his knuckles against the panel of the door. In the stillness of the desert night, it sounded as loud as a gunshot. "Mrs. Fairweather?"

The light winked out. Mr. Briarcliff raised his hand to knock again, but the cabin door burst open, banging into him.

A blinding flash of light seared across my eyes as the torch snapped on. Someone charged through the doorway, shoving me hard on the shoulder to force their way past. The beam of light waved wildly back and forth as Mr. Briarcliff and I bumped into each other. Then the torch went dark, and rapid footfalls pounded toward the saloon.

# CHAPTER 11

The upcoming inaugural Winter Olympics will be held in Chamonix, France. Athletes from 16 nations will compete in ice and snow sports, with Great Britain's curling team and figure skaters among those vying for medals.

—*The Standard*

M r. Briarcliff and I did an awkward dance trying to stay upright. "Are you all right?"

"Yes," I said. "You?"

"Fine, except for my pride." Mr. Briarcliff let go of my arm, and we both dashed toward the saloon. It was silent and empty. Mr. Briarcliff hurried to the door on the far side of the room. I paused to switch on a lamp. No one lurked behind the bookcase or the chairs.

Mr. Briarcliff returned. "They've gone to ground. It's as quiet as a church out there. Whomever it was either went into a cabin on this deck or slipped down the stairs to the main deck."

"Oh, your nose is bleeding."

Mr. Briarcliff pressed the back of his hand to his nose. When he took his hand away and saw the trace of red, he blinked and wavered a moment.

I took a step toward him.

He muttered, "A curse on all outward opening doors," as he shook his head, sniffed deeply, and pulled a handkerchief from his pocket. "I'd better check the Fairweather cabin. You needn't come along," he said with his head tilted back as he walked across the saloon to the door we'd entered through.

I turned off the light and trotted across the room as fast as I dared in the darkness. "You must be joking. I'm not going to my cabin now."

"Of course not."

The door to the Fairweather cabin hung open. When we stepped inside, Mr. Briarcliff flicked on his lighter, using it to illuminate his path to the bedside table, where he turned on the lamp. A few things had been disarranged in the cabin. A pile of toppled books and a fallen ashtray seemed to be the worst of it.

I straightened a crooked lampshade. "At least nothing's broken." I turned in a circle, noting that the desk did not appear to have been touched. "I wouldn't have thought Mr. Alexander would be able to get out of bed, much less rifle though another cabin."

"You think it was Mr. Alexander who was in here?" Mr. Briarcliff lowered the angle of his head and experimentally removed the handkerchief from his nose.

The bleeding had stopped, and he daubed at his nose a few times as I said, "Well, he was in my cabin and—"

I stopped short as I realized I couldn't say anything about

my speculation that it was Mr. Alexander who had been in Hildy's cabin because I'd promised not to tell anyone about her role as Amelia Wise. I bent to pick up the books to cover my gaffe, hoping Mr. Briarcliff wouldn't realize I hadn't finished my sentence.

"And?"

Of course he wouldn't miss something like that. I stacked the books on a shelf. "And . . . since he was in my room without permission, it's reasonable to assume the intruder here is the same person, isn't it?"

"Except Mr. Alexander was quite ill when I left his cabin. As you said, it's doubtful he's up and about." He folded the handkerchief and put it away, his frowning gaze fixed on me. "You have a peculiar expression on your face, Miss Windway."

"Me?" I returned the ashtray to a side table.

"Yes, you, Miss Windway." He stepped toward me and leaned down so that his face was level with mine. His gaze darted back and forth across my face. "In fact, you look as if you know something that you're not sharing."

I closed my eyes briefly, partly in exasperation but also to block out Mr. Briarcliff's intense stare. He was so close—uncomfortably close—and for some reason I felt short of breath. "I'm afraid I can't say anything else."

Mr. Briarcliff opened his mouth to argue, so I quickly added, "You have your secrets, and I'm bound by a promise to keep someone else's secret. Surely you understand I can't share something I've promised not to. That wouldn't be cricket."

He looked disgruntled but gave a little head bob of a nod. "Fine. I won't press you about it, but I imagine it would be prudent to look in on Mr. Alexander—make sure he's recovering from his fever."

"Excellent idea."

"Probably not a good idea for you to accompany me, though."

"Sadly, I agree with you." It wouldn't do for me to be spotted on another deck at such a late hour, particularly near a young man's cabin. "You'll tell me what you find out?"

"Why would I do that? You're not sharing information."

"Sworn to secrecy, remember." I gave him my best wide-eyed pleading look, and he sighed.

"Fine. First thing in the morning."

A NOTE WAS beside my breakfast plate the next morning. It was unsigned, but I knew the moment I unfolded it that it was from Mr. Briarcliff.

*Miss Windway,*

*I'm sure you'll be thankful to hear that I was not sworn to secrecy last evening and can report, as promised, what I've learned. Dr. Walsh was leaving Mr. Alexander's room when I arrived. The doctor confirmed he'd looked in on the patient and sat with him for about half an hour before I arrived. While I wouldn't trust Mr. Alexander's statements—I don't know the man—Dr. Walsh is upstanding, and I do believe him. So, Mr. Alexander couldn't have been the intruder.*

I put away the note and carried on a conversation with Hildy at breakfast, but all the while my thoughts were churning. Was there a *second* person on the steamer who was searching cabins? Perhaps I was wrong, and Mr. Alexander hadn't pinched a letter from Hildy's writing desk. Perhaps the name on the envelope had been Amanda, as I originally thought.

We had an excursion to the rock-cut tombs in the morning, but I wasn't able to give my attention to the site. I was too preoccupied with everything that had happened in the last day. We were a smaller party that made the trek to the tombs. Louisa and Miss Fairweather stayed behind on the steamer, and Dr. Walsh said Mr. Alexander, who hadn't appeared for breakfast, was still not feeling well and would spend the day in his cabin. I'd been disappointed to hear the news that Mr. Alexander wouldn't be joining us. I wanted to watch his reactions as Hildy and I interacted with him, but that would have to wait for tea when we returned to the steamer.

Honestly, I didn't take in much about the tombs. One of the illustrations of a corpse on a bier being transported to his tomb brought back thoughts of Mr. Fairweather lying dead on the floor of the saloon. From that moment on, I simply took photos of the colorful reliefs. I'd match up my pictures later with details from the guidebooks.

That afternoon we sailed to Asyut, passing many villages and more tombs cut into the rock, which were visible from the Nile. We went by Amarna and the palace ruins of the heretic pharaoh who shifted worship in Egypt to a single god. We cruised between islands, and then the mountains closed in on the Nile. Hassan had said this part of the river was dangerous because of sandbanks and the twisting course of the river. The caw of birds that nested in the cliffs along the river filled the air as swarms swooped to and fro. Eventually, the mountains receded and the turns of the river became less sharp as it widened into broad sinuous curves before we reached Asyut, where we had the option of going to the local bazaar. I went along and took some photos, then returned to the steamer before I was tempted to spend more money.

Soon we were underway again, and I worked in my cabin for the rest of the day, jotting down impressions of the sites we'd seen. I'd often found that if I worked on some other task, it seemed to free up my mind on some other level to unknot worrisome questions, but that was not the case today.

I went down to dinner still ruminating over the strange events of the previous day and night. Why had Dr. Walsh been collecting coffee cups? Could I casually ask Seffie about her husband's actions? Was there a way to drop that into after-dinner conversations? Probably not.

Why had Mr. Alexander been in my cabin? Had he been in Hildy's cabin and taken an envelope addressed to Amelia Wise? Did he now know that Hildy was an agony aunt? Hopefully, Mr. Alexander would be there this evening and either Hildy or I could talk with him and perhaps find some answers for his strange behavior.

Disappointingly, Mr. Alexander was again absent from dinner. Hildy and I exchanged a look as we were seated. "Odd that he's not left his cabin all day," she said.

I knew exactly who she was referring to. "I agree. You should talk to Seffie after dinner. She'd know if Dr. Walsh is still checking on him."

The Fairweather ladies were also absent from dinner, and it was a subdued evening. Hildy wanted to walk after dinner, so we made several laps around the steamer, and then I played patience in the saloon while she and Mr. Lister-graff battled it out at the chessboard. As I returned to my cabin that evening, Hildy caught up with me. "I just spoke to Seffie. Mr. Alexander is quite ill—worse than he was yesterday—so I may have to wait several days to speak to him."

"How frustrating," I said, then stifled a yawn and apologized. My late night the previous evening had caught up with me.

Hildy patted me on the shoulder. "You look done in. Go on to bed. I'm sure I'll get everything sorted out, even if I have to wait a few days."

I was up early the next morning and felt refreshed after a good night's sleep. I was the first and only passenger to sit down to breakfast in the deserted dining room. I found letters at my plate, which had been collected at Asyut, one of the stops where mail was sent for steamer passengers. The S.S. *Cleopatra* had a postbox, which had been emptied that morning. Any letters we'd put in the post would be sent by train to Cairo.

I used my knife to slit the envelopes. I had a request for a lecture from a ladies' group in England as well as a letter from Megs, my favorite governess. A few passengers arrived while I was eating, including Miss Entwhistle and Mr. Shaw. Since there was no sign of Hildy, who must have been either having a lie-in or had requested a tray in her cabin, and Mr. Alexander was again absent, I spent the morning writing replies to my letters and then attempting to photograph wildlife.

I had plenty of images of the Nile banks, the river traffic, and modern Egyptians. I snapped photos of water buffalo, some elegant egrets, and a heron, patiently watching the shallows for its lunch. Some vultures circled, their inky wings dark against the blue sky, but they were too high for me to get a good photo. That wasn't a problem, though. I doubted my ladies' groups wanted to see pictures of carrion-eating birds. They wanted to see something exotic, like a hippopotamus or crocodile, but when I'd asked Hassan about them, he'd told me the chances of sighting one of those animals was decidedly slim. He'd apologized as if it were his fault that the wildlife was limited to birds and water buffalo.

In the afternoon, needing something to fill my time until Mr. Alexander appeared, or I worked out how to ask either Seffie or Dr. Walsh about the coffee cups, I went along to the saloon. I sat down on the carpet in front of the bookcase and spent a good while searching through the magazines for the issue of *The Saturday Evening Post* that contained the continuation of the *Agony Column* story.

It was late afternoon when Mr. Briarcliff entered the saloon and stepped around one of the stacks of magazines I'd piled up on the floor around me. "Goodness, what's all this?"

I explained my quest. "I've found the issue with the second installment, but I had a look at the end, and the story concludes in the next issue. Unfortunately, I haven't been able to turn up the third part, and I've been through all the magazines. It's quite vexing."

"Yes, there's nothing more annoying than not knowing the solution to a mystery."

"Quite." I began restoring the scattered magazines to their place on the bottom shelf of the bookcase. "Rather like a certain recent nocturnal incident. Any news on that?"

"No." He picked up a pile of periodicals. "I spoke to Mrs. Fairweather. She had a look around. Nothing of hers is missing. Mr. Shaw said the items on the desk might have been shuffled around, but he's not sure. Nothing was taken as far as he can tell."

I glanced around to make sure the saloon was still empty, then reached up and took the stack from him. "What about

Mr. Fairweather? Did the authorities at Asyut take charge of his body?" I hadn't wanted to mention the subject to any of the passengers—rather unseemly to ask about a dead body —but I couldn't help but wonder if the body was still on board. I was sure the other passengers were wondering, too, but we were British and supremely talented at ignoring uncomfortable topics. However, Mr. Briarcliff wasn't a passenger, and after our nighttime conversation, I felt I could broach the subject with him.

"No, the officials insisted that we sail on to Luxor and let the authorities there take over. I suppose they're correct. Luxor is a larger city with a British cemetery where he can be buried."

So, Mr. Fairweather's body was still in the cold storage area on the steamer. I considered telling him about Dr. Walsh's collection of coffee cups, but I held back because Miss Entwhistle and Seffie entered the saloon. They settled on a sofa and rang for tea. Mr. Briarcliff nodded to the ladies, then wished me a good afternoon before departing. Shortly after he left, Louisa arrived with Mr. Shaw, who carried a briefcase. He trailed along behind her, his chin pressed into his collar, but his face wasn't his usual impassive blank stare. Was there a bit of a disgruntled look about him? I wasn't sure, because it was hard to see his full expression with his head ducked.

I hadn't seen Louisa since Mr. Fairweather's death. The death of her husband had clearly sapped her energy. She was moving without the usual bounce in her step, and her eyes were pink-rimmed and puffy. She gestured with a book she was carrying to one of the tables where the passengers played cards in the evening. "Have a seat there, Mr. Shaw. It will do you good to get out of that stuffy room."

Mr. Shaw set his briefcase on the table and pulled out the

chair that would put his back to the room as Louisa went and sat down with Seffie and Miss Entwhistle. I replaced the last of the magazines and went to join the ladies.

"How are you, my dear?" Seffie asked Louisa as I took a seat.

Louisa pushed her curls from her forehead. "Honestly, I'm devastated and flabbergasted. I still can't believe Ambrose is gone. It all happened so quickly. I keep expecting to see him walk through a door and say it was all a mistake." She gave her head a little shake as if to get rid of that image, then she reached out and patted Miss Entwhistle's hand. "But I can't impose on you for a moment more."

Miss Entwhistle said, "It's no bother at all, I assure you."

Louisa continued as if Miss Entwhistle hadn't spoken, "I do appreciate you letting me stay in your cabin, I really do. However, I can't impose on you any longer. I had my belongings returned to my cabin." She looked around as if truly taking in her surroundings for the first time. "I can't spend the rest of the trip in a cabin. I need fresh air—as does Mr. Shaw."

Her gaze went to Mr. Shaw, whose back was now curved over the table as he wrote, papers stacked around him. Louisa lowered her voice. "He's a bit nervy—aftereffects of the war, you know—and I thought it best to get him out of our cabin for a bit as well. I had no idea he was working away there at Ambrose's desk—as if Ambrose would look in on him at any moment to check his progress. When I arrived at the cabin, Mr. Shaw said he'd move down to his own cabin, but I think he'll do much better up here, where there's a good breeze and he's surrounded by people."

Seffie had brought some embroidery, and she was threading a needle with bright yellow thread. "It's so important not to isolate oneself. Being sequestered was the worst thing about the sanatorium. It was so grim and ghastly, being separated from my usual life." She pulled the fabric tight, and her needle flashed back and forth as she made tiny stitches. "But I came through it. I'm glad you've joined us here, my dear."

"You've all been so kind. I do appreciate it, all you've done—the checking in on me, the kind notes you sent." Louisa's face contorted as she was overcome with emotion, but she regained control of herself, drawing in a deep breath. "I think I'll just read now—or try to read. I haven't been able to do much of anything."

"Give it a try," Seffie advised, and Louisa put on a pair of gold-framed spectacles and opened her book.

Miss Entwhistle set her artist box on the table and took out a sketchbook and pencils. She angled her chair so that she could see the whole saloon and began making broad strokes on the page, capturing the general outline of the room. I settled in with the second installment of *The Agony Column*. I'd at least get to find out what happened in this part of the story.

A quarter hour or so passed in silence except for the scritch of Miss Entwhistle's pencil over the paper and the rustle of paper as I turned a magazine page. I was on the last few paragraphs of the installment when Louisa closed her book. "It's no use. I can't concentrate. I've read the same chapter twice, and I couldn't tell you even one character's name."

Seffie examined her stitches and added a few more to the row. "That's to be expected. It will take a while—probably a long while—before you're able to settle."

"My thoughts keep circling around and around. Was the heat too much for Ambrose? If we'd stayed in England, would he still be alive? If I hadn't insisted on this holiday . . ."

Seffie snipped the yellow thread. "Everyone asks those questions after a death. Most likely, the same thing would have happened if you'd been home."

"Ambrose seemed fine to me." Louisa lowered her voice, her gaze going to Mr. Shaw, who was still bent over the desk. "And I couldn't get more than a few words out of Mr. Shaw. He spent an hour with Ambrose immediately before he . . . passed on. I wish Mr. Shaw would tell me more about those last moments. If I knew more, it might ease my mind."

Miss Entwhistle's pencil, which had been moving rapidly back and forth as she shaded in the side of the saloon that was out of the sun, stopped. She studied Louisa with a look that I couldn't decipher. For a moment, I thought she seemed cross, but then her expression shifted to . . . pity? I must have been mistaken, though, because when Miss Entwhistle spoke it was in a bland, deliberate tone, with no trace of either anger or sympathy. "He was quite talkative immediately after."

"What?" Louisa put her book on a nearby table and turned to Miss Entwhistle. "I didn't realize you'd talked to him."

"I wasn't sure if you wanted to hear anything about those last hours, so I didn't say anything earlier." Miss Entwhistle looked over her shoulder to make sure we hadn't drawn Mr. Shaw's attention, then she said, "I simply listened while he spoke. I wouldn't call it a conversation. Shock does that to people. Sometimes they're quite verbose."

"What did he say?"

"He was extremely upset, of course. He said it didn't make sense because Mr. Fairweather had been fine when they were working."

Louisa scooted forward on her chair. "Anything else?"

Miss Entwhistle pursed her lips and moved them to the side, her unfocused gaze directed at the floor. "Let me think . . . Mr. Shaw said your husband was 'in a mood.' He was put out that they'd run out of stationery, and he was irritated because Mr. Shaw was taking too long with the business correspondence. Something about some shares that needed to be sold. Mr. Shaw said he was working on a long letter to one of the subsidiaries, and Mr. Fairweather became impatient and said he'd write the last letter himself. Mr. Shaw protested, but Mr. Fairweather insisted."

Louisa chuckled. "That sounds exactly like him. Patience was never one of his strengths. What else?"

Miss Entwhistle sat silent and erect for a moment with a tension in her body that seemed at odds with the conversation. Surely someone who had nursing experience wouldn't have difficulty describing the last moments of a patient to a family member? Had she and Mr. Shaw been close? She paused a moment and continued in her measured tone. "Oh yes, I remember one other thing. Mr. Shaw said they were in a rush because Mr. Fairweather knew you were in the saloon, and he didn't want to keep you waiting too long."

Louisa let out a little huff of a laugh. "Yes, that was Ambrose exactly, thoughtful and thoughtless at the same time."

"Then Mr. Shaw repeated himself quite a bit, about how it just wasn't possible. That's all, I believe."

"I see. Thank you. That does help a bit."

Seffie said, "And here's the tea. Perfect timing."

Mr. Shaw pushed back his chair. He'd quickly packed up his case, and a neat stack of sealed and stamped envelopes rested on the center of the desk. Louisa raised her voice. "Do join us for a cup of tea, Mr. Shaw."

"Thank you, but I'm not"—he pressed a hand to his chest —"feeling well." His words were labored. "I think, I'll rest . . . in my cabin . . ."

Miss Entwhistle slapped her sketchbook down and stood. "You're quite flushed, Mr. Shaw." She went to him and took his arm. "Have a seat—"

He gasped, clawed at his collar, then fell forward, knocking his head against the edge of the desk with a crack that made me wince.

# CHAPTER 12

Mr. P's demonstration of his steel-shaft golf clubs is the current topic of conversation among the sport set in Cairo. Leaving his wood clubs behind for his recent round of golf, he showed off the new swing the steel clubs require. The dramatic improvement in his game suggests his fellow members might soon follow in his footsteps.

*—About Town, The Nile*

Miss Entwhistle tried to catch Mr. Shaw, but she wasn't able to. He slipped through her hands and landed hard on the floor. The steward, who'd arrived with the tea, was passing by at that moment and swerved to avoid Mr. Shaw. The teapot and cups rained down in a clatter of shattering china.

I dropped the magazine and hurried over, crouching down near Miss Entwhistle, who was on her knees beside Mr. Shaw. She loosened his collar and pressed her fingers to his neck, ignoring the rivulet of blood trickling from a cut on his forehead. She drew her hand back from his neck.

"Can I help? What do you—" Her expression stopped me like a brick wall had been thrown up in my path.

Eyes wide and face as pale as the bits of porcelain scattered across the floor, she said, "He's dead."

I got to my feet and turned to the steward, who was gathering up broken crockery. "Find Dr. Walsh and bring him here immediately. Tell him to bring his medical bag."

Seffie had her arm around Louisa, who looked stunned and sat with both hands over her mouth, rocking back and forth.

Dr. Walsh arrived moments later, black bag in hand. He avoided the small pool of blood on the carpet near Mr. Shaw's head as he squatted on the opposite side of Mr. Shaw's body from Miss Entwhistle. A few seconds later he swiveled around on the balls of his feet, examined the desktop, then looked over his shoulder, still crouched low. "Who's been at this desk?" he demanded, his gaze going to each of us. "Who's been around Mr. Shaw?"

The sharpness of his tone startled me. Seffie's head snapped toward him. She'd been patting Louisa's back, and she continued to do so, but the look on her face as she locked eyes with her husband told me something was wrong. Seffie said in her usual calm tone, "I don't believe anyone was near him." She looked around our little group for confirmation.

I said, "He'd been sitting there alone for, I don't know, probably half an hour."

Miss Entwhistle had risen and moved a few steps back. She wiped her fingers on her handkerchief, leaving bright red smears. "I wasn't watching the time, but that sounds about right."

Dr. Walsh stood and placed his hands on his hips, then

his gaze went to the marks on Miss Entwhistle's handkerchief, and his eyebrows crinkled together. "Are you sure?"

The steward returned with a bucket and a mop, but Dr. Walsh threw up his hand, palm up, fingers splayed. "Stop. Don't come any closer."

Seffie stood up. "What is it, my dear? What's happened?"

"He may have been poisoned. We mustn't disturb the scene."

Louisa swayed, but Seffie caught her arm before she slipped off her chair. She pushed Louisa's head down and said in an unruffled voice, "Just breathe. Take a few moments and breathe."

Dr. Walsh checked his watch as he said, "We must leave everything in place so that the officials can investigate once we reach Tahta tonight." Miss Entwistle looked from her handkerchief to the blood that had soaked into the rug. Her voice was brisk as she said, "I don't see how that will be possible. We still have several hours until we dock tonight. The weather is quite warm. Even if we have the canvas panels lowered, we can't completely seal off the saloon. The heat, not to mention the insects . . . it wouldn't be healthy."

Louisa sat up slowly. "I'm all right now. I'm frightfully sorry. It's just too much."

Seffie said, "Yes, it is. Let's go rest in my cabin for a moment." Seffie put a hand under Louisa's elbow and helped her to her feet. They departed with Seffie murmuring, "It must have been food going off."

I turned to Dr. Walsh but kept my voice low. "Mr.—um— Cordial told me Mr. Fairweather's body is still on board because the authorities at Asyut wouldn't take charge of it. They said officials in Luxor would handle it. The same thing might happen in this situation."

Dr. Walsh pushed both hands into the droopy pockets of

his linen suit jacket and considered Mr. Shaw's body. "If that's the case, then we'll definitely have to move him." He reached down and ran his hand over Mr. Shaw's eyes, closing them before straightening and turning back to me. "Miss Windway, your camera. Do you have any film left?"

"Yes, several rolls." I had been carefully doling out my film. It was a delicate balance of taking enough photos so that I had several to choose from but not taking an over-abundance of photos and running out of film before I could purchase more during one of our excursions.

"Would you photograph this?" He waved his hand, encompassing Mr. Shaw's body and the surrounding area. "I'll purchase more film to replace what's used. If you don't feel comfortable doing it, I'll do it, but I imagine you have more skill with the camera than I do."

"I'm not squeamish. I'll do it," I said, but as I went to my cabin, my legs felt unsteady, as if I were walking on ice instead of the deck. I'd just seen a man die. The thought echoed around in my head. He'd been standing there, packing up his case, and less than a minute later he was sprawled on the floor, lifeless.

I drew in a deep breath and steadied myself. I'd told Dr. Walsh he could count on me. I'd take the photos and then have a restorative cup of tea. I retrieved my camera from my cabin and slipped the strap around my neck. I stopped on my way back to the saloon and rapped my knuckles on Hildy's door. She called out that it was open, and I stepped inside. "Hildy, something awful has happened."

She was seated at the desk and swiveled toward me as I came in. I told her about Mr. Shaw's death, and she put down her pen. "Goodness gracious. How terrible. Are you all right?" She came across the room and gripped my hands. "Gracious! You're icy."

"I'm—I don't know—gobsmacked, I suppose."

Hildy chafed my hands. "Let me ring for tea."

"I'll join you for a cup of tea later. I must return to the saloon. Dr. Walsh has asked me to take photos."

"Photos? Whatever for?"

"He said Mr. Shaw was poisoned, and his death must be investigated. He intended to leave Mr. Shaw's body where it was until we docked tonight, but Miss Entwhistle pointed out that wasn't practical with the heat. Dr. Walsh must suspect foul play of some sort. Seffie said something to Louisa about food going off, but it must be more than ptomaine poisoning since he wants photos. He didn't say anything specific, though."

"Of course not. Doctors are the worst people to pin down."

"I should get back to the saloon."

"But do you feel up to it?"

"Yes, I feel better just speaking to you about it. I think it will be better to do something at the moment, and I feel most comfortable behind the camera."

"Yes, action is often better than idleness. Can I do anything?"

"You might look in on Louisa. She seemed quite wobbly."

"Anyone would be. I feel a bit wobbly myself at the news, and I only spoke to the man a few times. Two deaths on this steamer!"

"Seffie took Louisa away from the saloon to her cabin—the Walshes', I mean."

Hildy blotted her letter and capped her pen. "I'll look in on them."

When I returned to the saloon, Mr. Briarcliff was entering through the other door. He scanned the room, but his gaze jumped away from Mr. Shaw's body. I couldn't see Mr. Briarcliff's expression because his spectacles caught the light, but he swallowed and ran a finger around his collar. He shifted his stance, turning away from Mr. Shaw's body and focusing on me. "Miss Windway," he began, his tone exasperated, "you can't—"

Dr. Walsh jumped in. "I asked her to take photos, Mr. Cordial, as it's not practical to leave things as they are with the heat and the time it will take to get to Luxor. We'll have to go on to Luxor with the body, correct? We won't be able to preserve the scene."

Mr. Briarcliff still had a scowl on his face as he looked at me, but he replied to Dr. Walsh. "Yes, I've just spoken to the captain, and that's what he's decided. We'll overnight at Tahta, then spend Sunday on the Nile as planned. We'll arrive at Luxor on Monday evening, skipping the planned excursion to Dendera. The Blue Lotus Line will either compensate the passengers for the missed excursion or arrange a visit to Dendera from Luxor."

Dr. Walsh nodded as he took out his pipe. "Then the Luxor officials will have no choice but to rely on photos." He said to me, "Go ahead, Miss Windway. Photos of everything in this area, please."

Dr. Walsh paused in lighting his pipe, stepped closer to Mr. Briarcliff, and peered up at his face. "You're quite pale, Mr. Cordial. Are you all right?"

Mr. Briarcliff drew in a deep breath. "Fine. I'm perfectly fine." He motioned for Dr. Walsh to follow him, then went across the room and turned so that his back was to me. They spoke in a quiet huddle as I snapped away. I took multiple photographs of poor Mr. Shaw's body from every angle I could manage, then I got closer shots of the items on the floor, including the broken teapot, the soggy sugar cubes, the shattered china, and the scattered spoons. I rounded off that set of photos with several of Mr. Shaw's briefcase, which had also fallen under the desk and was spattered with drops of tea.

Mr. Briarcliff left, his gaze on his watch as he strode from the room. I finished up with a few wider photographs of the whole saloon, then I went to Dr. Walsh. He'd taken out his little pencil and notebook, but he looked up as I approached and said, "I've probably taken far more photographs than are needed."

"Better to have too many than too few."

"Spoken like a photographer. What should I do with the film?" I removed it from my camera and transferred it to the small canister. "Should I give it to you for safe-keeping?"

"I believe Mr. Cordial should take charge of it until we arrive in Luxor."

I dropped it in my pocket. "I'll see that he gets it. Is there anything else I can do?" Two stewards had arrived with sheets and were using two long poles to create a makeshift stretcher.

Dr. Walsh considered for a moment, then said, "Miss Fairweather should be informed of the situation, I believe. Mr. Shaw was traveling with the Fairweather party."

"Yes, that's true. I can do that."

"I should stay here and oversee the removal of Mr. Shaw's body, but if she doesn't handle it well, do send for me. She was quite distraught over her brother's death. I can give her another sleeping draught if needed."

I put my camera away in my cabin and met Hildy as I came out again. I asked, "How is Louisa?"

"Still shocked, of course, but otherwise all right."

"It's completely understandable. Dr. Walsh asked if I

could break the news to Miss Fairweather about Mr. Shaw. Would you come with me?"

"Yes, of course."

"How much should we tell her?" I wondered. "Should I tell her Dr. Walsh thinks the death was poisoning?"

As we walked to the stern, where Miss Fairweather's cabin was located, the rhythmic churn of the steamer's paddlewheel grew louder. Hildy said, "I suppose it depends on how she takes the news of Mr. Shaw's death."

Miss Fairweather's cabin was in the second-class area on the opposite side of the steamer from my cabin. I tapped on the door, and when she opened it, I was shocked at her raw red nose and swollen eyes. The cabin was stuffy, with a stale, closed-up smell overriding the aroma of her usual floral scent. Her hair was flattened to one side of her head, and her gray dressing gown was tied with a saggy bow. The lapels gaped open over a lace-trimmed cotton nightgown with a high neck. Clearly, she was gutted over her brother's death.

Hildy exclaimed, "Oh my goodness! You look like you're having a difficult time, Miss Fairweather. Let me ring for some tea."

"No. I want to be alone."

Her words were whip sharp, and Hildy dropped back, the hand she'd extended to Miss Fairweather falling to her side.

Miss Fairweather was already swinging the door closed. I stepped forward and placed my foot on the threshold. "We'll leave in a moment, but we have some sad news that I'm sorry we have to share."

Hildy said, "Perhaps it would be better if you sat down, Miss Fairweather."

Miss Fairweather's grip tightened on the door. "No. What is it?"

I hesitated, reluctant to announce the news abruptly.

"Well, get on with it."

Abrupt seemed to be the only choice in the situation. "I'm sorry to tell you that Mr. Shaw has passed way. He collapsed in the saloon—"

"You disturbed me to tell me something about *Mr. Shaw?*"

"We thought you'd want to know. After all, he worked for your brother and was traveling with you."

"Mr. Shaw's death is of no consequence to me." Her gaze shifted to beyond my shoulder. "Yes?" she asked the steward, who stood a few steps behind me, his hands clasped together at his waist. He bowed, then straightened. "Pardon my intrusion. The captain requests all passengers attend dinner this evening. An important announcement will be made."

Miss Fairweather dismissed the man with a flick of her fingers. "Now, ladies, if you'll excuse me—"

"Wait." I flattened a hand on the door panel to stop its movement. "There's something more." With her vinegary attitude, I had no qualms about telling her everything. Despite her abrasive personality, I didn't want the news about the possibility of poisoning to be sprung on her in a room full of people this evening. "I'm afraid there's more bad news. Dr. Walsh believes that Mr. Shaw may have been poisoned."

Her chin angled down, and her lips flattened to a line. "The doctor thinks Mr. Shaw was poisoned? Silly man. That's the most absurd thing I've ever heard." I barely had time to step back before she slammed the door.

I turned away from the door. "I believe I'll have that cup of tea now."

THE DINING ROOM was almost full that evening. Even Miss Fairweather turned up and sat at the same table with Louisa. While neither looked their best, Miss Fairweather had tidied her hair. It was in its usual style, piled up on her head, and she'd powdered her face. Hildy and I were at the next table and couldn't help but overhear the few conversational gambits Louisa threw out. Miss Fairweather shut down any possibility of dinner chitchat with immediate one-word responses of *indeed* and *quite*.

After pudding was cleared away, Mr. Briarcliff entered the room. He nodded at Dr. Walsh, who pushed back his chair. Once Dr. Walsh reached Mr. Briarcliff's side, conversation died away.

"Thank you for joining us this evening," Mr. Briarcliff said. "I know it was an effort for many of you. First, let me say on behalf of the crew of the S.S. *Cleopatra*, our condolences to the Fairweather family." He inclined his head toward the table with the two ladies. Louisa pressed a hand to her chest and nodded. Miss Fairweather didn't move or acknowledge the sentiment. She looked as if she'd been turned to stone, a furious Medusa.

Mr. Briarcliff explained our new itinerary, which would take us directly to Luxor. No one grumbled about it, and I suspected that most of the passengers had anticipated the change in our schedule. "We will get to Luxor as quickly as possible," Mr. Briarcliff summed up. "Unfortunately, we've had a complication. Dr. Walsh," he said and stepped back.

Dr. Walsh cleared his throat. "You may have noticed that Mr. Alexander is not with us again this evening. He fell ill a few days ago. I can now confirm that he has scarlet fever.

Therefore"—a murmur rippled through the room, and Dr. Walsh raised his voice—"*therefore*, we will have to quarantine on the S.S. *Cleopatra* for three weeks."

# CHAPTER 13

King George V will open the British Empire Exhibition at
Wembley in April, showcasing the industrial and cultural
achievements of Britain and its colonies. The monarch will
take part in the opening ceremony, which will be broadcast
by BBC Radio, and it will be the first time royalty takes part
in a live radio broadcast.

*—The Illustrated Dispatch*

The murmur in the dining room became a noisy
buzz. I'd expected Dr. Walsh to talk about Mr.
Shaw's death, so I was as stunned as everyone else. I caught
snippets of conversations from the raised voices.

*That's impossible! Our schedule is already fixed. We're to
travel on to Aswan and then . . .*

*. . . but we're meeting friends in Luxor . . .*

*. . . and the rest of our tour departs from Luxor. What will
we do?*

Miss Fairweather surged to her feet. Her shrill voice cut across the babble. "I refuse to stay on this . . . this *death cruise* a moment longer. Once we reach Luxor, I'm departing this steamer."

Dr. Walsh, his tone mild, said, "That won't be allowed. I agree we are in a difficult situation." His gaze shot to Seffie, and I was sure he was thinking of her delicate constitution. She smiled at him in a reassuring way as he resumed, "But we must endure it. No departures from the steamer will be allowed. An outbreak of scarlet fever in a city such as Luxor —a crossing point of so many journeys—would be devastating. The disease could spread to other parts of Egypt. We must sacrifice a few weeks of our time and remain on the steamer for a bit longer than we planned. We were all exposed to Mr. Alexander before his symptoms presented, so there's no need for each of us to isolate. We can move freely about the steamer. That said, if anyone feels the least bit ill, please go to your cabin and let me know."

He looked toward Mr. Briarcliff, who stepped forward again. "The steamer line will compensate you for the change in itinerary. We're already working on rescheduling transfers and tours. Once we're in Luxor, we'll drop anchor some distance away from the dock. We've already arranged for food and medicine to be ferried out to us. There won't be any problem with supplies."

An uneasy silence had settled over the room. Miss Fairweather had gradually lowered herself back into her chair, but her hands were clenched into fists in her lap. Mr. Briarcliff tilted his head to one side and circled his chin, as if he had a crick in his neck. "Now another issue must be addressed."

He glanced at Dr. Walsh, who said, "It appears a poisonous substance caused Mr. Shaw's death."

Chatter broke out again, and the volume of conversations moved from muted to strident, like embers blown into flame. Miss Fairweather's strong voice sounded above the general din. "Poppycock! The man has been in poor health since the war."

Dr. Walsh fixed his attention on Miss Fairweather. "Be that as it may, he wasn't under my care—or any doctor's care, it seems. An unexpected death must be investigated." His firm tone quelled the babble of talk that had broken out.

Louisa leaned forward, a motion that rucked up the white linen tablecloth. "But wasn't it ptomaine poisoning?"

"That's a possibility, yes. I've inspected the kitchen and can assure you all the foodstuffs are in order at this time. Certain tests will be done once we reach Luxor, but for now the captain has directed Mr. Cordial to take initial statements from everyone regarding the deaths of both Mr. Shaw and Mr. Fairweather."

Louisa's brow furrowed. "About Ambrose as well?"

"Yes, it's also an unexpected death, so inquiries have to be made. Mr. Cordial, anything else?"

"One other thing." Mr. Briarcliff removed his black-rimmed glasses, folded them, and tucked them away in an inside pocket of his navy jacket. "I must confess that I haven't been completely honest during this journey."

Across the table from me, Hildy angled her head to the side for a second, then her eyes widened as her gaze pinged to me. She mouthed, *Rafe?*

I swallowed and nodded, mentally stiffening my spine as I prepared for a reproachful glare from her, but she only looked puzzled as she turned her attention back to Mr. Briarcliff.

He cleared his throat. "The name *Mr. Cordial* is a pseudonym. I took it on because I was employed by the owner of the Blue Lotus Line to travel incognito in the role of the steamer manager to assess the quality of service and the performance of the crew. Please accept my apologies for my deception"—he aimed those words at Hildy, then scanned the room—"and allow me to introduce myself properly. I'm Mr. Rafael Briarcliff, and I remain at your disposal. I will continue acting as the steamer manager. I'll do everything possible to smooth the way through this difficult situation."

Hildy said in an undertone, "Oh, what a delightful surprise—Rafe on the steamer with us! You knew?"

I flattened my lips into a line as I cringed. "Yes, I recognized him the day we boarded, but he asked me to keep his secret. I'm sorry I couldn't tell you sooner."

"Don't look so worried, my dear. If anyone understands about keeping secrets, it's me."

I was relieved that Hildy wasn't upset with me, and the low-level disquiet I'd been feeling about keeping Mr. Briarcliff's secret from her faded. I felt as if I'd been toting around a weighty suitcase and had been suddenly relieved of the burden.

I realized Mr. Briarcliff was still speaking and shifted my attention back to him. ". . . and if you have any information about Mr. Shaw and his activities today, please share them with me. I'll speak to each one of you individually tomorrow. Since I'm not an officer of the law, I suggested to the captain, and he agreed with me, that a second person should join me in collecting information so that everything will be established by two witnesses. I suggested someone who has proved to be both impartial and observant in the past." He extended a hand in my direction and, to my astonishment, said, "Miss Windway."

I blinked as heads turned my way. Surely I'd misheard. I'd expected him to say that it would be Dr. Walsh assisting him. I leaned over and whispered to Hildy, "What did he say?"

"Rafe complimented your perceptiveness, my dear, and he wants your assistance."

"How strange." My brain seemed to have stalled out. Mr. Briarcliff had said something admiring about me *and* had singled me out to help with the inquiry into the deaths? But he thought I was a nuisance and a flibbertigibbet. Had I stepped through the looking glass?

Hildy tapped the table, pulling me out of my reverie, and said with a little smile, "Don't look so flabbergasted. You're well up to the task."

I felt the weight of the stares from the passengers as the hiss of whispered questions eddied around me. Seffie bent her head toward Louisa, and I had no doubt they were talking about me. And was Miss Entwhistle frowning at me? A familiar panicky sensation seized me. My heartbeat surged, and I pressed my suddenly clammy palms against my skirt.

I didn't want to be the center of attention again—not questioning, speculative attention like this. I'd had enough of gossip and cutting glances to last a lifetime, but Mr. Briarcliff had brought it about again. Didn't he realize his announcement would set tongues wagging? Indignation prickled through the fretful and uneasy feelings that were swamping me. How high-handed of Mr. Briarcliff. He hadn't even bothered to ask me if I'd help. Instead, he'd broadcast the news to the whole steamer.

Miss Fairweather didn't bother lowering her voice. "A fake name—how gauche. I've never heard the like! Whomever he is, it's clear he only wants a secretary to take notes. Why doesn't he just say so? Either that or he wants an excuse to spend extended, unchaperoned time—"

Hildy sent her a glare and spoke over Miss Fairweather, drowning out her words as she announced, "Blix is an excellent choice."

Mr. Briarcliff said, "We'll begin collecting statements in the morning after breakfast. A crew member will inform you when we're ready to speak to you. Good evening."

Chairs scraped back, and Hildy came around the table to me and put her hand on my arm. "You look quite alarmed."

"Everyone is staring at me and whispering and speculating."

Hildy glanced around, then drew me to the side of the room. "May I give you some unsolicited advice?"

Her tone was quite serious and drew my attention away from the passengers. I focused on her face, which had a concerned expression on it. "Yes, of course."

"To be blunt, I doubt anyone is interested in you at the moment—that's what Amelia would tell you."

"But Seffie and Louisa had their heads together, and Miss Entwhistle's expression . . ."

Hildy glanced around. "Look again. I believe Seffie was letting Louisa know her shawl had fallen to the floor, and Miss Entwistle was trying to fight off a sneeze."

I swept around. Louisa was shaking out her shawl, and Miss Entwhistle held a handkerchief to her face. Bits of conversation floated to me from the passengers gathered in little clumps as they prepared to leave the dining room.

*Three weeks' quarantine!*

*. . . rather like having a spy among us! So thrilling . . .*

*How incredibly inconvenient . . .*

I drew in a breath and let it out slowly. Hildy was correct. No one was focused on me. "Oh, how foolish of me."

Hildy gave me a sympathetic look. "Now, as your friend, let me add that I know you have good reason to be wary of gossipmongers, but don't let what happened in the past taint today. Most people are occupied with their own thoughts and problems. They have little time to speculate or cause trouble for someone else. Chin up!"

I realized my shoulders were curved forward in an imitation of Mr. Shaw's usual posture. I straightened my spine.

Hildy gave me an approving nod, then said, "I'm sorry if I overstepped, but I don't want you to feel ill at ease."

"You shared some words of wisdom. I'll try to remember them."

Mr. Briarcliff had threaded his way through the tables to us. "Hildy, might I have a word? I apologize—"

She waved a hand. "Not to worry, Rafe. I'm not the least bit upset that you were traveling incognito. We all have certain things that we must keep quiet about. I do understand. Believe me, I really do."

I watched their exchange, arms crossed.

Mr. Briarcliff nodded, relief evident on his face. "Thank you for being so gracious."

When he turned to me, he stepped back and blinked, clearly taken aback. "You look rather annoyed, Miss Windway. You're not pleased? You don't want to participate?"

"Of course I want to be involved, but I should have been asked in person, not have it sprung on me. Common courtesy dictates one ask a lady before volunteering her."

Hildy said, "I must speak with Louisa," and melted away.

Mr. Briarcliff didn't look contrite at all as he said, "I only received permission from the captain to include you moments before I spoke to the room. I didn't have time to clear it with you. And I knew you'd dog my heels throughout the questioning. I thought it would be more efficient to have you along rather than to try to keep everything from you."

"So, I'm an annoyance."

"I didn't say that."

"Yes, you did."

He let out a sigh and shifted his weight from one foot to another. "I didn't phrase that well. I meant you're persistent. I stand by what I said earlier. You have excellent observation skills, Miss Windway, and I thought you'd be helpful. I'm sorry I didn't consult you before announcing it to everyone."

His conciliatory tone surprised me. It was unlike him. My ire drained away. "Well . . . um . . . thank you."

"I'm sorry for putting you on the spot."

"I'm surprised you didn't pick Dr. Walsh."

"Dr. Walsh is already run off his feet, and if anyone else falls ill, he'll be even busier. He needs to conserve his energy."

"Then what about Mr. Listergraff?"

His lips pressed tight, turning down at the corners. Mr. Briarcliff said quietly, "He's German. With the majority of the passengers being British, I believe there would be objections."

"Sadly, you're probably right about that." Since the war, there was still quite a bit of negative sentiment directed at Germans. Despite Mr. Listergraff's ebullient personality, those prejudices might come to the fore if he were tasked with interviewing passengers.

Still speaking lowly, Mr. Briarcliff held my gaze. "There are two additional reasons I suggested you, Miss Windway. I did take into account the fact that you're a woman, which I hope will put some of the ladies at ease. I imagine Miss Fairweather in particular might kick up a fuss if I interviewed her alone. But that aspect pales in comparison to the one paramount qualifier you have."

"What is that?"

"A person who recently solved a murder case. That would be you, Miss Windway. You will join me, won't you?"

I matched his posture, leaning in as I gave him a small smile. "Now that you've asked me personally—and so nicely—yes, I will." Even though it meant having to endure his vexing qualities, I couldn't resist the opportunity to find out what was really happening on the steamer. Were the deaths on the steamer murders? That was the primary question, but dozens of others sprouted along with it. However, it appeared our discussion had to end, because Mr. Listergraff was approaching. "I have more questions and something that I must tell you," I said, "but I don't think this is the time."

"Shall we meet on the deck later? Same spot as last evening?"

"A half hour from now?" The timing would give us a measure of privacy as most passengers would be mingling in the saloon for after-dinner coffee.

"I look forward to it," he said, and I moved away as Mr. Listergraff slapped Mr. Briarcliff on the back.

"It will be good to call you Rafe, my friend."

I JOINED Miss Entwhistle for coffee in the saloon and passed a half hour with her, Hildy, and Mrs. Walsh, then I excused myself. The deck was quiet. The clouds were gone, and the sliver of moon illuminated a figure at the railing. The height and broad shoulders narrowing to a trim waist could only be Mr. Briarcliff.

His deep voice came out of the darkness. "Good evening, Miss Windway."

I returned his greeting and said, "Hold out your hand."

"Excuse me?"

"Give me your hand."

The white of his cuff was visible in the dimness as he reached out. "Miss Windway, I didn't expect anything so forward from you." His tone was lightly mocking.

"Don't be a goose. This is about Mr. Shaw." I took his hand and rotated it. I put the film canister in his palm and closed his fingers over it. "Dr. Walsh said you should take charge of this." I patted his closed hand. "Don't drop it. It's the roll of film I took this afternoon in the saloon." My fingers rested lightly on his for a second, and I noticed how warm his hand was and how large it was compared to mine. What strange thoughts to trace through my mind—and about Mr. Briarcliff, of all people.

"Ah. I see." He pulled his hand back quickly.

I was suddenly aware of the chilly night air. I fisted my hands and shoved them in my pockets. "Don't lose it."

"I won't."

"Your voice sounds odd. You're not coming down with something are you?"

He cleared his throat, then fabric whispered as the white cuff disappeared for a moment. I assumed he was putting the canister inside his suit coat. "No. Although I must admit that I coughed after dinner, and my thoughts immediately went to fever, rashes, and being confined to my bed for days."

I let out a sympathetic huff of a laugh. "I had the same experience when my throat felt dry. Of course, I was fine after I had a drink of water."

We stood there in silence for a few moments, then I

turned toward him and leaned an elbow on the railing. "Since we'll begin taking statements tomorrow, I want to share something with you. I think Dr. Walsh is concerned about Mr. Fairweather's death, that it might be more than just a dicky heart."

"Why do you think that?" He slipped his hands into his pockets. In the faint light, his silhouette moved slightly as he rocked back and forth on his heels.

His guarded tone told me that he already knew of Dr. Walsh's suspicions. I drew a breath, then paused at the sound of footfalls on the deck. We both waited until the faint patter of feet descending the stairs faded.

"A steward returning to the main deck after handling a call from one of the cabins, I imagine," Mr. Briarcliff said, but he spoke more softly than before. "You were saying?"

"Right." I stepped closer to his silhouette. He bent his head, and I described seeing Dr. Walsh collecting cups in the saloon around the area where Mr. Fairweather had died.

His breath whispered beside my cheek as he let out a shallow laugh. "And this is exactly why I asked you to be involved. Yes, Dr. Walsh did have some . . . concerns, let's say, about Mr. Fairweather's death, but he has no proof."

"What does he suspect?"

"Cyanide poisoning."

# CHAPTER 14

Dear Amelia,

My fiancée insists on a grand wedding at St. George's, Hanover Square, but I'd prefer a quiet ceremony in our village church. How can I convince her without dampening her spirits?

Dear Flustered Fiancé,

Marriage is all about compromise—consider it practice for the years ahead. Perhaps suggest a London ceremony followed by a reception back home? That way, you'll have the best of both worlds, much like a perfect Sunday roast with Yorkshire pudding.

*—Ask Amelia, The Illustrated Dispatch*

I jerked back. "Cyanide?"

Mr. Briarcliff twisted around and listened. Since we'd stopped for the night, the steamer's paddle wheel was still, and the only sound was the whisper of a breeze through the palms on the shore and the low, steady slap of water against the steamer. He continued in the undertone we'd used before I raised my voice. "Yes, I'm afraid so. That's why he collected the cups, but he could find no trace of the poison."

I kept my voice down this time. "He was able to check for that?"

"Dr. Walsh is quite a resourceful man. He has an interest in that sort of thing. He told me there's a newish test that shows the presence of cyanide. He was able to find the necessary items to conduct the experiment, but none of the cups contained traces of cyanide. Dr. Walsh informed the captain of his suspicions, but the captain is reluctant to call the death a murder. The captain decided that until evidence is found to prove otherwise, he would consider Mr. Fairweather's death a natural death."

"But Dr. Walsh still suspects Mr. Fairweather was poisoned?"

"Yes. He described it as one of those hunches a medical man gets, and he can't shake off the idea."

"And then Mr. Shaw died. Does he suspect cyanide there as well?"

"More than suspects. He's quite sure Mr. Shaw was poisoned—something to do with the color of the blood along with the speed of his death."

"Yes, the blood was bright, almost a cherry color, especially the marks on Miss Entwhistle's handkerchief where she wiped her fingers. It stood out so brightly against the whiteness of the fabric."

"Quite," Mr. Briarcliff said. "But again, Dr. Walsh couldn't locate the source of the poison."

"What about ptomaine poisoning? Couldn't it have been that?"

"No, Mr. Shaw didn't have any of the symptoms associated with that type of poisoning. Dr. Walsh was thorough. He questioned the stewards. Mr. Shaw took his meals in the dining room and hadn't requested any food be delivered to his cabin. Dr. Walsh also examined the galley and said there was no sign of any food that had gone off."

"And no one else has fallen ill, which I suppose is another indication that it wasn't the food."

"Dr. Walsh pointed that out as well. The time frame we're interested in is quite narrow. In the case of cyanide, Dr. Walsh informs me, death is extremely quick, often within a few moments, but sometimes up to a quarter of an hour."

"And Mr. Shaw was seated at the desk for much longer than that. Tea was just being brought in when he died, so he didn't have anything to eat or drink—at least nothing that I saw."

"Dr. Walsh examined Mr. Shaw's pockets, his case, and the desk. He didn't find any food."

"But if he didn't have anything to eat, then how was he poisoned?"

"That is the question. According to Dr. Walsh, cyanide can be swallowed, inhaled, or absorbed through the skin. Dr. Walsh examined Mr. Shaw's case and his clothing but couldn't find any trace of a foreign substance."

I rested my elbows on the railing and stared down at the gently moving water. The faint light caught an occasional tiny swell among the undulating water, picking out the edge of the wave as it broke against the hull. "Did Mr. Shaw smoke or chew gum? I don't remember seeing him do either, but I wasn't paying attention to that sort of thing."

"It doesn't appear so. I had a look at his cabin. I didn't

see a pipe or any trace of cigarettes or cigars. No chewing gum either. And there was no sign of anything like that in his pockets. Dr. Walsh would have found it if there had been. Perhaps something will come to light as we speak to the passengers."

"This sounds quite complicated."

"We'll take statements and then add in background information and see where that gets us."

"We'll be looking for any snag or thread that we can pull at. Yes, I see exactly what you're aiming to do."

Mr. Briarcliff turned his head toward me. "And now I have something to tell you. Mr. Fairweather wasn't a stranger to me. I had a prior acquaintance with him. It's another reason that I want you involved."

"Really?"

"I met him twice—once at a dinner party and another time at my club in London."

"He was a casual acquaintance, then."

"I wouldn't even call him that."

Mr. Briarcliff seemed to be choosing his words carefully, and I wondered why he felt the need to share that detail if there was nothing more to it than such a brief connection. However, I decided I wouldn't press at that moment. My mind was still boggled with the thought of cyanide.

"Are the police involved? Do they know about the possibility of cyanide?"

"Not yet. I need more information before I go to the police—or Mr. Martin—with any accusations."

His cuff moved, a bright flash of white, as he patted his chest where he'd stashed the roll of film. "The photographs that you took today, could you develop them if you had the appropriate equipment?"

"I've developed photos in the past, but it was years ago. Now I send them out."

"Right. We will get them developed once we reach Luxor, then."

"What time do we start in the morning?" I asked.

"Let's say nine o'clock. The captain has put his cabin at our disposal. It's on the main deck." He pushed away from the railing. "It's quite late. Shall I see you to your cabin, Miss Windway?"

"There's no need. Good night, Mr. Briarcliff. I'll meet you at nine."

AFTER BREAKFAST THE NEXT MORNING, I followed the steward's directions to the captain's quarters on the main deck. Mr. Briarcliff opened the door for me when I knocked. "Good morning, Miss Windway."

Not only were his black-framed glasses still absent, but he was now smooth-shaven. He wasn't in the steamer uniform either. Instead, he wore white trousers and a navy double-breasted suit jacket with a pale gray tie. It was a clever choice. The civilian clothes echoed the steamer uniform he'd been wearing. I wondered if it had been an intentional selection, or if he didn't like wearing a uniform.

"Do you plan to join us, Miss Windway?"

"Oh. Right." I stepped across the threshold. "Your change in appearance threw me off."

He rubbed his hand across his jaw as he closed the door behind me. "Can't say I'm sorry to see the last of the beard."

The captain's spacious cabin was divided in two. The portion where we stood was a sitting room with large windows and a round mahogany table, where pens and pencils were aligned next to a stack of notebooks. An easy chair with an ottoman and gooseneck reading light completed the furnishings. A closed set of sliding doors in an interior wall hid what was probably the captain's sleeping quarters. Built-in wooden cabinets, with a geometric wood inlay in a repeating diamond shape, covered the walls on both sides of the sliding doors.

The captain, a tall man who wore a turban with his uniform, came around the table and inclined his head as he greeted me. I tipped my head forward in return as I said, "Good morning, Captain Farouk."

"Thank you for assisting with the statements," he said in French-accented English. "The Blue Lotus Line is indebted to you, and I apologize for the inconveniences you are experiencing on your Nile cruise."

"I'm happy to help in any way I can."

"Excellent." He glanced from me to Mr. Briarcliff as he said, "Mr. Briarcliff tells me he's informed you of the suspicion of poison in Mr. Shaw's death." I nodded, and he studied my face for a moment, then said, "No vapors or feminine hysteria. Good."

Irritation flared through me at his assumption that I'd react emotionally to the news. Of course, I'd been emotional last evening when I learned about the possibility of poisoning, but who wouldn't be worried and frightened at the thought of a fellow passenger being poisoned? "I'm sure all the passengers will be upset when they learn of the details around Mr. Shaw's death."

Captain Farouk said, "And that is why we are keeping it quiet. Now, for clarity, let me go over your remit." With a wave of his hand that included me and Mr. Briarcliff, he continued, "You are to carry out the shipboard investigation into the deaths of Mr. Shaw and Mr. Fairweather. Mr. Fairweather's death was, it seems, a natural death—unfortunate that it happened on the steamer—but we must provide details that will satisfy police officials in Luxor and eliminate the fuss the passengers would have to endure regarding an investigation. Interview the passengers and collect all the details around his death so that the police will have no additional questions and won't bother Mrs. Fairweather or the man's sister. In the case of Mr. Shaw, the situation is different. Collect statements from the passengers and any other evidence you deem necessary or of interest."

"What about the crew? Are we interviewing them as well?" I asked.

"That won't be necessary. I've questioned the crew myself. I'm confident none of them were involved. Mr. Briarcliff was with me during the questioning and can confirm the crew is in the clear. None of them had any interactions with either Mr. Fairweather or Mr. Shaw immediately before the men died."

Mr. Briarcliff added, "At the captain's request, I double-checked the details of the crew members' movements, and I don't believe any of them are involved in either death."

The captain resumed speaking. "You must focus on the passengers and establish their whereabouts and any motive they may have in regard to Mr. Shaw. Carry out the questioning of the passengers, and we'll hand everything over to the officials in Luxor. I'm sure you both understand that an ideal outcome would be to find the person responsible for Mr. Shaw's death and to have firm evidence to prove guilt."

As he'd spoken, my irritation at his assumption that I'd have the vapors on hearing the disturbing news of a poisoning faded and a simmering apprehension took its place. "I thought we were to take statements."

"Yes, but you must realize that a completed investigation with a guilty party identified is the optimal result. Especially since we'll be isolated on the steamer for weeks to come. Questions will ferment like mold in the tropics unless clear answers can be found. I sent a telegram to Mr. Martin, informing him of the situation."

Mr. Briarcliff's brow lowered into a frown. "That's not what we discussed yesterday. We have no results to share."

"You'll send those shortly. Mr. Martin has officially put you in charge of the investigation. He'll sort out your position as a liaison with the police in Luxor."

Mr. Briarcliff's jaw worked, and he seemed to be holding back from speaking, so I said, "This is a much bigger task than simply taking statements. You want us to find a murderer."

"Yes. I expect you to bring clarity to this situation." He said it as if the task were as simple as brewing up a pot of tea. "Now I must be off. You and Mr. Briarcliff have access to this room at any time you need it."

He removed a set of keys from a pocket and unlocked one of the cabinet doors with the geometric wood inlay, opening it to reveal a shelf that contained Mr. Shaw's case. Paper bags lined the shelf above it. "I had Mr. Shaw's belongings from the saloon brought here along with the coffee cups that Dr. Walsh collected, which I gather from Mr. Briarcliff you already knew about, Miss Windway. I understand you have an appointment with Mr. Fairweather's widow shortly, but I'm sure you'll want to examine these items. Please create an inventory of them and include it with your final report."

He handed the key to Mr. Briarcliff. "If you collect any

other evidence, please add it to this cabinet for safekeeping. Feel free to use this area for any interviews, if needed. I expect a preliminary report this evening."

After the door closed behind him, Mr. Briarcliff bounced a clenched fist lightly on the back of one of the wooden chairs. "And *this* is why I work alone."

# CHAPTER 15

Visitors to Helwan will be pleased to note improved train service and the promise of better road conditions between Cairo and the desert town famous for its sport—golf and tennis—as well as its baths.

—*The Illustrated Dispatch*

"*I* couldn't agree more," I said.

Mr. Briarcliff, lost in his own thoughts, was saying in an undertone, "You make one exception . . ." He blinked. "I'm sorry. What?"

"Working with people can be quite trying."

"Especially when they go over your head. I detest hierarchy, Miss Windway."

"I've noticed."

"And I hate political maneuvering."

"Another reason to avoid hierarchal organizations. So why did you take on the role of manager?"

Mr. Briarcliff sighed. "A personal reason, Miss Windway, which I'm discovering is a very bad reason." He squared his shoulders. "Nothing to be done about it now. This is turning into much more than I realized. Would you prefer to bow out?"

"You won't get rid of me so easily." He gave me one of his lightning smiles, and a little dart of happiness pinged inside me as the gloomy expression on his face lightened a touch. To cover my surprise at the zing of emotion, I picked up a notebook and pen. "How are we to go about this?"

"What questions to ask, you mean? Let's start with everyone's movements at the crucial times, interactions they'd had with Mr. Fairweather and Mr. Shaw, that sort of thing."

"And if they had any connection with either man in the past," I said, then added, "And we should also examine everyone's passports."

"Why?"

I leveled a glance at him. "In case someone is traveling under a false name."

He let out a huffing laugh. "Point taken."

"Thank you. Now who will take notes? If you're planning on me being only a scribe, think again."

"You have atrocious handwriting, do you?"

"My governesses knew their job, otherwise my father would have sacked them. I have beautiful penmanship, but I think we should take turns."

"Exactly what I was thinking, Miss Windway."

"You see, it will be better—wait, did you agree with me?"

"Strange, isn't it?" He selected a notebook and pencil for himself. "I thought we'd trade off, with me asking the men the questions and you taking notes. Then we'll switch when we interview the women. I believe the women will be more comfortable answering questions coming from you."

"All right." I certainly wasn't about to point out that with two of the men on the cruise having passed away that left him with the majority of the note-taking duties. I tucked the notebook in the crook of my arm. "Shall we?"

Louisa had sent a message asking us to meet her on the deck outside her cabin. She was seated at a small table in a rattan chair near the railing. A book with lined pages was open on the table. She wore a wrinkled gray linen dress with a black scarf knotted at her neck. She didn't notice our approach. The steamer was moving at a good clip, and a strong breeze blew a strand of her gingery hair across her face. She sat unmoving, gazing across the water to the hazy ribbon of greenery along the distant shore. All the verve and excitement she'd had at the beginning of the cruise seemed to have drained out of her.

"Hello, Louisa," I said, and she jumped as if she'd been stung by a bee.

"I'm sorry. I didn't mean to startle you."

She patted her chest and tucked her hair behind her ear. "It's not your fault. I was lost in thought." She gestured to the chairs. "Do you mind if we speak out here? I don't enjoy being in the cabin alone."

"Not a problem at all." Mr. Briarcliff held a chair for me, then took a seat on the other side of Louisa.

"You keep a diary?" I asked, hoping to put her at ease before I launched into my questions. She'd written the date at the top of the page and the words, *Sailing. No stops today.* The rest of the page was blank, and her pen rested in the gutter of the book.

"An old reporter's habit." She ran her hand across the empty page. "I tend to jot things down. Events, people, places we visited. It's quite boring, really. But I can't seem to find the energy today." Louisa removed the pen and closed her diary. "How can I help? What would you like to know? Goodness, this feels odd." She gave a little smile. "I'm more used to being the questioner, not the questioned."

Mr. Briarcliff opened his notebook and took a pencil from an interior jacket pocket. "First, let us get the details down from your passport."

"Oh, of course." Mr. Briarcliff stood as she pushed back her chair. "Just give me a moment." She disappeared into her cabin and returned seconds later. She handed her passport over to me as Mr. Briarcliff resumed his seat. I took a quick look, then gave it to Mr. Briarcliff, who noted down the information as Louisa asked, "What would you like to know?"

I said, "Tell us when you were in the saloon yesterday afternoon. What time did you arrive?"

"I suppose it would've been around two or three. I'm not sure."

"Did you speak to Mr. Shaw earlier in the day?"

"Yes, when I learned he'd been working for several hours at the desk in our cabin, I convinced him to come up to the saloon. I made him pack up his things right then and accompany me."

"Why was that?" I gave her a quick, encouraging head bob. "Of course, I know. I remember what you said in the saloon, but we need to get it down on paper."

"Right. I see. Well, I knew Mr. Shaw would say he would be along soon, but he'd stay put in that stuffy room. As I mentioned yesterday, Mr. Shaw had some difficulties after the war. He was nervous and had a tendency to become quite morose if he didn't get out and about. I noticed it at Nobilis

Domus. He did much better if he rambled about the estate occasionally. I didn't think it was good for him to remain in a cabin all day, so I insisted he come up to the saloon."

Mr. Briarcliff's pencil was still moving, so I paused to give him time to catch up with his notes. As he wrote the last word, he gave me a little nod.

"Did you see anyone else come into the saloon between the time you and Mr. Shaw arrived and when the steward brought in the tea tray?"

"No, no one."

"And how was Mr. Shaw handling Mr. Fairweather's death?"

Louisa laced her fingers together and rested them on top of the diary. "I don't really know. I didn't see any changes in his manner."

"Were he and Mr. Fairweather close?"

"No, surprisingly. As much time as they spent together, one would think they'd have developed a rapport, but it was very much a formal relationship. I don't think there was much chitchat between them. Ambrose wasn't the sort to do that, and Mr. Shaw preferred to keep to himself."

I waited a few moments until Mr. Briarcliff stopped writing. "How did Mr. Shaw seem yesterday? How were his spirits?"

"He seemed to be in his usual temperament, which is to say a bit melancholy and timid—completely normal for him."

"I see." I waited a few beats as Mr. Briarcliff's pencil scratched across the page. When he paused, I turned back to Louisa. "Just a few more questions, this time about your husband. I'm sorry I have to ask you these things—"

"I understand." She drew in a breath and closed her eyes

briefly. "As the captain said last evening, the formalities must be observed."

"If I remember correctly, you and Mr. Fairweather dined together that evening along with Mr. Shaw?"

"Yes, he joined us. Mr. Shaw said he'd take a tray in his room, but I insisted. After dinner, they went back to our cabin to finish some correspondence. Apparently, it was important to get it in the post when we arrived at our next stop. They completed what needed to be done and then came to the saloon about . . . oh, let me think . . . probably three quarters of an hour later. Miss Entwistle can tell you a little bit more about what they worked on."

"Yes, I remember what she told you earlier. We'll talk to her later. So, Mr. Fairweather came into the saloon . . ."

"Ambrose sat down at the chair beside me. There was a bit of shuffling around." She motioned to me. "You left for the promenade deck. Miss Entwhistle came over and refreshed her coffee about the same time as when Hildy poured a cup of coffee for Ambrose. She handed it to Seffie, who passed it to Ambrose." She went quiet and looked over the railing. The steamer sluiced through the water, and a trail of foamy waves fanned out behind us. "I asked Ambrose if he'd completed the work that needed to be done, and he said they had. Seffie asked me a question about pruning, and it was when I was talking to her that it happened. I heard a funny noise, a gasp or a gargling sound." She shuddered. "I turned my head, and Ambrose's face was as pink and flushed as when he played golf in the awful heat last summer. He came home looking like a lobster. I was quite worried about him and sent him off to have a cool bath right away. But this was even worse." She put a hand to the neck of her dress. "He was clawing at his collar and then—" She patted her pockets and sniffed. Mr. Briarcliff handed her his handkerchief. She wiped her eyes as she said, "It all happened so quickly. He gasped and fell out of his chair and then . . ." She shrugged. "And then he was gone. It happened so suddenly that it's still difficult to comprehend."

"I'm so sorry it happened." I gazed at the sunlight sparkling on the water for a moment to give Louisa time to compose herself. "Just a few more questions and then we'll be done." I glanced at Mr. Briarcliff, and he gave me a quick nod as he closed his eyes, indicating I should keep going.

"Did Mr. Fairweather know anyone among the passengers before we departed? Were there any prior associations?"

"Not that I'm aware of. Except Mr. Shaw, of course." She seemed to relax, settling back into her chair, now that we weren't talking about her husband's death. "Ambrose did have a wide range of acquaintances, but he didn't mention anyone he knew specifically on the steamer."

I looked across the table. "Anything else you'd like to ask, Mr. Briarcliff?"

He looked at the notes, then asked, "Did you know Mr. Shaw's family?"

"No, he had a nephew, who worked in London, and a distant uncle, who lived in Canada—or was it Australia?— I'm afraid I can't remember."

"Mrs. Fairweather, is there . . ." Mr. Briarcliff paused as he frowned at his notes, then rolled the pencil between his palms. "This is quite a delicate question. I apologize in advance for asking, but did Mr. Fairweather leave a will? The police will need to know, and we hope to spare you having to answer their questions once we're out of quarantine."

I didn't turn my head, but I sent Mr. Briarcliff a look out of the corner of my eye. It was quite an outrageous thing to ask, but Louisa replied matter-of-factly. "Yes, he did. It's with our solicitors in London. Everything goes to me, with Millicent receiving a generous stipend each quarter and continuing to live at Nobilis Domus. I told Ambrose it was quite absurd. If anything happened to him, Millicent and I would not live in the same house, but he wouldn't hear of any change to the will. Once he made up his mind, he was implacable."

"Why wouldn't you and Miss Fairweather continue to live at Nobilis Domus?" I asked.

She snorted. "Because Millicent hates me."

I was tongue-tied, but Mr. Briarcliff nodded and murmured mildly, "That is a shame," as he made a note. "Thank you for answering my presumptuous question, Mrs. Fairweather."

I blinked at the smile Mr. Briarcliff sent Louisa's way, and she dropped the handkerchief she was folding. "Oh no," she said as Mr. Briarcliff reached for it. "Let me see that it's washed."

He wouldn't hear of it and tucked it away in a pocket. I scooted my chair back, and we all stood. Louisa reached for her diary, turned away, then turned halfway back, a hesitant move.

I said, "Was there something else?"

Her brow was crinkled, and she looked like someone who couldn't decide if they wanted to step onto a ferry wheel ride or not. "Well . . . possibly. There is one thing that's happened that's quite strange. I don't see how it could be related to Mr. Shaw's death, but since he worked with Ambrose . . . yes, I do believe I should tell you. Ambrose received some odd letters, not exactly threats, but they upset him greatly."

"What sort of letters?" I asked.

"Anonymous letters."

# CHAPTER 16

Cairo society waves farewell to the Hon. Reginald Biggers and his American bride, who have checked out of the Continental-Savoy after a honeymoon that included a grand tour of the ancient sites.

— *Arrivals and Departures, The Nile*

*L*ouisa opened the diary and took several envelopes from between the end paper and the cover at the back of the book. "They're quite strange." She handed them to me. "I don't know what to make of them."

The envelopes all had *Mr. Ambrose Fairweather* written on them, but nothing else. I took out the contents of the first envelope. A newspaper clipping and a photograph of a young man with a lopsided grin and a swath of hair falling over his forehead were nestled in the single sheet of white paper. The page was blank except for a name centered in the middle of the paper, written in neat copperplate. "Who is

Henry David Anderson? Is he the young man in the photograph?"

"I have no idea who he is, and neither did Ambrose. He didn't recognize any of the names."

"Any?" I asked. "I don't understand."

Louisa gestured to the other envelopes I held. "He received several of these recently. The first ones, he threw away, but after the third or fourth one, I began to pluck them out of the rubbish and save them. I tried to convince Ambrose he should go to the police, but he wouldn't do it. It was what we were arguing about in the tomb during our first excursion. So embarrassing that we put you in such an awkward position that day."

"Mr. Fairweather didn't want to go to the police about them? Why not?"

"He said it was just some barmy person trying to bother him." She held her diary against her chest, her arms crossed over it. "I didn't agree, but Ambrose was as obstinate as an old ox. I saved the most recent letters without Ambrose knowing about it. He did receive odd mail—threats and vicious letters. I don't know what corporate entity doesn't, but these are different," she said as she shifted her gaze at the rest of the envelopes. "They're not really threats. They're just . . . peculiar. Ambrose said they weren't malicious." Louisa shook her head, and her shoulders twitched up in a little shrug. "But the way they kept arriving, it was . . . disturbing somehow."

The newspaper clipping was an obituary for Henry David Anderson, who'd died during the war. I skimmed it, then turned the photo over. *Henry at Sutherton, May 1914,* was written on the back. "I agree with you. It's bizarre."

"I'd decided to take them to the police on my own once we reached Luxor, but then Ambrose . . . passed, and they went completely out of mind. I only thought of them just now when you began asking about Ambrose."

I glanced at Mr. Briarcliff, trying to catch his eye to see if he had any thoughts to share or questions to ask about them, but his gaze was concentrated on the photo and the obituary.

Louisa added, "They came in a pattern. They didn't arrive together." She tapped the paper. "An envelope with a single page with the name first, then the photograph, and then the obituary. Each thing arrived in separate envelopes with only Ambrose's name on them."

"So the clipping and the photograph were sent separately?"

"That's right. I consolidated things, putting the clippings of the obituaries and photos with the page with the name— an old reporter's instinct to categorize and sort information."

I fanned the envelopes out. There were several more. "You've received this sort of thing about four other people?"

"Yes. It's been going on since we arrived in Cairo. One was propped against a cup of coffee at Shepheard's. Another was tucked inside his newspaper. Another was in his luggage."

"These last two are different." I'd been opening each envelope, examining the contents.

"They were left at the same time. I saw them when we came back from dinner that first evening on the steamer. They were on Ambrose's desk. He didn't even open them, just tossed them in the rubbish, but I retrieved them later. Each one contained a page with a name and photo."

"But no obituaries?"

She shook her head.

Mr. Briarcliff asked, "Did Mr. Shaw know about them?"

"I don't believe so. They were left in places that Ambrose

would find them—our cabin or at our breakfast table and the like."

I returned all the items to the envelopes. "Do you mind if we keep these?"

"Please do. It's a relief to hand them off."

I looked at Mr. Briarcliff and raised my eyebrows. He shook his head, then said to Louisa, "Thank you for speaking to us today."

"Of course."

I put the envelopes in my notebook, thinking that I needed to speak to Hildy. If other people on the steamer were receiving strange correspondence, perhaps it was linked to the anonymous letters she'd received. However, I couldn't tell Mr. Briarcliff about Hildy's secret. She had to be the one to do that.

Mr. Briarcliff put his pencil inside his jacket pocket. "Shall we speak to Miss Fairweather next?"

"Speaking to the people most closely associated with Mr. Shaw makes sense," I said as we walked to the second-class cabins, having decided to approach her ourselves instead of sending a steward to fetch her. I patted my notebook, where I'd stowed the envelopes Louisa had given us. "What do you make of the strange correspondence? Why would someone do that?"

"I really couldn't say."

Most passengers opened their cabin windows during the day to catch the breeze as we sailed along, but Miss Fair-weather's windows were closed, and the drapes were drawn. I tapped on her door. "It doesn't look as if she's in."

I was surprised when I heard her faintly call out, "Come in."

I poked my head in to announce myself but didn't speak, because the cabin appeared to be empty. Then fabric swished and an arm appeared from what I'd taken to be a pile of blankets on the bed. Miss Fairweather was curled into a ball, swathed in blankets, with a pillow half covering her face. The arm waved toward the little dressing table by the curtained window. "Leave the tea."

"Miss Fairweather, it's Blix Windway and Mr. Briarcliff. We'd like to speak to you. Shall we return in, say, a quarter of an hour?" I wanted to give her time to freshen up. I certainly wouldn't want to speak to my fellow passengers from my bed.

Miss Fairweather surged up, sprang out of bed, and crossed the room. Her gaze was so ferocious that I took a step back and bumped into Mr. Briarcliff. She grabbed the door and shoved it at me. Through the inch of space that she left open, she said, "No, you may not come in. I will not have my privacy invaded."

Mr. Briarcliff said, "As you heard last evening, the captain has instructed us to speak to everyone about the deaths of Mr. Shaw and your brother."

"I'm certainly in no state to do that now." She slammed the door.

I turned away. "Perhaps we can return later."

Mr. Briarcliff added, "And send a steward to fetch her next time."

"Definitely. I'm tired of her shutting her door in my face."

"This happened to you before?"

"Yesterday when Hildy and I went to inform her of Mr. Shaw's death, she nearly took off my nose when she closed the door." I spotted a figure over Mr. Briarcliff's shoulder. In an effort to make sure he didn't suggest we interview Hildy next—I wanted to speak to her first—I said, "Look, there's

Mr. Listergraff. Let's see if he can speak to us now." I waved and called out to him.

Mr. Listergraff was striding along with two wooden poles. I caught up with him. "Do you have a few moments to speak with Mr. Briarcliff and me?"

"One always has time on a cruise for a chat. Shall we go to the stern? There are some empty deck chairs there."

Once we reached the back of the steamer, Mr. Briarcliff tilted his head toward the poles Mr. Listergraff had propped up against an empty chair. "What are those for, Henry?"

Mr. Listergraff pulled another chair toward the two Mr. Briarcliff was rearranging. "Miss Entwhistle has decided that since we will be confined to the S.S. *Cleopatra*, we had best have some activities. She's taken on the role of games mistress. She's currently chalking a shuffleboard pattern on the promenade deck and tasked me with producing something we can use for cues." He took several empty food tins out of his coat pocket along with pliers, gloves, some beat-up forks, and a length of twine. "I'll fashion these mop handles into something that we can use for cues."

"Ingenious," I said.

"Thank you. It was Miss Entwhistle who came up with the idea." He returned everything to his pockets. "How can I help?"

# CHAPTER 17

The Egyptian Institute appeals for funds to conduct borings near the Great Pyramid, hoping to locate the fabled subterranean canal mentioned by Herodotus.

*—The Nile*

With the chairs in a little semicircle at the stern, Mr. Listergraff, Mr. Briarcliff, and I had an excellent view of the water frothing out behind the steamer. In the distance, a few steamers plowed through the water along with some barges. Five pelicans flapped their way across the river, the shadows of their huge wingspans skimming across the water in dark pulses.

I sat down in one of the deck chairs, but as I opened my notebook, I realized I didn't have anything to write with. I must have left the pen on the table when we'd spoken to Louisa.

Mr. Briarcliff took his pencil from his pocket and handed

it to me as he asked Mr. Listergraff, "Do you happen to have your passport on you?"

Mr. Listergraff reached inside his suit. "Even in such luxurious surroundings as this, it's always a good idea to have one's documents on one's person." He handed the passport to Mr. Briarcliff, who gave it a quick glance, then handed it to me.

It was in German, but I had no trouble translating the relevant parts. I jotted down Mr. Listergraff's name and the passport details, then returned it.

Mr. Briarcliff said, "Let's get some basic details first, if you don't mind. Were you in the saloon when Mr. Shaw passed away?"

"No. I was reading in my cabin." He added, "And before you ask, yes, someone else can confirm that. My cabin steward brought me a drink."

My pencil skimmed over the page as Mr. Listergraff continued, "Not sure of the time, but it was shortly after that—maybe ten minutes—that I finished my book and was on my way to return it to the saloon when one of the stewards blocked my way and said no one was allowed in. When I questioned him about it, I learned it was on Dr. Walsh's orders."

I felt Mr. Briarcliff's gaze on me. I nodded, and he looked surprised. "You got all that?"

"Yes, of course." He sent me a look one might bestow on an opponent in a card game if cheating were suspected. "Please continue." I made a little rolling motion with my hand.

Mr. Briarcliff turned his attention back to Mr. Listergraff. It took him a moment to regain his train of thought. "Did you know Mr. Shaw before the tour on the steamer began?"

"No, I met him on our first excursion. I'm sure your next

question will be about Mr. Fairweather, because the captain directed you to ask about him as well. I didn't know him either. I hadn't had the pleasure." I smiled at the hint of sarcasm in his tone, but I kept my head down and focused on my notes. Mr. Listergraff continued, "I'm sorry I can't be more helpful, Rafe."

"It's fine. Every detail is important," Mr. Briarcliff said. "Where were you when Mr. Fairweather died?"

"I was on the promenade deck, which Miss Windway can verify."

"That's correct," I said, as I finished writing down his words.

Mr. Briarcliff asked, "Had you been in the saloon earlier?"

"Yes, Miss Honeyworth and I played chess after dinner." He sighed. "Fiendishly clever woman. She took my rook, and that was the end for me."

"Was Mr. Fairweather in the saloon during this time?"

"No. I don't know when he arrived. Once Miss Honeyworth trounced me, I went to the promenade deck to lick my wounds. I believe she joined the other ladies. I'm not sure. I was out there quite a while. Once I got my pipe going, I lingered to see if the clouds would clear for some stargazing."

"Did anyone else join you?"

"Not until Miss Windway appeared."

"I see," Mr. Briarcliff said. "Going back to Mr. Shaw for a moment. Do you know of anyone who had any grudge against him?"

"No, I didn't know the man well enough to have any knowledge of his friends or enemies. But he didn't seem to be the kind to inspire great emotion of any kind, whether positive or negative."

"Quite a milquetoast chap," Mr. Briarcliff said, which I left out of the notes. "What about Mr. Fairweather? Any grudges or enemies there?"

"Nothing I know with confidence."

I looked up. His tone had changed. It was charged with a hint of a question. Mr. Listergraff had taken out the twine and was winding it into a neat coil.

A crease appeared between Mr. Briarcliff's eyebrows. "What do you mean?"

"One hears rumors." Mr. Listergraff shrugged a shoulder. "Nothing specific. Only hazy hints and insinuations."

"What sort of hints?" Mr. Briarcliff asked, and I gave him a second glance. Was his jaw clenched?

"Shady business practices of his company. Things that aren't necessarily illegal but would be frowned on if made public. Perhaps I shouldn't have said anything since I can't provide specifics. You Brits would say that's bad form, wouldn't you?"

"In polite society, yes," Mr. Briarcliff said, "but rumors are a different matter in an investigation. Anything else, Miss Windway?"

I said I didn't have any additional questions, and Mr. Listergraff set off with the mop handles under his arm and the metal tins jangling in his pocket. "Perhaps we should speak to Miss Entwhistle next. She spoke to Mr. Shaw after Mr. Fairweather died, and she was the first to check on Mr. Shaw after he collapsed." Mentally, I added, *And then we can leave Hildy until after lunch.*

"Excellent idea. Let's do that."

As we walked to the promenade deck, Mr. Briarcliff said, "You seemed to have no trouble at all keeping up with your notes, whereas I was quite the laggard."

"I used shorthand."

He stopped walking and turned to me, hands in pockets and elbows flared out. "You know shorthand?"

"Yes. Is that so surprising?"

"For a lady of your background, it is."

"Well, as I said earlier, my governesses were an interesting lot. In addition to all the ladylike arts, I can also take shorthand, drive a motorcar, and defend myself."

He gave a thoughtful nod, and we resumed walking, but then he paused again. "But you'll have to transcribe them eventually."

"I'll do that when I type them up."

He swiveled to look out across the water, but I glimpsed the corner of his mouth inching up before his back was turned. "And touch typing is also in your repertoire. Why am I not surprised?"

"If the Blue Lotus Line doesn't have a typewriter, then I can ask to borrow Mr. Alexander's."

"There's one in the purser's office," he said as we passed through the saloon, where Mr. Listergraff was already at work banging the food tins into a new shape. The mop poles were propped up on a chair beside him, and the twine and some tools were spread across the table in front of him. He gave a salute to us as we passed through. Mr. Briarcliff opened the door to the promenade deck, and a gust of wind sent my hair flying.

It was much breezier at the bow of the ship, and Miss Entwhistle's skirt fluttered as she crouched down, marking the long boundary line of the shuffleboard court.

She stood up, dusting her hands. "I suppose you've come to ask me questions. Just give me a moment, please. My things are over there." She waved toward a row of tables under the awning at the back of the deck. I spotted her artist box on one of the tables and led the way to it. While Mr.

Briarcliff took his notebook from a pocket and sharpened his pencil with a penknife, Miss Entwhistle numbered the spaces on the shuffleboard court. She stood back and checked her work, with her head tilted to one side, before joining us.

She settled into a chair across from us and took a round saddle soap tin out of the pocket of her wide-legged trousers, which today were a pale pink. They matched her pink linen top that was piped in ivory around the Peter Pan collar. "I almost tossed this in the rubbish yesterday when I used the last of it on my leather artist box. Now I'm glad I didn't." Miss Entwhistle popped the lid off the tin, then took out a change purse from her other pocket. "I cleaned the tin out, and I intend to make this into a shuffleboard disk." The coins jangled as she dumped them into the tin.

She swished the tin back and forth to level the coins, then fastened the lid in place. "Let's see how it does." She gave it an experimental push across the table. Mr. Briarcliff caught it before it went off the edge. He tested the weight in his hand before sending it back across the table to her. "That should do nicely."

"Excellent. Now we just need to find seven more tins and more change."

"Very innovative," I said.

"When one is a teacher, one must be creative."

She set everything aside. "I suppose you have some questions for me about Mr. Shaw."

As Mr. Briarcliff turned to a fresh page in his notebook, I said, "We do, but first, do you have your passport with you?"

She scooted her chair back. "No, but I can get it." She was back within a few minutes. There was nothing out of the ordinary about the American passport, except that her middle name was Grey. When I asked her about it, she said, "It was my mother's maiden name. She was quite fond of it and wanted to pass it on. It is a bit odd."

I handed the passport over to Mr. Briarcliff to jot down the details and said, "I think it's lovely. Let's begin with what happened with Mr. Shaw. If I remember correctly, you were seated in the group with me when it happened."

"Yes, I was sketching. Mr. Shaw had come in with Louisa earlier and taken a seat at one of the tables to work while Louisa joined us. Louisa had some questions about what Mr. Shaw said after Mr. Fairweather collapsed."

"Right. I remember. We'll come back to that in a moment. Did you leave our group or the saloon?"

"No." Her expression changed to a look you'd give someone if you were wondering if they were right in the head.

"I remember, but I'm asking so we'll have all the details down on paper." I glanced at Mr. Briarcliff, who was bent over the notebook.

"I see." Miss Entwhistle twitched her shoulders.

I wondered if she didn't like the idea of her words being recorded. "Did you see anyone else enter the room or stop by Mr. Shaw's table?"

"No. I don't think anyone else came into the saloon during that time. Well, except for the steward when he brought the tea, but that was about the same time Mr. Shaw had his attack."

"And you went over to Mr. Shaw right away?"

She nodded.

"I remember you saying you had nursing experience. Can you describe in detail for us what happened?"

"Mr. Shaw was flushed and pulling at his collar. His breathing was labored. I reached out when he collapsed. I tried to catch him but wasn't able to. He hit his head on the desk." She looked away, down at the deck. "I was going to apply pressure—I could see blood welling from the cut on his head—but I realized as soon as I knelt down that he was dead. I could tell immediately."

I glanced at Mr. Briarcliff, and he must have felt my gaze because, though he didn't look up, he nodded.

Remembering how tense she'd been when she spoke to Louisa, recounting what Mr. Shaw had told her about Mr. Fairweather's last moments, I asked, "Did you have any prior acquaintance with Mr. Shaw before we departed on the steamer?"

"I didn't know him at all."

Her response was immediate and nonchalant. She didn't blink or break eye contact either. So much for my half-formed theory that they'd known each other. "Did you have any conversations with him?"

She shook her head. "None. He kept very much to himself."

"And you know no one who had a grudge against him or anyone who felt any ill will toward him?"

"No. I never spoke to the man except to say hello or goodbye."

Out of the corner of my eye, I watched Mr. Briarcliff's pencil. I paused until it stopped moving and then asked, "You're aware the captain has asked us to also gather information about Mr. Fairweather, so tell me about that evening he died. When did you arrive in the saloon?"

"I went there directly after dinner. I glanced through a few magazines, then I played solitaire after you kindly passed the cards over to me until Mr. Fairweather had his attack."

"What did you see when that happened?"

"I wasn't in the immediate group around him. I only heard the commotion. I went over, and he was lying on the floor, his hand clenching the lapel of his suit. Mrs. Fairweather was at his side as well as Mrs. Walsh, so I wasn't able to see much else. Mrs. Walsh called for a steward to send for Dr. Walsh, but I realized Mr. Fairweather was beyond anything I could do. After a moment, Mrs. Fairweather realized he was gone and began to cry. I noticed Mr. Shaw looked incredibly pale. I was afraid he might pass out. I made him sit in a chair and brought him a glass of water."

"I remember you later told Louisa what he said during this time. Can you repeat that?"

"Not verbatim, but I can tell you in general what he said. He was talking about Mr. Fairweather and what they'd been doing and how shocked he was that he'd died."

"And what did Mr. Shaw say they'd done before arriving at the saloon?"

"They had correspondence to deal with after dinner, papers that had to be signed and letters that had to be written. He mentioned it was something to do with shares. Mr. Shaw said Mr. Fairweather was 'in a mood.' He was annoyed because they'd run out of stationery and was impatient with how long Mr. Shaw was taking with the letters. Mr. Fairweather took over writing one of the letters himself. I was quite surprised to hear he even fetched some envelopes from Louisa's portable writing desk and sealed up the letters while Mr. Shaw sorted the stamps. Mr. Shaw was perturbed about the stationery. He was rather fixated on it. People often do that in a traumatic situation—ramble on about something inconsequential. Apparently, the steamer hadn't been resupplied with envelopes, and he hoped the ones he borrowed would be enough to last until Luxor, where he could get more. He also talked a bit about how Mr.

Fairweather was in a hurry to get to the saloon because he knew his wife was waiting for him. Mrs. Fairweather found that detail comforting."

"Did you know Mr. Fairweather before this journey?"

"No."

I had mentally gone on to the next question, but her tone, which wasn't flat but had more of a considering lilt to it, made me pause. "It sounds as if there's more to that sentence."

Miss Entwhistle was running her finger along the edge of the tin. With her gaze fixed on it, she said. "I knew of his wife."

"Louisa?"

"When she was Louisa Lancaster."

"You'd read her articles?"

She let out a scoffing laugh. "You could say that."

# CHAPTER 18

The sudden departure of Mr. and Mrs. Theodore Crofterson from the Semiramis has set tongues wagging. Could it be related to that unfortunate incident in the ballroom last Tuesday night? Time will tell!

—*About Town, The Nile*

*I* glanced at Mr. Briarcliff, who was flexing his fingers. His eyebrows flared a tiny bit, a subtle movement that conveyed he wasn't sure what to make of Miss Entwhistle's statement, but he was intrigued. I was too.

He picked up his pencil as I said, "I sense there's more to this than reading Louisa Lancaster's articles."

Miss Entwhistle shoved the tin away and stood. She paced across the promenade deck and stared out at the water, arms crossed, the breeze lifting her hair away from her face. Mr. Briarcliff drew a breath. I had no doubt he was about to command she return to the table, but I put a hand on his arm. He jerked away, leaving a slash across the note-book page.

Miss Entwhistle dropped her arms and strode back. She gripped the back of the chair. "I'm a straightforward sort of person. I don't see any use in beating around the bush. Do you remember an article Louisa Lancaster wrote after she worked under an assumed name as a factory girl?"

"No, but I heard about her articles from Hildy. She said Louisa exposed the difficult working conditions."

Her fingers flexed, digging into the rattan on the chair back. "My uncle owned that factory. I was his ward. I went to live with him after my parents died in a train accident when I was ten. Because of that article, his business went bankrupt. He'd been too trusting, he told me, and had given his factory manager free rein. He jumped off the roof of the factory the day he declared bankruptcy."

"Goodness. I had no idea. I'm sorry." I'd been completely wrong about the source of tension I'd sensed in Miss Entwhistle. It wasn't linked to Mr. Shaw, but to Louisa.

Miss Entwhistle gave a mechanical nod. "I was nineteen at the time and self-sufficient enough to survive on my own. I had a teaching certificate and found work at the school where I teach now." She released the back of the chair and straightened. "So yes, I did know of Louisa. Looking back, I can see that things did need to change at the factory, but I believe it could have been done in a different way. Louisa Fairweather is still responsible, in a roundabout way, for my uncle's death." She pulled out the chair and sat down, letting out a tremendous sigh. "However, once I found out that she was on the steamer, I decided there would be no use to behave with animosity toward her now. I can't change what happened, and I bear no ill will toward her."

We sat in silence for a moment, the only sound the pulse

of the awning in the wind and the faint scratch of the pencil on paper. "That's very practical," I said. "I'm not sure I know many people who would be that forgiving."

Miss Entwhistle had picked up the tin and was turning it over, setting the coins rattling inside it. "Oh, I haven't forgiven her. I didn't say that. I was extremely angry for years." She placed the tin gently on the table and put her hands in her lap. "But I've learned that my anger and rage, while directed at her, was harming me, not her. I could live my life consumed by those emotions, or I could let go of it. It *was* a practical choice. When I saw her name on the passenger list, I made a decision not to snatch up that anger again. Of course, you may have noticed that I don't go out of my way to speak to her. There are limits to what one can handle."

"And yet you still insisted she sleep in your cabin the night her husband died."

"I couldn't in good conscience avoid it. Mrs. Walsh is rather fragile, and I knew if I didn't offer, she would. I was afraid it might tax Mrs. Walsh too much."

"You also shared Mr. Shaw's recollections of Mr. Fairweather's last moments with Louisa."

"Believe me, I considered keeping quiet. But I know grief very well. Could I hold back what might provide a small portion of comfort?" She closed her eyes a moment. "I couldn't. Now, if you'll excuse me, I have to find Mr. Listergraff and see if he needs help with the shuffleboard cues." She picked up the makeshift disk.

I twisted around in my chair. "Wait, Miss Entwhistle. One more question." She halted at the door to the saloon. "Did you send any correspondence—letters or anything of that type—to Mr. Fairweather?"

"Of course not. Why would I do something like that? I

wanted as little contact as possible with Mrs. Fairweather and her husband." She opened the door smoothly and didn't slam it behind her, but her stiff movements conveyed her agitated state.

Mr. Briarcliff put the pencil in his pocket and closed the notebook. "Well. I didn't expect that."

"Indeed. I did notice Miss Entwhistle seemed uncomfortable and somewhat conflicted when she spoke to Louisa about Mr. Shaw, but I had no idea of the link between the two women."

"And it sounds as if Louisa has no idea either."

The canvas flapped in the wind, and I studied the swirl of water several yards away as the Nile churned around a sandbank. "Do you believe Miss Entwhistle?"

"That she didn't send the letters? I do."

I let out a shallow laugh. "You're so confident in everything you say." I sobered. "But in this case, I believe her too. She's a phlegmatic sort, and I don't see her sending mysterious notes with only a name and then following them up with photos and obituaries. If she wanted revenge or a confrontation, I think she'd be more the type who would face one head-on."

Mr. Briarcliff made a humming sound and looked toward the bow, squinting into the distance. "And why would she send something like that to Mr. Fairweather? Mrs. Fairweather would make more sense as a recipient."

Were the letters to Hildy linked somehow to the strange missives Mr. Fairweather had received? I shifted in my seat. It was imperative I speak to Hildy and convince her to share the details about the letters she'd received. I consulted my watch. "It's almost luncheon. Shall we plan on speaking to Hildy, Dr. Walsh, and Seffie after luncheon?"

"Yes. If it's agreeable to Hildy, shall we meet at her cabin after luncheon?"

I pushed my chair back. "Let's plan for that. Then we'll have spoken to everyone except Mr. Alexander."

"You've forgotten you and me. We should interview each other."

"Oh yes. I suppose you're right. Even if we are the captain's designated investigators, our statements must be included as well."

"Exactly. No one is above suspicion."

Anticipation continues to build as Howard Carter prepares to open Tut-ankh-Amen's sarcophagus in the Valley of the Kings. The momentous event, eagerly awaited by Egyptologists worldwide, has faced delays due to tensions between Carter's team and Egyptian authorities over excavation rights and artifact ownership.

—*The Standard*

On our way into the dining room, I caught up with Hildy and threaded my arm through her elbow. I had to give her a warning about the letters. I wasn't sure how she would take my advice, but I tamped down a flutter of unease and launched right into it since time was of the essence. "Mr. Briarcliff and I would like to speak to you directly after luncheon in your cabin, if that's a good time for you."

"Yes, of course."

"Then Mr. Briarcliff will meet us there. And, although I know you won't want to, you must mention the anonymous letters you've received."

She pulled back from me. "Why would I do that?"

"I can't say more now." We entered the dining room, and I gave a significant look at the passengers flowing into the room behind us. She gave a little nod, and we sat down on opposite sides of our table. We didn't speak of the topic during the meal. The tables were close together, and our conversation would be easily overheard. But we weren't silent. After all, we were two British women and had no trouble filling the time with inconsequential discussions about the weather, plays we'd seen, and latest fashion trends. As I sipped my soup, I tried to detect if Hildy was upset with me, but her manner seemed perfectly normal. When the final course was removed, we were the first to leave the dining room. Once we were striding along the deck, she asked, "What do you mean I have to talk about the letters?"

I glanced over my shoulder to make sure no one had caught up with us. "You're not the only one to receive anonymous letters. We need to figure out if there's any link between your letters and the others. I'm sure Mr. Briarcliff will keep your secret—unless it's critical to reveal your identity as Amelia Wise to apprehend the poisoner, of course."

"Dear me. What an unexpected turn of events, more anonymous letters. You didn't inform Mr. Briarcliff about the letters I've received?"

"No, not at all. It's your secret to tell."

Hildy patted my shoulder. "Poor Blix. It must be wearisome to carry so many secrets. First Mr. Briarcliff's and then mine. I'm sorry to put you in this position."

The knot of worry inside my chest loosened, and I looked

away from her sympathetic face. My throat suddenly felt prickly. She tilted her head and looked closer at me. "What's wrong? Your eyes look glassy."

"It's the wind."

"Are you sure you're all right? Is taking statements too arduous? It has put you in a difficult position."

I dabbed at the inside corner of my eye with a finger. "Nothing's wrong. I just appreciate you being understanding."

"Here. Have my handkerchief." She shook her head impatiently. "One should consider the feelings of others."

I blotted my lower eyelids quickly and handed the handkerchief back. I kept my voice light as I said, "I so rarely encounter kindness from those closest to me that I don't know how to receive it."

Hildy's expression changed again, and she looked both sad and fierce at the same time. "I should like to have a long talk with your parents. They have a lot to answer for."

"Father would never sit down with anyone who wanted to tell him off."

Hildy raised her chin. "It's a challenge I'd relish. Ah, look. Mr. Briarcliff is waiting for us." Hildy opened the door of her cabin and invited us in.

She motioned to the notebook Mr. Briarcliff held. "It looks like you will be the note-taker, so why don't you have a seat here?" Hildy's spacious first-class cabin was completely paneled in glossy dark wood with gilded molding and had a sitting area with two plush armchairs with an occasional table between them. In my cabin, a small arrangement of lotus flowers was refreshed every day, but in Hildy's cabin vases of lilies, lotuses, and birds of paradise were dotted around the room. I brought over the chair from the desk while Hildy took a seat in the other armchair.

Mr. Briarcliff balanced his notebook on his knees, took out his pencil, and gave me a nod. I asked for Hildy's passport. She retrieved it from a drawer in the large wardrobe. I gave it a quick glance before handing it across to Mr. Briarcliff. Once he'd noted the details, he handed it back to her.

I said, "Let's talk about Mr. Shaw first. You weren't in the saloon when he passed?"

"No, I was here in my cabin. I didn't know about it until you arrived and told me."

"And did you speak to Mr. Shaw that day?"

"No. I actually never had any direct conversation with him, other than a passing greeting."

"When did you first become acquainted with Mr. Shaw?"

"On the first day of the journey. But, as I said, I never really had a conversation with him."

"Then let's move on to Mr. Fairweather." I glanced at Mr. Briarcliff to see if I needed to pause, but he seemed to be keeping up. "You were in the saloon in the group around Mr. Fairweather. Can you describe exactly what happened from your point of view?"

"Well, it was all very sudden and traumatic. One moment he was sitting there speaking to Louisa, and in the next he was gasping and tumbling onto the floor."

"Did you see anyone hand him anything?"

"No. Well, except for the coffee."

"Tell us more about that."

"Minute by minute? All right." Hildy's brow furrowed, and although she was looking at the bird of paradise arrangement on the table, her gaze was unfocused. "Let's see . . . Blix, you left when Mr. Fairweather and Mr. Shaw arrived."

"Yes, I went to the promenade deck."

"Mr. Shaw took your seat, and Mr. Fairweather went to

the empty chair near Louisa. She asked if he'd completed everything he needed to do that evening, and he said he had. I asked the men if they wanted a cup of coffee, and they both said yes. The tray was nearest me, and I poured out two cups and handed one across to Mr. Shaw and passed the other one to Seffie, who handed it to Mr. Fairweather."

"They didn't take anything in their coffee?"

"No, both of them wanted it black."

"I see."

"And did anyone else approach your group at that time?"

Hildy closed her eyes a moment, then they popped open. "Miss Entwhistle, who was seated at a nearby table playing patience, came over and refilled her coffee cup. I remember it was right before the men took a seat because I thought there might not be enough coffee, and I thought I'd have to summon a steward, but there was enough coffee for two more cups."

"And what happened after the coffee was passed along to them?"

"I remember this part quite clearly. Seffie and Louisa had been talking about pruning trees—they're both avid gardeners—and Seffie asked Louisa a question about a Japanese yew she'd pruned, but before Louisa answered, a horrible gasping sound came from Mr. Fairweather. He dropped his cup, coffee spattered everywhere, and he collapsed, falling out of his chair to the floor. It was so very shocking. I think we were all stunned for a few seconds. Then everyone jumped up, and we all spoke at once."

"Did you hear anything that Mr. Shaw said during that time?"

"No. Miss Entwhistle rushed over and had a look at Mr.

Fairweather, but he was already gone—it happened so swiftly—and then she took Mr. Shaw to the chairs on the other side of the little bookcase and had him sit down. But I couldn't hear what they were saying."

"And were you acquainted with Mr. Fairweather or Louisa prior to departing on this cruise?"

"No. I was aware of who he was and knew of Louisa's time as a stunt-girl reporter, but I'd never met him or Louisa."

"Do you know of anyone who disliked Mr. Fairweather or Mr. Shaw?"

She lifted her shoulders in a *who knows* kind of gesture. "Businessman often have animus directed toward them, so I assume there was some of that, but I know of nothing specific."

"I see. That's all the questions around Mr. Fairweather and Mr. Shaw. I believe you have something to share?"

She gave a little half laugh. "Yes, apparently I do." She turned so that she faced Mr. Briarcliff directly. "This is not something that I would normally share, but Blix told me that it could be helpful. Please keep this amongst the three of us unless it becomes impossible to do so."

Mr. Briarcliff looked like he'd been asked to converse in a language he didn't know. "I'm sorry, but I don't follow."

"If it becomes necessary to share this information with the authorities to apprehend the culprit who poisoned Mr. Shaw, then I'll understand, but if what I'm about to tell you isn't related to that, I ask that you keep my secret."

"Your secret?" Mr. Briarcliff glanced at me, and I gave him a quick bob of my head. His glance pinged between Hildy and me. Then he said to me, "You obviously know about this." He sounded a little put out that he wasn't in on the secret. "You agree that this is something that can be kept quiet?"

"Yes. You'll see why in a moment, if you'll agree."

# CHAPTER 20

Dear Amelia,

I long to bob my hair, but I'm afraid it will shock Grandmother. How can I be fashionable without causing her distress?

Dear Rapunzel,

Fashion and family harmony can be as tricky to balance as a new cloche hat in a strong wind. Why not start with a modest trim, a shorter cut that's not quite the full bob? You'll be stylish without causing poor Grandmother to reach for her smelling salts. And remember, dear, hair has the marvelous habit of growing back.

*—Ask Amelia, The Illustrated Dispatch*

*M*r. Briarcliff crossed one leg over the other, closed the notebook, and balanced it on his knee. "All right. I give my word, but with the condition that if it's related to the poisoning, we'll reveal it."

"That's fine. I'll deal with it if that happens." Hildy went to her travel trunk, unlocked it, and took out her broken writing desk. She said over her shoulder, "I've received some rather vitriolic anonymous letters."

Mr. Briarcliff's foot jerked, and his notebook fell to the floor. "You have?"

Hildy returned to her chair and settled the writing desk on her lap.

"The first one arrived the day we departed from Cairo. I threw it away, but Blix saw it because it was delivered to her room instead of mine."

I picked up the notebook and held it out to Mr. Briarcliff as he asked, "The first one?"

Hildy nodded. "I've received two, but discarded them."

Mr. Briarcliff took the notebook, and I cleared my throat. "I was worried about you, Hildy, so I saved the second note." I took the crumpled note I'd rescued from the waiter's tray from my pocket. "Both notes were typed on the steamer's stationery, sent in a blank envelope."

Mr. Briarcliff's forehead wrinkled at my statement. "But then perhaps the first note was intended for you?"

I raised my eyebrows. "Are you insinuating that I'm a more appropriate recipient for threatening letters than Hildy?"

"Well, even you have to admit you're quite trying at times, while Hildy has such a sweet nature."

Hildy chuckled. "Thank you for the compliment, but because of their contents, I believe both were intended for me."

I smoothed the wrinkled note. "I've been carrying this around with me for several days. I don't feel comfortable leaving it in my cabin. You'll understand why in a moment." I handed it to him. As he scanned it, I said, "I insisted Hildy tell you about these because she's the second person receiving anonymous letters. Perhaps it's linked to the other letters that were sent to another passenger."

Mr. Briarcliff open his mouth, then closed it. He shifted in his chair and reread the page again. "This is quite vile. Was the other the same?"

"Yes, the same tone and the same insinuation that time was running out."

Mr. Briarcliff finally looked up from the note. "Whoever wrote this is threatening to expose a secret of yours, Hildy?" He gave a little laugh, indicating he thought that was an absurd thing, but Hildy didn't smile in return.

In a matter-of-fact tone, she said, "They're threatening to reveal something I'd rather not be public knowledge. I arrived back from dinner a few nights ago and found someone had pried this open. You see, I have a secret identity, just as you did, Rafe. Although mine is much more long-standing than yours."

Mr. Briarcliff looked as if he had suddenly found himself in a maze and wasn't sure how to get out.

She took out a packet of letters and handed them to him. "Do you know who Amelia Wise is?"

"The name sounds familiar." He returned the wrinkled note to me and took the bundle of envelopes Hildy held out to him, but he continued to stare at her.

She flapped her hand. "Take a look."

He gingerly flipped through the envelopes, then his gaze hopped back to her.

"Go on. Read a few."

The envelopes were already slit open, and he took out a letter. His gaze skimmed down the page, then he looked at the next one, the furrows in his brow deepening. "Dear Amelia? *You're* Amelia Wise?"

"That's correct." Hildy's tone was that of a teacher pleased with a student's answer. She sat back, hands folded in her lap. "My contract with my publisher requires I keep my role as Amelia secret."

Mr. Briarcliff readjusted his position in the chair, opened his mouth, closed it, and then shifted again and finally said, "Well, you've certainly done an excellent job of that so far. I had no idea." He returned the agony letters to their envelopes.

A smile broke across her face. "Neither did Blix. I didn't realize I excelled at subterfuge."

Mr. Briarcliff looked so gobsmacked that I added, "I just learned a few days ago. I was as shocked as you are."

He made a little head-shaking motion as he regarded Hildy. "I'm seeing you in a whole new light."

"Don't be silly, Rafe. I'm still exactly the same. I just have employment that I keep quiet about. If anyone should understand that, it should be you."

"Indeed," he said with one of his quick smiles that flashed across his face, then he turned serious as he picked up the anonymous letters. "Why would someone want to expose the writer of an agony column?"

Hildy said, "I don't know. Perhaps I gave advice to someone and they're disgruntled. Or it might be a family member who didn't approve of the counsel I gave to someone they loved. Another possibility is that it could be someone from another newspaper out to expose me. After all, I am an old maid who often dispenses advice about love and marriage. If that detail became known, it could discredit the paper."

Mr. Briarcliff scoffed. "Surely not."

"Oh yes, indeed. The *Ask Amelia* column is one of the biggest draws for the paper, along with the crossword and the comics. A rival newspaper might be quite happy to disparage me and perhaps draw people to their agony column. *Joyce's Jottings* has been gaining quite a following over at *The Independent Herald*."

"I had no idea the world of agony aunts was so cutthroat."

"I hope you will keep this to yourself. If it must come out, then so be it. I no longer have to depend on the agony column to pay the bills, but I do enjoy it. I don't see how my publisher would let me continue to do it if I broke the contract."

"Well then, we'll do our best to keep it under wraps, won't we, Miss Windway?"

"That was my plan."

He nodded to the writing desk. "Have you informed anyone of the damage?"

"No. I thought the fewer people who knew about it, the better."

"Quite."

Mr. Briarcliff checked his watch. "I spoke to Dr. Walsh on my way to luncheon. He's able to give us a few moments at the top of the hour, Miss Windway." Mr. Briarcliff braced his hands on his knees. "We should be getting on . . . unless we have any other secrets to discuss?"

Both Hildy and Mr. Briarcliff looked at me, and I gave a little laugh. "Don't look at me. *I* don't have a secret identity."

# CHAPTER 21

The London Underground continues to update station exteriors and platform nameboards with the red roundel designed by calligrapher Edward Johnston, who also created the typeface used by the London Underground. Architect Charles Holden has been retained to design new stations.

*—The Standard*

Mr. Briarcliff closed the door to Hildy's cabin behind us. "Dr. Walsh will meet us at the stern," he said, and we turned in that direction. "Thank you for convincing Hildy to share about the anonymous letters she's received. It's very concerning."

I tilted my head so that I could see his face better. "Yet you didn't seem worried about the letters Mr. Fairweather received, and they were decidedly strange."

"The letters sent to Mr. Fairweather didn't contain

threats, while Hildy's do. Very vicious language in hers too —at least the one you saved."

"Do you think it's the same person sending letters to both Hildy and Mr. Fairweather?"

"Why would it be the same person? The letters are completely different."

"You sound almost personally offended. It's a question that has to be asked. Both Hildy and Mr. Fairweather received anonymous letters while on this steamer. Surely there aren't two different people sending threatening"—I caught his expression and realized he was about to protest my word choice—"or *strange* letters to passengers?" I strolled along, hands behind my back, holding my notebook, my gaze focused on the steamer deck. "You'd think blackmail would be the purpose of the letters, but those directed at Hildy seem to be only intended to frighten her."

"Perhaps fright is the initial tactic before a demand of money."

"Mr. Fairweather's letters, on the other hand, aren't scary at all. Just perplexing." We'd reached the stern, but it was empty. Mr. Briarcliff walked over to the starboard side and glanced toward the bow. "I believe that's Dr. Walsh heading for the stairs." He jogged off, and I followed at a quick walk. The figure that was striding purposely toward the stairs set midway between the bow and stern was indeed Dr. Walsh, pipe smoke trailing behind him as he paced away.

When I caught up with the two men, Dr. Walsh held his pipe in one hand and his other hand was palm up, as if he were a bobby stopping traffic. "Don't come any closer, Miss Windway. I've just come from Mr. Alexander, and I'm trying to keep my distance from all the passengers."

I stopped even with Mr. Briarcliff, who stood about six or

seven feet away from Dr. Walsh. "We were to meet at the stern so we could ask you a few questions."

Dr. Walsh let out an exasperated breath. "I'm sorry. It completely slipped my mind. I'm afraid I can't speak to you now. I'm on my way down to visit one of the stewards who isn't feeling well."

"Oh, that's not good news."

"No. It's not. That's why I don't want you to be close to me."

For a few hours, I'd forgotten about the possibility of a scarlet fever outbreak on the S.S. *Cleopatra*. Even though I wasn't feeling sick, I couldn't help thinking back over the morning for any small indications—a cough or scratchy throat—that I might be coming down with something. Thankfully, I didn't pinpoint any telltale indications of an infection.

Mr. Briarcliff said, "We won't keep you, then."

Dr. Walsh took a few steps down the stairs, then trotted back up. "On second thought, I doubt I'll be less pressed for time in the next few days." He returned to the deck but remained several feet away from us. He put his hands in his pockets and spoke around his pipe. "If it's just a few questions, I can spare you five to ten minutes now."

I opened up my notebook, propped it on the stair rail, and nodded at Mr. Briarcliff to go ahead. He said, "I don't think this will take us too long. We'll need to see your passport."

"It's in my cabin."

"That's fine. We can ask Mrs. Walsh to retrieve yours when we get the particulars of hers. You were not near either Mr. Shaw or Mr. Fairweather when they passed, correct?"

Dr. Walsh took out his pipe. "No, I wasn't. I was in Mr. Alexander's cabin attending to him when Mr. Fairweather passed. When Mr. Shaw expired, I was in a deck chair on the port side, making a few notes in my travel journal." He patted the bulging pocket of his suit jacket. "And before you ask, yes, someone can verify my time on deck. A steward brought me a cup of tea."

"Excellent. Thank you for your concise answer," Mr. Briarcliff said. "Now about the deaths themselves, you had suspicions about Mr. Fairweather's passing?"

"I wish I hadn't, believe me. A medical man doesn't like to go poking bears, but if one doesn't, then . . . well, the situation can become worse if it's not investigated. There was nothing specific about his death that I could point to, other than it was exceptionally fast and that he'd not displayed any symptoms beforehand. I felt I should do due diligence since I was the only medical man on board."

"So, you gathered the coffee cups because you thought he might have been poisoned?" Mr. Briarcliff asked.

"It was a possibility. An issue with his heart was another option."

"But you found no evidence of poison?"

Dr. Walsh shook his head as he looked out at the Nile. "No. But my methods of testing are somewhat limited here on the steamer."

"I expect so. It sounds as if you've been quite innovative. And you suspected a certain poison, didn't you?"

"Yes, cyanide. However, even cyanide doesn't always have an immediate visible effect, although that's often the case. It's quick, but whether or not a person has eaten and how the poison is administered can cause variances in the onset of symptoms. Even the size of a person plays into it." He waved a hand in an apologetic manner. "Sorry. I tend to get carried away with the details. Suffice it to say, even with a fast-acting poison, it could be immediate or a quarter of an hour later before there are symptoms."

"And Mr. Shaw?"

"Now in his case, I'm quite sure it was cyanide poisoning. The devil of it is, I can't figure out how it was done. The man hadn't had anything to eat or drink in over an hour, and there was no trace of poison."

Mr. Briarcliff checked to see how I was doing with the notes, and I nodded for him to continue. He turned back to Dr. Walsh. "And did you know of any enemies either man had?"

"No." Dr. Walsh took a step toward the stairs.

Mr. Briarcliff added, "And did you send any passengers any notes or letters?"

Dr. Walsh let out a guff of a laugh. "No. I'm not much of a correspondent when it comes to letters." He took out his pocket watch. "Excuse me, I really must check on the steward."

He started down the stairs, and I leaned over the railing. The earthy smell of pipe smoke floated up as I called out, "We also need to speak with Mr. Alexander. When will that be possible?"

He paused and cranked his head back. "He's not up to visitors, and he's still contagious. I won't feel comfortable allowing visitors for several days."

"But the captain wants all the statements before we reach Luxor."

Dr. Walsh drummed his fingers on the railing. "I suppose if you give me a list of questions, I can ask him and jot down his answers."

"That would be very helpful," I called to his retreating back. He waved a hand in acknowledgment as he disappeared down the stairwell.

Mr. Briarcliff perched on the end of one of the deck chairs and opened his notebook to a blank page. "Let me make a list of questions for Dr. Walsh to ask Mr. Alexander."

Once he'd finished and torn out the page, he sent a steward to deliver it to Dr. Walsh.

I said, "Let's see if we can talk with Seffie next."

"I believe at this time of day she's normally in her cabin."

As we set off down the deck, she emerged from her cabin carrying knitting needles and yarn. I called out, "Seffie, do you have a few moments to answer some questions for us?"

"Yes, of course." The door to her cabin was still partially open, and Mr. Briarcliff reached out to hold it open for us, but Seffie shut the door firmly. "Let's go to the saloon. I've had quite enough of being in my cabin. I always rest in the afternoon, but it's purely to humor my husband." We moved to the saloon at her slow pace. "Edmund's quite concerned I'll have a relapse, but I'm in excellent health—hale and hearty, even."

I said, "I'm glad to hear it."

We entered the saloon, and Mr. Briarcliff asked, "Sun or shade?"

"Sun for me," Seffie declared, and Mr. Briarcliff dragged three rattan chairs over to the sunny side of the deck. Once we were settled and he had his notebook and pencil ready, Seffie lifted her face to the sun, then closed her eyes for a moment. She was so small that her feet barely touched the floor. Her eyes popped open. "Now what can I tell you about Mr. Fairweather and Mr. Shaw?" She arranged her yarn in her lap and began knitting, the needles clicking softly with her swift movements.

I said, "Let's start with Mr. Fairweather since you were in the group around him when he passed away. Tell us what you remember from the time he and Mr. Shaw entered the saloon."

"Well, let me think . . ." Her hands stilled as she looked out at the sparkling river, then she said in her usual measured cadence, "Mr. Fairweather sat down by Louisa and said something to her—or perhaps she asked him a question. I don't remember exactly. Hildy asked the gentlemen if they wanted coffee. They both did, and they both preferred it black. Miss Entwistle came over around then and refilled her cup." She sent a pitying look toward Mr. Briarcliff, whose pencil was racing across the page. "Is this too much detail?"

"No, it's perfect," I said. "Please continue."

She resumed knitting. "Well, there's not much more to tell. Hildy poured out the coffee, gave one to Mr. Shaw, and handed another one over to me, which I passed to Mr. Fair-weather."

I gave Mr. Briarcliff a moment to turn the page, then asked, "And what happened next?"

"Mr. Fairweather had sort of a fit and fell from his chair, clutching at his chest." She demonstrated, gripping the fabric of her dress. "Then Miss Entwhistle hurried over to him. I moved out of her way. She nursed during the war, you know. I sent a steward for Edmund. Everything was at sixes and sevens. I wasn't able to see anything else."

"And then with Mr. Shaw, what happened?"

"I was here in the saloon when he and Louisa arrived that afternoon. Mr. Shaw took a seat at one of the tables, and Louisa came over to sit with our group, which included Miss Entwhistle and you." She leaned toward Mr. Briarcliff and clarified, "For your notes, that's Miss Windway I'm referring to." She untangled a knot in her yarn as she continued, "We chatted a bit, but there was also silence when I did my needlework, Miss Entwhistle sketched, and Miss Windway and Louisa read. Then tea arrived."

"Did you see anyone else enter the saloon before the steward brought in tea?"

"No, it was very quiet until that moment. I remember quite clearly that Mr. Shaw stood up and was packing up his case at that point. Louisa invited him to join us for tea, but he said he wasn't feeling well. Then he gasped and fell, and seconds later Miss Entwhistle said he was dead. It was just an appalling and awful shock."

The measured tempo and the pattern of her word choices seemed to echo in my mind. I sat for a moment, lost in thought, then realized Mr. Briarcliff had spoken to me. "Yes?"

"Don't you have a few more questions for Mrs. Walsh?"

"Right. Yes. May I see the notes for just a moment?" I asked to buy myself time to think. He handed me the notebook, and I looked at it carefully, studying the bold strokes that made up the words *appalling and awful*. Something clicked over in my mind, bringing back the memory of the words I'd overheard about Mr. Fairweather in the tomb during the Saqqara excursion.

I handed the notebook back and swiveled quickly to Seffie. "You and your husband were acquainted with Mr. Fairweather before this trip, weren't you?"

# CHAPTER 22

Sir Edgar Ridgemont, the eminent archaeologist, departs today for Luxor. He joins the excavation team at the Valley of the Kings. We wish him luck and hope for the discovery of another golden tomb.

*—Arrivals and Departures, The Nile*

The rhythmic click of the needles stopped as Seffie's hands dropped to her lap. She looked stunned, as if someone had doused her with a bucket of cold water. I could feel Mr. Briarcliff's heavy gaze on my profile, but I didn't look his way. I kept my attention fixed on Seffie.

She began knitting again, but this time her movements were jerky instead of smooth and rote. "No, that's incorrect. Neither my husband nor I ever met the man." She spoke more quickly and more adamantly than I'd ever heard her. Her shoulders were drawn back, and there was something guarded about her posture as well.

"But I overheard you during the Saqqara excursion. I didn't mean to, but sound carried in the tomb. You were in the lower level, and I was at the top of the stairs. You said Mr. Fairweather was horrible—*vile and vicious* were your words, I believe. They stuck in my mind because they were so vivid and a rather severe choice of words. You also said you'd have chosen another steamer if you'd known Mr. Fairweather was among the passengers. You're fond of using alliteration in your descriptions, aren't you? *Hale and hearty. Appalling and awful. Vile and vicious . . .*"

She dropped her knitting again and leaned forward, putting her elbows on her knees and resting her forehead in her hands. I could practically feel the daggers from Mr. Briarcliff's eyes piercing my flesh. "Miss Windway," he began in an admonishing tone, but Seffie sat back, shoulders slumped.

"Miss Windway is partially correct." She sounded quite regretful, and her words silenced Mr. Briarcliff. "It's true that we hadn't met the man," she infused the last two words with a tone usually reserved to describe vermin, "personally, but we certainly knew who he was."

"Why did you think he was vile?"

"It's quite a small, petty thing, and now that he's dead, well, does it matter? It's Mr. Shaw's death that will be under investigation."

I glanced at Mr. Briarcliff. He was staring at Seffie like she was a creature from another world. He shifted his gaze to me and gave a little nod as if to say, *Go on with the questions. I'm with you now.*

"It is important," I said to Seffie and waited.

Her words came even more slowly than before. "You're aware I'm quite fond of gardening. I wrote a series of articles for my local garden club circular about rock gardens and . . ." She twitched her shoulders. "No. Let me start another way." She put her knitting aside, tucking it between her leg and the arm of the chair. "I believe you said you visited Nobilis Domus?"

"That's right. I gave a travel lecture there."

"Did you perhaps see the gardens?"

"I didn't have time. I heard they're sensational."

Seffie let out a snort, and Mr. Briarcliff looked up from his notes. Clearly, he hadn't expected her to make such an indelicate sound. "What an apropos description, especially if you mean sensational in the sense of the *sensational* topics in the illustrated newspapers that focus on stunts and tittle-tattle with evocative headlines."

I felt we were getting a bit off track. "So, you visited the gardens of Nobilis Domus?"

She nodded. "And they're exactly what you'd expect from Mr. Fairweather. He was a rather showy sort, if you know what I mean."

I thought back to the gilt, the lush fabrics, the Rococo and Baroque furnishings of the mansion. It had been rather over the top. Even the name itself was ostentatious. "The house certainly doesn't adhere to modern aesthetics of simple lines and less ornamentation."

Seffie chuckled and smiled briefly. "Imagine his ostentatious style applied to a garden. I have specific opinions about gardens. Perhaps I'm a little too rigid in my thinking, but I believe a garden is a place where one appreciates the beauty of the natural world. It should be a respite. It should rejuvenate and refresh one's soul."

"I see." I spoke the words, though in reality I wasn't sure what gardens had to do with Mr. Fairweather, but Seffie was so soft-spoken and deliberate in her speech that I didn't want to interrupt her.

"Mr. Fairweather had an interest in cultivating plants. You'll notice I don't call him a gardener—he didn't deserve that title. When he and Louisa married, she convinced him to let her take over the gardens immediately around the house. She's been renovating them, converting them to pleasant landscapes people can enjoy for years to come, probably decades. But Mr. Fairweather refused to hear of any changes to the areas farther afield from the house, his *showpieces*, as he called them. He'd produced a blight of absurd vignettes on the estate grounds."

"I'm not sure I follow."

"Ha! I didn't understand it either. Let me explain." She inched forward on her chair, her words flowing quickly now. "He attempted to recreate a desert with pyramids to scale." She threw out a hand toward the stern of the boat. "You saw the pyramids. There's no vegetation around them, and yet he planted acacias and palms and had the gardeners ruthlessly weed out any plants or grasses native to England. There's a topiary garden with plants trimmed into life-size elephants, hippos, and giraffes. He brought in masons to create caves with manufactured stalactites and stalagmites and a tunnel with waterways and an underground grotto. In another area, he had a cottage built to look aged. And he employs someone to live there and act the part of a hermit!" She huffed. "It's just absurd. And that's not even mentioning his gnome and pixie garden."

She'd worked herself up into quite a state, becoming more passionate the longer she spoke, but now she crossed her arms and dropped back against the chair, like a top that had stopped spinning. "I'm getting worked up about it now, even though I know it's such a small matter compared to the seriousness of his death and the poisoning of Mr. Shaw, but I don't see how anyone could *not* think his actions are a detriment to gardening."

Mr. Briarcliff's lips were twitching. I sent him a severe look. He dipped his head deeper over the notebook as I said to Seffie, "I think I understand. You believe his actions cause people to ridicule gardeners?"

"Exactly! It's quite difficult to gain respect for home gardeners and our little cottage gardens. Some in the Royal Horticulturist Society see us as dabblers. Silly women prattling on about our pretty flowers, when some of us are creating hybrids and writing papers for journals. It's fine for Mr. Fairweather to indulge in the fanciful, but his actions impact the community of gardeners as a whole."

She tossed her head in a way that if her hair hadn't been pinned up, she would have flung it over her shoulder. "His fantastical approach is a travesty. I said as much in a series of articles I wrote for our local gardening circular." Seffie became focused on a loose thread on her sleeve. Her tone was more subdued as she said, "Someone must have sent it to Mr. Fairweather. He didn't like my opinion. The Royal Horticultural Society didn't want to offend him, so because of his maneuvering, I lost my position on a committee. My draft of a book about rock gardens, which was slated for publication, has been returned to me. The publisher withdrew and canceled the contract—after a lengthy lunch with Mr. Fairweather."

She tucked the thread under her cuff and met my gaze. "It's all a very small drama around what some consider a hobby, but there you are. That's why I said he was vile and vicious. He was also uncouth and uncultured. He didn't like that I criticized his garden, and he made sure I was shunned by the gardening community."

"Goodness," I said. "I'm surprised you get on so well with Louisa. You two seem quite friendly."

"Oh, I have no quibble with Louisa. As I mentioned earlier, she wasn't fond of Mr. Fairweather's horrible outdoor displays. It wasn't difficult to avoid speaking to Mr. Fairweather. He rarely deigned to speak to anyone but Louisa. I didn't like the man, but I assure you, I did not harm him." I must have looked surprised because she added, "I sensed that Edmund had some questions about Mr. Fairweather's death. He never said anything to me, of course. He never does, but a wife can tell when her husband is troubled. If there was foul play involved in his death, it certainly wasn't on my part. I didn't like the man's choices when it came to his landscaping and vegetation. On the face of things, it's quite a silly reason to be upset—over the appropriate display of plants. But people do become entangled in these petty arguments, and it does lead to quite a bit of animosity, but I'd never go so far as to physically harm someone."

# CHAPTER 23

Dr. Alary left Cairo last week for England to visit to his sick mother.

—*Arrivals and Departures, The Nile*

*I* believed Seffie. She looked so earnest. With her elfin build and delicate air, it was hard to imagine her intentionally hurting someone. However, a voice at the back of my mind whispered, *That's why she'd use poison.* She was also an avid gardener. Compared to Seffie, my knowledge of gardening was sketchy, but even I knew plenty of poisonous plants could be found in gardens and in the wild.

Mr. Briarcliff cleared his throat, pulling me out of my reverie. "Just a few more questions, Mrs. Walsh. Have you or your husband received any unusual letters or notes lately? Perhaps something unsigned?"

"No, nothing like that."

I pulled my thoughts back to the present moment and

asked, "And have you sent any letters or notes to any other passengers?"

"No. There's no need to do that. We see each other so often. If I have something to say to someone, I just wait until I see the person. It's such a small steamer that we run across each other several times a day."

"That is true," I said. "And finally, do you know of anyone who had a disagreement with either Mr. Fairweather or Mr. Shaw?"

"No. Other than the, um, tiff between myself and Mr. Fairweather, I don't know of anyone specific. If his behavior toward me was his usual manner, then I would imagine there would be quite a few people angry with him, but I don't know of anyone specific. As for Mr. Shaw, I didn't know the man well enough to say."

"Thank you. I believe that's all we need." I looked at Mr. Briarcliff to see if he had anything to add.

He put the period at the end of a sentence with a flourish. "All that's left is that we need to jot down the particulars of your passport and your husband's."

"Let me get them for you now."

Once her light footsteps died away, I turned Mr. Briarcliff. "What a peculiar quarrel."

He sat back, stretching out his legs. He crossed his ankles and folded his arms over his chest. "I must say, I'm learning more about women on this steamer than I ever have in my entire life—and I grew up with a sister. Who would have imagined it?" He dropped into a whisper. "One woman hiding a pen name"—he returned to his normal conversational level—"and another in a feud—over gardens!—with one of the most successful businessmen in Britain."

"Could it possibly be that you just assume older women are boring and insipid?"

He pursed his lips to the side and tilted his head back and forth slightly as he weighed my comments. Before he answered, Seffie returned with the passports. We examined and recorded the details as she wound her loose yarn.

"If that's all you need from me, I believe I'll spend some time on the promenade deck. Hildy just invited me to join her and Mr. Listergraff in a game of shuffleboard."

As she left, a steward entered and said something to Mr. Briarcliff in a low voice. Mr. Briarcliff nodded and stood. "I'm needed on the main deck. It shouldn't take long. I'll return as quickly as I can."

"I'll wait for you here." He paced off, following the attendant's fluttering robe. I opened my notebook, intending to look back over the statements from Mr. Listergraff and Dr. Walsh, but when I cracked the book open, the notes Louisa had received slipped partially out from between the endpaper and the back cover.

I read through the obituaries. I reached the last one, and a little spark of excitement flared. Hadn't I seen that phrase *Section Twenty* before? I was looking back through the newspaper clippings when another steward arrived and handed me an envelope. "From Dr. Walsh," he said with a little bow and left. Both my name and Mr. Briarcliff's were written on the envelope. It was sealed. I tapped it on my knee as I debated whether to read it right away or go in search of Mr. Briarcliff.

Mr. Briarcliff's phrase about "two witnesses" came to mind. I let out a sigh and returned the notes and clippings to the proper envelopes, then put them back in my notebook.

"You weren't thinking of opening that without me, were you?"

I jumped at the voice that emanated from just behind my shoulder. I slammed my notebook closed. "Of course not. I was having a look at Louisa's notes, waiting for you to return. The envelope is from Dr. Walsh." He took a seat beside me as I ran my finger under the flap and took out two sheets of paper and a British passport.

The handwriting on the first page was a hurried scrawl. I read the short note aloud.

"Dear Mr. Briarcliff and Miss Windway, Mr. Alexander's answers to your questions are on the following page. I located his passport in his suitcase and enclosed it as well."

I caught the faint woody scent of his shaving lather as Mr. Briarcliff leaned across the arm of his chair and read over my shoulder as I skimmed the second page.

The answers were brief. "Mr. Alexander says he was in his cabin at the time of both deaths."

Mr. Briarcliff said, "Nothing remarkable there," his breath tickling the side of my neck.

"Don't loom so." I handed the pages to him. "He said he didn't know either man before meeting them on the steamer. May I borrow your pencil to take down the details of his passport?"

He handed it to me as I flicked the cover of the passport back and scanned over it. Then I dropped the pencil and sat forward, tilting the passport as I read it again.

Mr. Briarcliff looked up. "What is it?"

I turned toward him slowly. I couldn't keep the grin off my face. "I told you we should examine everyone's passports." I held the passport like a placard and waved as if I were showing off a beautiful painting or an *objet d'art*. "Mr. Alexander is traveling under a false name."

"What?" He dropped the papers, and I handed him the passport.

I pointed to the two names. "His surname isn't Alexander. That's his *given* name. His name is actually Alexander Howard."

"But he's listed on the passenger roster as Howard Alexander," Mr. Briarcliff said.

"Well, both Alexander and Howard are names that could be either a given name or a surname. Perhaps someone in the offices of the Blue Lotus Line made a mistake and reversed the order."

Mr. Briarcliff didn't look pleased. "If they did, it's a serious error. It's critical we have the correct information about each passenger on the manifest. Passengers present their travel documents before departure. It should have been noted correctly."

"But if there was an error—mistakes do happen—why didn't he point it out? It was printed on the card listing all the passengers that was placed in the cabins on the day we departed. Surely that was the time to bring attention to the error. Either then or when people began to address him by the wrong name."

Mr. Briarcliff murmured a sound that I took to be agreement as he angled the passport so the sunlight hit the paper directly. He ran a finger across the letters.

I continued, "Perhaps Mr. Alexan—I mean, Mr. Howard wanted the names switched on the passenger list. Could he convince someone to do that? Perhaps he persuaded the steamer official who compiled the list to change the order . . . ?"

"A bribe, you mean." His face was troubled. "Yes, that's possible. There would only be one person who'd have to be paid off. The Blue Lotus Line doesn't examine passports once steamers depart. All that is done in Cairo. The name itself hasn't been tampered with." He splayed the pages of the little book into an acute angle and examined the binding.

"It doesn't appear he replaced the entire page either." He looked through the stamps on the pages, then the front and back cover. "It looks authentic to me. If it's a forgery, it's quite well done." A smile flashed across his face. "I owe you an apology, Miss Windway. Sorry I doubted your instinct to check everyone's passports." He handed the booklet to me. "But why would Mr.—er—Howard travel with his names reversed?"

"Alexander Septimus Howard," I said, reading off the full name. "His family must have been fond of the classics."

Mr. Briarcliff blinked and looked as if he were trying to identify an unfamiliar sound. "That name rings a bell, but I can't think why."

"Perhaps he traveled on another Blue Lotus steamer? Do you see the passenger lists of all the departures?"

"No, I don't, so it couldn't have been that." He sat back and tapped the arm of his chair.

"Did you hear it in conversation? The full name is rather unique."

The tapping stopped. "I saw it in print."

"A book?"

"No, it was a newspaper." By the time he finished the sentence, he was striding across the saloon to the bookshelves.

He retrieved a stack of newspapers and deposited them on the table.

Hands on his hips, he regarded the publications, then said to himself, "I read *The Standard* most often, but I do occasionally glance through *The Illustrated Dispatch*." He began to methodically sort them into separate piles.

# CHAPTER 24

The final weekly sports meeting in Aswan concluded
Saturday with a splendid regatta. Under the expert guidance
of Mr. and Mrs. Fleming, the event drew enthusiastic visitors
to the Cataract Hotel's terrace and gardens overlooking the
picturesque river scene.

*—About Town, The Nile*

I surveyed the two stacks of newspapers Mr.
Briarcliff was making. Each pile already contained
at least a dozen or so papers, with Mr. Briarcliff tossing more
by the second. Like the magazines, the newspapers available
on the steamer were a random mix of publications that had
been left by passengers.

Even with the task narrowed down to two newspapers, it
could take hours to look through all the papers for the
mention of the name Alexander Septimus Howard.

"Couldn't we just ask Mr. Alexander why he's traveling with his names switched around?"

"Dr. Walsh won't let us speak to him, and I doubt Mr. Howard will be very forthcoming with us, especially if we have to ask through an intermediary. I *know* I've seen the name recently. Any information we can discover about Mr. Howard will give us an advantage, which we can leverage later when we are able to speak to him."

"You're sure you read the name recently? Sometime since we departed Cairo?"

"Positive. I borrowed a few of the more recent editions to read in my cabin. I distinctly remember seeing that name, and I had the same thought you did—his parents must have been quite keen about the classics."

"Then couldn't it be in your cabin?"

The sorting completed, Mr. Briarcliff took a newspaper from the top of the tallest of the stacks he'd created. "I always return the newspapers here so other passengers can enjoy them."

He unfolded the newspaper but turned to look at me, holding it poised in front of his face. "I went along with your idea of checking passports. Now it's your turn to go along with my idea."

I didn't bother to stifle a sigh and pulled out a chair. I took a newspaper off the stack of *The Illustrated Dispatch*. "I hope this turns out better than my search for the final install-ment of *The Agony Column* story in *The Saturday Evening Post*."

Head swiveling as he scanned across the front page, he asked, "No luck on that quest?"

"None. I'll never know how that story ended."

"Perhaps you can find it when we reach Luxor."

"Doubtful. I've resigned myself to living without knowing how it ends."

For a while, the only sound in the saloon was the crack of newsprint as we turned pages and the exclamations that filtered to the saloon from the promenade deck, where the shuffleboard game was apparently still in progress. After about an hour, I stretched and rubbed my eyes. "Time for tea, I think. My vision is going blurry." I poured us each a cup after it arrived. Mr. Briarcliff drank his, his focus on the lines of text. I went back to skimming the narrow columns.

A while later, I rotated my shoulders and noticed the sun was sliding toward the horizon, coloring the sky a vivid gold edged with pink. "The sun will set soon." Mr. Briarcliff glanced up, grunted an acknowledgment, and went back to his task. Usually, some passengers gathered in the saloon to watch the sunset, but the shuffleboard game was apparently the main attraction this evening, because voices continued to filter in from the promenade deck, and no one came into the saloon.

I shifted three more editions before the fringe of palms on the bank became a silhouette against the bright disk of the sun as it sank lower. I was so immersed in my search that I didn't realize the steamer had stopped for the night until I finished with one of the newspapers and put it in the "completed" pile. I looked up, trying to put my finger on what had changed, and noticed the absence of the constant breeze created from the steamer's forward progress.

When the sun finally set, we moved a lamp to the table. Even though it felt like late evening, we still had nearly two hours until dinner would be served. The stewards arrived and lowered the canvas panels that blocked out the darkness and some of the insects.

I was grateful I had the illustrated newspaper, which

contained more photographs than the staid *Standard* that Mr. Briarcliff was trudging through. I finished looking through another edition, then took a lap around the room, angling my head from side to side to stretch my neck. I sat back down and opened the next newspaper. "Are you *sure* it was in a newspaper? Perhaps it was in a book?"

"I'm sure." The pages rattled as he folded a newspaper and placed it on the growing pile of newspapers he'd looked through. He shook out the next newspaper.

I read on, skimming down the columns, but after a few moments I realized Mr. Briarcliff was sitting absolutely still, his hand suspended motionless as he held a page half-turned.

"Did you find it?"

He released the page, and it settled onto the desk as he pointed with an ink-smudged finger to an article. I moved around the table and read over his shoulder, "Famous Psychic Exposed as Charlatan." I couldn't keep the incredulity out of my voice as I read on, "By our Special Correspondent Alexander Septimus Howard." I stepped back, hands fisted at my waist. "He's a *reporter*? Not an archaeologist?"

Mr. Briarcliff shushed me, his gaze shooting to the door to the promenade deck. The muted conversation about strategy indicated the game was ongoing and the players hadn't overheard me.

"Apparently." Mr. Briarcliff's voice held a grim note.

"If he's a reporter, a special correspondent, even, then there might be more articles."

"Possibly."

I abandoned *The Illustrated Dispatch*, and we divided the remaining newspapers from Mr. Briarcliff's stack.

Within an hour, we'd completed the search. It went much

faster when one only had to look at bylines instead of combing through all the articles. We lined up the articles written by Special Correspondent Alexander Septimus Howard. I read over the headlines, my hand curled into a fist with my knuckles pressed to my mouth. Mr. Briarcliff stood beside me, his hands braced on the back of a chair.

*Socialite's Scandal: Charity Funds Embezzled*
*Fraudulent Financier Flees: Investors' Money Missing*
*Art Dealer's Authenticity Under Scrutiny*
*Famous Psychic Exposed as Charlatan*

I pulled my knuckles away from my mouth. "He must be on the steamer to get a story. Why else would he travel under a different name?" My voice sounded just as flinty as Mr. Briarcliff's had.

He picked up the stack of *The Illustrated Dispatch* and headed for the bookshelf to return them to their place. "I agree. Who was his target? Mr. Fairweather? He's the most prominent person on the passenger list, but Mr. Howard said he didn't know Mr. Fairweather before embarking on the S.S. *Cleopatra*."

"He wouldn't have to know Mr. Fairweather to write an article about him." I paced a few steps away, then turned back. "Or else he's focused on another story."

"I doubt he's interested in a tiff between gardeners." Mr. Briarcliff squatted and set the newspapers on the lowest shelf.

"I was thinking of Hildy."

He pivoted on the balls of his feet to look at me. "The notes she received were typed . . ."

". . . and Mr. Howard has a portable typewriter. We must check and see if the notes were typed on that machine."

# CHAPTER 25

The Nefertiti Bust, which was excavated in 1912, will be displayed to the public for the first time as part of the Egyptian Museum of Berlin's newly created Amarna Courtyard.

*—The Illustrated Dispatch*

I paced in a small circle, my thoughts whirling about what Mr. Howard's plans might be. "In fact, Mr. Howard could have sent the anonymous letters to both Mr. Fairweather and Hildy."

Mr. Briarcliff stood up after stowing the newspapers on the shelf. "Why would he type letters to Hildy and then handwrite letters to Mr. Fairweather? Why use two different formats?"

"To make it *appear* as if they came from different people."

"No. The senders are two different people."

Irritation sizzled through me. "You say that with such

assurance—but then again, you have complete confidence in everything you say. You could be wrong."

"Not usually." His tone was flat, as if he were sharing common knowledge, such as the detail that the earth orbited the sun.

"How can you say that? You're incredibly annoying when you take that matter-of-fact tone." It was more exasperating than if he'd taken on a braggadocio attitude.

"In this case, I'm quite sure."

His words were laced with . . . chagrin? Regret? I wasn't quite sure what the emotion was, but it prevented me from replying with another sharp comment.

"I'll explain," he said as he checked his watch, "but it will have to be later. It's almost time to change for dinner. We must speak afterward. I apologize for being an annoyance to you. Will you meet me in the captain's quarters after dinner, if the captain will allow us to work late?"

"Since you've apologized, yes, I will." My tone was grudging, but it didn't seem to bother him.

"Thank you. I'll ask Dr. Walsh to bring Mr. Alexan—um —Mr. Howard's typewriter to us."

"We can say we need to type up the notes tonight, which we will need to do."

"Excellent idea. I'll bring the typewriter from the purser's office. Those are the only two typewriters on the steamer that I'm aware of. We can check if either machine was used to type the letters to Hildy."

"And the typing will go much faster with two typewriters."

What might have been a grin flitted across his face. "You obviously haven't seen me type."

～

WHEN I ARRIVED in the dining room, Miss Fairweather was moving through the tables, which reminded me that she was the final person that Mr. Briarcliff and I needed a statement from. I quickened my step and caught up to her. "Good evening. Are you feeling more the thing tonight? Perhaps Mr. Briarcliff and I could speak to you after dinner?"

"I assure you I have nothing of significance to contribute, and I intend to retire immediately after pudding."

"But we do need to speak with you. The captain has required a statement from each passenger."

She looked as if she wished I were a fly that she could swat away, but she drew her breath, flattening her lips into a line. "Fine. Despite it being a waste of time, I'll give you five minutes after dinner." She whirled around and walked away.

Mr. Briarcliff didn't usually join the passengers for dinner in the dining room, so I sent a message to him through one of the stewards to meet me in the dining room immediately after dinner, as Miss Fairweather had agreed to give us five minutes—and five minutes only—to take her statement.

The atmosphere of the dining room had altered. Bursts of laughter and animated discussion, typical of our early days on the Nile, were absent. Instead, an undercurrent of tension filled the room, an unseen but palpable counterpoint to the low and restrained conversation over dinner plates.

Hildy and I spoke of how we would spend our time on the steamer once we arrived in Luxor. I said, "It will be quite frustrating to be so close to so many interesting sites and not be able to see them."

Hildy buttered a roll. "We'll be able to see them eventually. It will just be a pause while we wait."

"That's true, but I'm not looking forward to being shut up on the steamer for weeks."

"Neither am I." Hildy put down her butter knife. "I just hope no one else falls ill."

Worry stabbed through me. "Are you not feeling well?"

"I'm feeling perfectly fit. And I'm sure the time will go much faster than we think. That's how it is with things we dread. Often the reality isn't nearly as awful as our imagination. Miss Entwhistle is planning more activities."

"That's a good idea. Three weeks is a long time to fill. There are only so many books to read on board. I suppose I could work on my sketches. Compared to Miss Entwhistle, I'm quite rubbish at drawing, but it would be something to do."

Hildy said, "I may ask if I can order yarn and needles and join Seffie in knitting. Although creating scarves and mittens while sitting in the heat of the Egyptian sun seems rather absurd. Oh, I finished the crime book I told you about called *Whose Body?* I'll bring it to your cabin. I think you'll enjoy it."

Mr. Briarcliff appeared in the doorway as the plates were cleared away and people began to push back their chairs. He caught my eye, and I gave him a nod. We moved through the passengers and converged on Miss Fairweather.

# CHAPTER 26

Experienced nurse (speaks English and French), highly recommended by English families, offers services in return for passage to Europe or America. Write, "Nurse," c/o "The Nile." P.O.B. 732, Cairo.

*—The Nile*

The muscles along Miss Fairweather's jawline flexed, and I wondered if she was gritting her teeth.

I said, "Shall we go to your cabin for the interview?"

"No." She flung her hand at a table that had already been cleared. "Here will do. This ridiculous formality will only take a moment."

Since she clearly wouldn't budge about going back to her cabin, I headed for the table, sending Mr. Briarcliff a side-glance with widened eyes. He gave a little nod, as if to say *we must work with what we have*, and went to hold a chair for Miss Fairweather.

Her hyacinth scent wafted in her wake as I followed her to the table. "We need to take down the details of your passport," I said. "Do you have it with you?"

"I'll send it to you later via a steward."

I was surprised to see Mr. Briarcliff had brought his notebook. We'd locked everything in the cupboard in the captain's quarters before dinner. As he took a seat, he said to me, "I had the captain retrieve my notebook from the cupboard and send it along."

Once Mr. Briarcliff had his pencil at the ready, I turned to Miss Fairweather. "I'm sorry to go back to such a painful subject, but we do need to get everything down correctly. Please tell us where you were when your brother passed."

"I hadn't been feeling well and retired to my room early. I went there directly after dinner and stayed there until Miss Entwhistle arrived and told me what had happened."

The stewards continued to clear the tables. The clink of glassware, the rattle of crockery, and the swoosh of fresh tablecloths being flung out went on in the background, but the crew stayed clear of our table. "And when Mr. Shaw passed, where were you?"

"Again, I was in my cabin. As I said earlier, this is all quite useless." Her words were as sharp as the edges of palm fronds. She placed her hands on her chair and pushed it back. "If that's all—"

"No, it's not," I said quickly. "We have a few more questions about both men, and you're the ideal person to answer them because you knew both of them well."

She sniffed and crossed her arms. "I did not know Mr. Shaw well."

Mr. Briarcliff looked up from his notes, gripping the

pencil so tightly that I hoped he didn't snap it in half. "You lived in the same household."

Miss Fairweather moved her shoulders as if she were shrugging off a coat. "He was an employee of my brother's. I really had no interaction with him at all."

I put my hand on the table near Mr. Briarcliff, hoping he'd realize it was a signal to back down. Miss Fairweather would only give us a few more minutes, and I wanted to make the most of it. I made my tone as bland as possible as I took over the questioning again. "Do you know anyone who had any grudge or animosity toward either your brother or Mr. Shaw?"

"I don't see why you're asking about Ambrose. I'm offended that you've included him with Mr. Shaw when asking such a thing."

It almost sounded as if a low growl came from Mr. Briarcliff's throat. I hurriedly scooted my chair forward, partially blocking him from Miss Fairweather's view. "It's something that we've asked everyone. The police will want to have all the details. If you'd rather speak with them, then I suppose we could stop here."

She looked like she'd bit into something sour, then said, "Very well." The cadence of her words was slow, as if they were being dragged from her. "Many people did not like my brother. He was quite good at business. In his field, there's always competition, so it goes without saying that there were people who were not fond of him—jealous of his success, of course. As for Mr. Shaw . . ." Miss Fairweather looked up into the corner of the room, and I thought for a moment she felt sorrow, but then she blinked and pulled at the corner of her eye. "The grit in the air here is absolutely abominable. The least the stewards could do is dust more often, but this is one of the many areas that I've found the Blue Lotus Line sadly lacking."

Mr. Briarcliff drew a breath—whether to apologize or chastise her, I wasn't sure—but before he could speak, Miss Fairweather snapped her head toward me. "As I said, I didn't know the man. He occasionally dined with us at Nobilis Domus, but not often. When Mr. Shaw joined us for meals, he rarely spoke, and the rest of the time he kept to himself."

"I understand he was in the war?"

"I don't know. He was at the appropriate age, so it's possible."

I knew I only had a few more minutes, so I moved on. "Have you received any unsigned letters or notes while on the steamer?"

Her brows descended into a perplexed look. "No, have other passengers?"

I didn't answer her query. Instead, I asked, "And finally, have you sent any letters to other passengers?"

"No, I've been too overcome with all that's happened."

"Thank you so much for speaking with us," I said as Mr. Briarcliff closed his notebook with a snap. I added, "You're returning to your cabin now? Wonderful, we'll send a steward along to collect your passport."

"I expect it back immediately."

In unspoken agreement, Mr. Briarcliff and I waited a few moments, then followed Miss Fairweather out of the dining room. He held the door for me. "I received word from the captain that both typewriters are waiting for us in his cabin. He'll be busy for a few more hours and said we should feel free to use his quarters."

We climbed the steps to the upper deck. "Excellent. Let me change out of my evening gown into another frock."

"All right. I'll meet you—" He put a finger under his nose, then turned away and sneezed. "So sorry." He took a handkerchief from his pocket and wiped his nose.

We reached the door to my cabin, but I paused, hand on the doorknob. "Are you unwell?"

He returned the linen square to his pocket. "No. It was the floral scent in the dining room. Certain flowers set off my hay fever."

"Are you sure that's it?" I stepped closer to him. "Your eyes look rather glassy." I pressed my palm to his forehead.

He backed up a step and bumped into the doorframe. "What are you doing?" he asked, the back of his head pressed against the wood.

His forehead was cool, and I took my hand away. "Checking to see if you have a fever, but you don't. We can't be too careful. Hildy and I were just talking about it at dinner—how distressing it would be if anyone else came down with scarlet fever."

He pulled at his jacket lapel, straightening it. "I assure you, I'm fine. The scent of flowers often makes me sneeze."

"Sorry to have startled you. I'll see you in the captain's cabin momentarily."

A few moments later a tap sounded on my door, and Hildy called out. "It's me, Blix."

I was sitting in a chair, fastening my T-strap shoes. "Come in."

"Here's the book I told you about. I think you'll enjoy it."

"Thank you. I'm sure I will." I moved the threatening note Hildy had received from my handbag to my skirt pocket. "I won't be in the saloon this evening. Mr. Briarcliff and I must finish a few things."

She put the book down on the bedside table. "What's wrong with Rafe?"

I was brushing down my skirt but paused at her words. "Did he look ill? He sneezed, but he insisted it's only hay fever."

"Ill? No, I don't think it's that at all. He was standing outside your door with his hand on his chest, breathing deeply, as if he'd been running."

"That's odd."

"Isn't it?"

"He and I just walked back from the dining room."

"Indeed."

I drew back from her. "Why are you looking at me like that?" I went to the mirror. "Do I have a blemish?"

"No, dear. It's nothing like that."

I shrugged into my tweed jacket. "The notes Mr. Briarcliff and I have taken must be typed so we can hand them off to the police when we arrive at Luxor tomorrow."

"Ah, yes. That must be done."

"What do you mean? Why are you using such a cryptic tone?"

"Never mind, my dear. I'm sure it will all become clear later."

I didn't know what to make of Hildy and her secret smile, but I put it out of my mind for the moment. There were lots of notes to type, but more importantly, I wanted to compare the output of the two typewriters to the letter Hildy had received. Hopefully, we'd have definitive proof that Mr. Howard had typed the threatening notes.

I was the first to arrive at the captain's quarters. A steward was waiting outside. He handed me Miss Fairweather's passport, then unlocked the door and gave me the key. The cabin was empty, but two typewriters sat on the round mahogany table, along with a stack of pristine white paper. I glanced through Miss Fairweather's passport, which contained exactly the information one would expect. I put it down on the table along with the key.

I recognized the Remington Portable I'd seen in Mr. Howard's cabin. I took a sheet of paper and rolled it into place around the platen. Then I removed the crumpled note Hildy had received from my pocket. I smoothed it out and positioned it beside the typewriter. I would put it in the locked cupboard tonight after we finished comparing it to the notes typed on the two typewriters. After a short tap on the door, Mr. Briarcliff came in.

I said, "I'm just getting started, typing up the text of the note Hildy received so we can compare it to the original. Oh, and Miss Fairweather sent her passport."

"Any more surprises?"

"No. Nothing interesting there."

He picked up the passport, then he caught me examining his face and leaned away, the open passport pressed to his chest. "Why are you staring?"

"I was checking to see if your eyes are still shiny."

"As I said earlier, there's nothing to worry about. I feel fine. Not under the weather at all. Absolutely fine."

"Glad to hear it." I went back to typing, and the clack of the keys filled the room as I retyped the disturbing lines.

*Fraud!*
*Ticktock, time is running out.*
*Your deception won't stay hidden much longer.*

I banged out the last few words.

I felt the weight of Mr. Briarcliff's gaze and looked at him. "What is it?"

"You're quite an aggressive—er—typer."

"Just working off my anger at whoever wrote those horrible words to Hildy."

I hit the return lever a few times, and the words inched higher as the platen turned. Mr. Briarcliff came around the table as I pulled the paper from the typewriter and placed the copy beside the original note Hildy had received. I repeated the process with the purser's typewriter and put that typed sheet on the other side of the original note.

We both leaned over the table, my arm brushing against Mr. Briarcliff's sleeve. He took a step away.

"Why are you so skittish? I promise I won't check to see if you have a fever."

He cleared his throat. "Sorry."

We went back to studying the freshly typed pages. "The page from the purser's typewriter doesn't match at all."

"I agree, but the note from the Remington does have some similarities. The uppercase letter *F* seems to have a gap in the ink."

I tapped the original note. "It's here as well, a tiny clear diagonal space right at the point where the stroke should meet it."

"And the exclamation point sits below the line on both as well."

I went back to the Remington, added a new sheet of paper, and typed the uppercase letter *F* a few times and then some random letters with exclamation marks interspersed among them. I rolled the paper up. "Each letter *F* has a tiny diagonal section missing ink, and the exclamation points are lower than the other letters on the line."

We turned toward each other as I said, "So it *was* Mr. Howard who sent these notes to Hildy."

Mr. Briarcliff nodded. "The stewards would have access

to his cabin, but I doubt one of them would have risked their job to threaten a passenger."

"He must be trying to expose her role as Amelia Wise. As she said, she's never been married and gives advice on dating and marriage. I imagine the *Special Correspondent*" —I gave the words a sarcastic twist—"would classify that as deception and fraud."

Mr. Briarcliff pushed off of the table and crossed his arms. "It doesn't seem like much of a secret to expose, though."

"Perhaps Mr. Howard has a personal agenda. Remember what Hildy said about someone taking her advice and things not going well. Perhaps that happened to Mr. Howard. We really need to speak to him."

"Dr. Walsh won't allow anyone near him for several days. He told me he'd locked Mr. Howard in his cabin."

"Really? That's rather extreme, isn't it?"

"Dr. Walsh takes quarantine very seriously."

"Hmm . . . where is Dr. Walsh now? Do you know?"

"I nodded to him just now. He was on his way to the crew's quarters to check on the ill crew members."

"Then this is the perfect time."

# CHAPTER 27

Despite light winds hampering the excitement of the sailing races for local boatmen, the regatta proved a rousing success. The program, cleverly interspersed with rowing and swimming races, ensured a lively atmosphere throughout, culminating in the enchanting Venetian Fete held in the evening at the Cataract Hotel.

—*The Nile*

*I* snatched up the two freshly typed pages and the original note. "Come on. Now's our chance to speak to Mr. Howard."

Mr. Briarcliff said, "For someone worried about people falling ill, you're quite keen to get into the sickroom."

"I never said we'd enter the room. His cabin has a window, doesn't it?" Even the cabins on the main deck each had a small window by the door. "The windows don't completely block out all sound. I can hear people talking as they pass my window. We can speak to him from the other side of the glass. Surely Dr. Walsh won't quibble with that."

Mr. Briarcliff picked up Miss Fairweather's passport. "All right, but let me jot down the particulars of this passport so we can send it back to Miss Fairweather. I'm sure she'll send the steward to fetch it if she doesn't get it back soon."

A few moments later I rapped sharply on Mr. Howard's window. Mr. Briarcliff raised his voice. "Mr. Howard, we need to speak to you."

There was no response, and Mr. Briarcliff banged on the window frame. "Mr. Howard? Draw back the curtain."

A few seconds later the fabric of the curtain jerked away, and Mr. Howard appeared in his pajamas, his face flushed and his hair untidy. "You have the wrong cabin. I'm not Mr. Howard."

Mr. Briarcliff had brought along Mr. Howard's passport. He pressed it against the glass. "Oh, I believe you are."

I added, "We know you're not an archaeologist, but a reporter. In fact, you're *The Standard*'s Special Correspondent, Alexander Septimus Howard."

Mr. Howard rubbed his hand across his eyes and sank down on the side of the bed, where he'd thrown the sheets back. I positioned the threatening note Hildy had received on the glass beside the passport. "We know this was typed on your Remington Portable. Why are you sending threatening notes to Hildy?"

He must not have had any trouble hearing me through the glass because he surged up, swayed a moment, then dropped back down to the bed. "That woman is an old maid." His words were a bit muffled, but I picked up on his bitterness quite clearly. "She has no right to tell someone to break off an engagement."

Mr. Briarcliff put the passport in his pocket. "Ah. And

you were the jilted party. I see. It's beginning to make sense in a twisted sort of way."

Mr. Howard rubbed his hand across his forehead and up into his hair, which made it stand on end even more. "Can't a man make one mistake?"

I said, "I suppose it depends on the kind of mistake."

Mr. Howard continued as if I hadn't spoken. "I was in my cups." He picked at the cuff of his pajamas. "I wasn't myself. And I didn't hit her hard, not really."

A coldness washed over me as I realized the cause of his broken engagement.

Mr. Briarcliff leaned closer to the glass. His voice went quiet. "You struck your fiancée?"

Mr. Howard didn't respond. I closed my eyes and drew a deep breath to steady my suddenly racing heartbeat. I made a fist and concentrated on the sensation of my nails biting into my skin to distract me from my memories.

A current of air brushed my cheek, and I opened my eyes to find Mr. Briarcliff was pacing away to the railing. He returned swiftly. His index finger punched at the glass as he emphasized each word. "It's a good thing Dr. Walsh has you locked in there." Mr. Briarcliff glanced at me out of the corner of his eye, then turned to look fully at me. "You look extremely pale, Miss Windway." He swooped down and picked up the paper I'd dropped. I hadn't even realized I'd moved my hand away from the glass and it had fallen to the deck. "Are you not feeling well?"

I straightened my shoulders. "I'm perfectly fine." I took the paper back and put it up to the window, letting my anger at what he'd done to Hildy push away my panicky feeling. "So this is revenge."

Mr. Howard stood and reached for the curtain. "I don't have to tell you anything."

"Would you rather speak to the police?" I said quickly.

Mr. Howard's hand stilled, and Mr. Briarcliff added, "I'm sure they'd be interested in why you're traveling under a false name. Better to tell us everything, wouldn't you say? After all, the game is up."

The skin on Mr. Howard's chin puckered as he stuck out his lower lip in a mulish expression. A sinking feeling came over me. The captain had asked everyone to cooperate with us, but Mr. Howard could refuse. He didn't have to talk to us. Then an idea jolted through me.

I waved Mr. Briarcliff back from the window. "You've heard of Casper Denby of *The Nile* newspaper, haven't you? I'd assume that a newspaperman like you would know your competition. I'm sure you've read his column. Everyone in Cairo does. He's a good friend of mine. I know he'd be extremely interested to hear how you deceived the passengers. A story about a fraud always sells papers. You know that well, don't you, Mr. Howard? And with the details about the threats," I shook the paper, "it would fly off the newsstands. It might even get picked up back in England, wouldn't you think, Mr. Briarcliff?"

"I imagine so. A juicy story like that—deception, poison-pen letters, unsavory behavior toward one's fiancée, not to mention the unexpected deaths on the steamer—that's the salacious stuff the public wants to read."

Mr. Howard rubbed his hand through his hair again, then jabbed his finger at the paper I held. "I only typed a few little notes. Nothing more than that."

"Really?" I asked. "It's difficult to know what's true and what's a lie with you, Mr. Howard." I emphasized his last name.

His gaze pinged from me to Mr. Briarcliff. "If I tell you

what happened, you won't go to Mr. Denby—or any other reporter?"

"I won't." As much as it galled me to agree to it, I did it.

He dropped his grip on the curtain and returned to sit on the edge of the bed. He crossed one leg over the other. "I have a contact at the newspaper that publishes the Amelia Wise column. He told me there was a change in the way they sent letters to the agony aunt and the way she replied. Recently, she'd been sending the letters from different places than where they were usually posted. Foreign places. The most recent batch of letters had come from Cairo. I convinced my editor to let me travel there. My contact wired me when a new bundle of letters was posted, so all I had to do was watch the front desk at Shepheard's to see who picked up the letters. Of course, when you picked them up, Miss Windway, I trailed you back to your suite, and that's when I realized there were *two* women staying there. I wasn't sure if it was you or the old hag—or perhaps both of you were acting as Amelia Wise."

"That's why you delivered the first note to my cabin instead of Hildy's."

"Yes, but when I saw you scurry over to the old maid's cabin with the letter, and then she shredded it and threw the scraps overboard, I was pretty sure she was Amelia Wise."

"Then why did you search our rooms and break her writing desk?"

His gaze slid to the corner of the room, then back to me. He twitched his shoulder. "You can't prove that."

"You were looking for definitive proof, the letters addressed to Amelia. Otherwise, you'd have already turned in your story to your editor during one of our overnight stops or during an excursion. But then you fell ill, and Dr. Walsh confined you to your cabin, so you haven't been able to do that. But now . . ." I tapped the window, pointing to the desk, which was covered with newspapers, books, and papers. "Is there perhaps a story in that messy pile about Hildy? Perhaps Dr. Walsh will run across it when he next visits you?"

"No, I haven't been feeling well enough to concentrate." He did look rather ragged with his watery eyes, flushed skin, and mussed hair. The unyielding expression came back again, but then he waved a hand. "I promise I won't write the agony aunt story as long as you two keep this quiet. No tattling to Mr. Denby—or anyone else."

"Agreed. I won't say a word to any reporter. No promises, though, about the police. Did you send anyone else letters or notes?"

"What? No. I only wanted revenge on that old hag." He studied our faces for a moment, then his eyes widened. "You think I had something to do with that secretary bloke's death?" He surged to his feet. "I didn't. I swear. I'll swear on a stack of Bibles. I didn't have anything to do with it."

"Unfortunately, even if Mr. Howard swears on a stack of Bibles, his word isn't very good," I said as we walked away from Mr. Howard's room. The main deck was quiet and empty, while lights glowed from the saloon on the upper deck, and the low hum of voices carried faintly on the breeze.

Mr. Briarcliff said, "Mr. Howard is a rotter and a cad, but I don't think he's a murderer."

"How can you be so sure? He could have sent the other notes to Louisa. He said he didn't, but he could be lying."

Mr. Briarcliff opened his mouth, then paused until a

steward passed us. We'd reached the captain's cabin, but Mr. Briarcliff didn't open the door for me. "Miss Windway, do you mind if we keep walking? It sounds as if everyone is upstairs in the saloon, so we shouldn't encounter any of the passengers. I have something to tell you, and it will be easier if I'm in motion."

"You sound as reluctant as if you were going to the dentist."

"I think this may be more painful than a tooth extraction." We paced around the bow of the steamer, crossed the foredeck, and walked along the port side in silence. Finally, I said, "You had something you wanted to tell me?"

"Yes, regarding the notes Louisa gave to us . . ." He sounded more subdued and hesitant than I'd ever heard him. He cleared his throat, then jutted his chin forward as if his collar was tight. "Dash it all," he muttered, "this is more difficult than I thought it would be."

We crossed through the passageway to the starboard side in another bubble of silence. Finally, I said, "I've been meaning to talk to you about those notes as well. I had another look at the obituaries yesterday, and it seems all the young men were in Section Twenty. I would have mentioned it, but I noticed it shortly before you remembered seeing Mr. Howard's full name in a newspaper. We became immersed in the newspaper search, and it completely went out of my mind."

As we reached the captain's cabin, Mr. Briarcliff stopped walking. "I was wrong. Movement doesn't make a confession easier." He took something from an interior pocket and handed it to me.

It was a photograph. I angled it so that the shiny surface caught some of the light emanating from the saloon on the upper deck as he said, "They were under my command."

I was so surprised it took me a moment to respond. "What?"

He opened the door and said, "You'll be able to see it better in here." He switched on some of the lamps in the cabin. I went to the table beside the easy chair and held the photo under the light.

Sandbags lined the sides of a trench, and several men in tin hats, coats, and gloves were busy. One man held a bayonet as he stood on what looked like a wooden riser that ran along the bottom of the trench. It raised him up so that his eyes were just above the top of the sandbag wall. Another young man's attention was on a stick that was fixed on top of the sandbags and protruded a few feet in the air. Behind the two men in the foreground ranged four or five more soldiers.

Mr. Briarcliff pointed to the man who was looking up at the stick. "That's Sid. Sid Hughes. He had the best eyesight, so we had him use the trench mirror."

"Like a periscope," I said.

"Exactly. We could mount them on our bayonets, but Sid liked to have his in place all the time, so he rigged up a stand for it. That's Albert peeking over the top. Morrison always was impatient and had to see for himself."

His words were infused with fondness as his finger moved to the other men in the background. "Dougie Northton, Rick Archer, and Henry Anderson. I'm surprised you can see Henry's face. Usually, he was hunched over, whittling away on a tiny piece of wood. Walt and Toffee aren't in this photo. Walt was probably off somewhere sleeping, and Toffee was most likely cleaning his boots. He nearly always managed to look like he'd stepped out of *The Spectator*. Don't know how he did it with all that mud."

I looked up from the photo. "Henry Anderson. Wasn't

that one of the names on the notes Mr. Fairweather received?"

"Yes," he said, still staring at the photo.

"Oh. I read his obituary today. I'm sorry."

He nodded an acknowledgment, the muscles in his jaw working. "I sent those notes to Mr. Fairweather."

I suppose I should have been shocked, but I wasn't. His resistance to even considering that any of the passengers had sent the notes made sense now.

He looked absolutely wretched, and I realized how he'd been apprehensive about the notes. Somehow, I must have picked up on a hint of his worry that seeped through his facade without realizing fully what role he'd played in the notes.

I swallowed, thoughts whirling. From our first meeting in Cairo, when we'd gotten off on the wrong foot, I'd been reluctant to welcome him into our group. His self-confidence and arrogance grated on me, but an irritating manner was a long way off from murder. Was it possible he was involved in the death of either Mr. Shaw or Mr. Fairweather? Hildy always gave Mr. Briarcliff the benefit of the doubt, and my instinctive answer to that question was *no*, but I didn't want to be foolish.

I moved around to the opposite side of the table from him, which put me closer to the cabin door and increased the distance between us. Mr. Briarcliff seemed preoccupied as he gathered his thoughts and was unaware of my movements.

I finally asked, "Why did you do it?"

His head was bent, his chin almost resting on his tie, as he studied the photo. He cut his gaze to me without lifting his head. "No recriminations? No shocked outrage?"

"Maybe later. It depends on why you sent them. It has something to do with the war, doesn't it?"

"Are you sure you don't want me to call for a steward who can summon the captain? I can't be involved in taking statements when I've sent anonymous letters myself."

"It's a little late for that. The time to step down was when Louisa produced the letters this morning."

"You're right. That's what I should have done," he said flatly without even a hint of derision.

I stared at him for a moment. "You never think I'm right. Are you sure you're not coming down with something?"

A hint of a smile traced across his face at my quip. "Ah, Miss Windway, how is that you can always make me smile?"

"I thought I made you glower rather often." One of his quick smiles came and went. I pulled at my cuffs, straightening my sleeves as I added, "Don't misunderstand me. I am irritated, but," I sighed, "we have too many questions that need answers for me to dwell too much on your vexing behavior. And I have a feeling it wasn't done for your personal gain." Mr. Briarcliff was many things—irritating and vexing being among the descriptors that came to mind first—but money-grubbing wasn't one of them.

"We do indeed have many questions. As soon as Louisa brought the envelopes out, I saw how my actions could be misconstrued, but I took the cowardly way out of not saying anything. To be fair, though, I didn't expect us to uncover so many secrets among the passengers."

"It has been rather a Pandora's box of poison-pen letters and hidden identities." I crossed my arms. "I suppose we can extend you the same courtesy that we've extended to other passengers and keep your actions quiet—as long as it isn't connected to the deaths."

"I assure you I had nothing to do with that."

"Then why did you send the notes to Mr. Fairweather?"

He scrubbed a hand over his mouth, creating a scratchy

sound as his palm rubbed against his slight stubble, then he let out a long, regretful sigh. "It was an error in judgment. I see that now, but originally it was part of a very specific plan that made excellent sense in Cairo when I came up with it. Now that two people have died, it's unraveled in the worst possible way."

# CHAPTER 28

*In the Land of Tut-ankh-Amen*, now showing at the Metropole Cinema in Cairo, marks a milestone in Egyptian cinema. The groundbreaking production is the first to be screened by an Egyptian company and features local actors, generating considerable excitement among audiences.

*—The Nile*

"*I*s that where it started, in Cairo?" I asked.

"No, farther back than that." Mr. Briarcliff placed his hands on the chair back. Shoulders slightly hunched, he looked up. How familiar are you with Fairweather Rubber Manufacturing?"

"I know they make hot water bottles and sink plugs."

"They make a lot more than that. They began in footwear in the early 1800s, then moved into tire production. When the war came, they supplied parts for gas masks. When we were in the trenches, we received a shipment of new masks.

There wasn't quite enough to go around, so I had the new ones distributed to my men, and I kept an old one. We came under an attack later that week, and that was when we learned that the rubber seal that connected the metal rims of the eyepieces to the mask itself was defective." His words were crisp and controlled, as if he were giving a report, but along with the precise cadence of his recital, there were faint notes of grief and anger underlining every word.

"How ghastly."

He moved his head in a tiny nod. "It was horrific. It was terrible when the German gas reached us, but to not be able to trust the equipment supplied by *good British companies . . .*" Sarcasm infused the last three words. He drew a breath, calming himself. "Many men died that day because of the mistakes that were made with seals on the gas mask. It wiped out my section. The obituaries I sent to Mr. Fairweather were of the men who died that day. Sid and Toffee survived but were gravely injured and haven't recovered. It is quite difficult for their families."

"But surely the military addressed it?"

He let out a bitter laugh. "If by *addressed it* you mean swept it under the rug, then, yes, that's exactly what happened. There was an inquiry. The failure was pinpointed in the report, but nothing was done. Absolutely nothing."

I was beginning to understand his lack of trust in large organizations and his insistence on being a *free agent*, as he called himself.

"I made it my goal to see that Mr. Fairweather took care of the two men who are still alive. It's all I can do for them now. If I had the finances, I'd do it myself, but the Briarcliff coffers are rather low."

"I see. And the notes were part of that plan?"

He pushed off from the chair and crossed his arms. "Oh

no. They were my last-ditch effort. I first approached Fairweather Rubber Manufacturing years ago. Long letters that never received a reply. I consulted solicitors but was told basically there's nothing to be done. I visited Fairweather Rubber Manufacturing, but Mr. Fairweather, after one meeting, refused to see me again. He also blocked any approach I made via correspondence or in person. He threatened to bring legal proceedings if I didn't drop the subject, so I backed off."

"But didn't give up."

"Of course not."

"Remind me never to get on your bad side."

I'd said the words lightly, but he replied soberly, "I know you don't admire me, Miss Windway, but I am loyal."

"I never said I didn't admire you, Mr. Briarcliff. You just annoy me."

That statement brought out another of his flashing grins that was gone as quickly as it appeared. He turned and paced to the small window behind him, looking out the small square of blackness. "I backed down."

"A strategic retreat to regroup," I guessed.

"Precisely. I knocked around Europe for a bit, but I couldn't stick it anywhere. I ended up in Cairo. I came here with a friend on a holiday. He returned to England. Then I heard that the *renowned* businessman, Mr. Fairweather, was set to visit, and I decided to stay. I found work with Mr. Martin and settled in."

"Like a spider spinning a web."

He drew a breath, seemingly to protest, then turned the corners of his lips down and tilted his head from side to side in agreement. "I suppose that's apt. Very apt, actually. Unfortunately, last year Mr. Fairweather had to postpone his trip, but I knew he had a fascination with Egypt. Well, more accurately, he saw himself as one of society's great benefactors—ironic, isn't it? He wanted to finance a dig and produce a treasure as alluring as Tut's Tomb, so I bided my time. When I finally saw his name on the VIP list that Mr. Martin circulates to us, I knew I had a chance. I decided to approach him differently. I wouldn't do it directly this time."

"The notes," I said. "Psychological warfare." He'd spent time in the trenches in the war, but I had a glimmer of what his plan was, and it made me wonder if he did other . . . tasks . . . during the war.

Mr. Briarcliff turned his head sharply.

"I've heard the term. And I see exactly what you were trying to do by sending him the notes with just the names, then delivering the photos and obituary clippings. You were piquing his interest and creating an air of mystery. They weren't specifically threats, but they did have an ominous air to them. And now I understand your disguise as well."

"I couldn't risk him recognizing me, but I needed to be the one to leave the notes. I didn't want to involve anyone else. If things went awry, the blame would rest solely on me." He pulled out a chair and sat down. "I realize how incriminating my actions appear, but I wasn't near either Mr. Shaw or Mr. Fairweather when they died. In fact, I hadn't even been into the saloon that afternoon before Mr. Shaw died. I've already told you I did know Mr. Fairweather before we departed, but I had no previous acquaintance with Mr. Shaw."

A metal click sounded, then the door swung open, and Captain Farouk strode into the cabin. He stopped short. "Pardon me. I assumed you'd have finished for the day."

Mr. Briarcliff stood, closed his notebook, and picked up the photograph. "No, we should be apologizing. Let us clear this up and we'll be out of your way."

I looked at my watch. "Goodness, it's nearly ten. We lost track of the time. So sorry."

"No need to apologize. I'm glad you're still here. Any progress?"

Mr. Briarcliff and I exchanged a glance. He put his things on the table and stood at attention, hands by his sides, shoulders back and chin up. He opened his mouth, but I jumped in quickly. "We've interviewed all the passengers and uncovered several interesting facts, but we haven't reached any definite conclusion. We haven't had an opportunity to compare all the statements or examine Mr. Shaw's belongings. Don't you agree, Mr. Briarcliff, that we need a bit longer before we present any findings?"

He hesitated. "Ah . . ."

I sent him a pointed look and gave a tiny shake of my head. Now was not the time to confess to his scheme, not unless we wanted to get into all the anonymous letters that we'd discovered, which included Hildy's letters, and that would reveal her identity as Amelia Wise.

Mr. Briarcliff must have had the same train of thought because he hesitated a moment, then cleared his throat. "Ah, yes. Best course of action at this time is to wait until we have a clearer understanding."

I added, "I believe we'll have a report for you by Monday with our findings, Captain."

"Very good."

AFTER WE LEFT the captain's cabin, Mr. Briarcliff fell into step with me as I climbed the stairs to the upper deck. "Thank you."

I paused and turned to him. No one else was near us, so I

said, "We agreed to only expose secrets that are related to either Mr. Shaw's or Mr. Fairweather's death, and while I don't have definitive proof that you aren't involved, I'm a fairly good judge of character. You're exasperating, but I doubt you're a murderer. You seem to be a man of good character."

"I'm happy to hear I've risen in your estimation since our first meeting in Cairo."

"And Hildy thinks the world of you. If you've deceived her, I'll be the first to turn you in."

"I don't doubt it. Nevertheless, I appreciate your patience in not outing me right away."

I resumed climbing the steps. "I'm only extending to you the same courtesy that we've extended to all the other passengers. You're not receiving special treatment."

We reached the upper deck and exchanged nods with Miss Entwhistle as she passed us. After a few paces, I said, "I thought that in taking statements we'd uncover some detail that would show us how Mr. Shaw was poisoned, but nothing has come to light."

"Well, as you said to Captain Farouk, we need to comb through the statements and compare them."

"Yes, that is true." We were at my door, but instead of going in, I turned to the railing and drew in a deep breath of the chilly night air. "And it's good that we stopped for the night. My brain is a ragbag of scraps of conversations and random observations."

I expected him to wish me a good evening and continue on down the deck, but he put his hands in his pockets and leaned his back against the railing, facing the cabins.

After a bit, I said, "You could approach Louisa."

He turned and looked at me over his shoulder. "What do you mean?"

"Louisa will inherit Mr. Fairweather's wealth, and she's also a former reporter. She might be interested in righting the wrongs where your men were concerned."

"I hadn't thought of that."

"One does tend to become focused on one approach. Sometimes there are other paths to the same point."

"Unless we discover she murdered her husband."

I dipped my head. "There is that to factor in. Perhaps don't speak to her about it until we've cleared up the questions we have about the deaths."

"Why are you suggesting options for my difficulties, Miss Windway?"

"I know what it is to be in an impossible situation and feel like there's no way out."

He turned around and rested his arms on the railing, mirroring my posture. "Mr. Howard's statements seemed to distress you."

I flicked a glance at him and saw his face was serious and possibly . . . concerned?

"If someone is troubling you in that way," he continued, "please don't keep it to yourself. I—or someone else—can intervene."

"Nothing like that is happening."

He turned his head and pinned me with a look that was definitely solicitous, but it contained a measure of anger as well. "I mean it. Don't endure that."

I looked away, up to the sweep of stars that blanketed the sky. I could tell he wouldn't be fobbed off with a vague reply. I gripped the railing. "A few years ago, I was involved in an incident—nothing as bad as Mr. Howard's actions—but sometimes memories of it catch me unaware." I released the railing and leaned forward to study the swish of the Nile's tiny waves. "I was devastated at the time, but I'm perfectly fine now. I appreciate your concern."

He nodded but remained silent. "You're sure it's ended? It's not something that's happening on the steamer?"

"Not at all."

He didn't look convinced, so I looked back out at the Nile. "Because you look so doubtful, and I don't want you hovering over me, I'll tell you the full story. You've told me your secret about your missives to Mr. Fairweather, so I'll tell you a secret of mine. I suppose you know society calls me the Jilter."

"I never pay much attention to gossip."

"You and Hildy are two of the only people who don't, apparently." I glanced at Mr. Briarcliff. "I'm sure you've heard the story."

"No."

Still gripping the railing with both hands, I leaned back, elbows locked. "Oh. Well, then. Only one part of it is actually a secret. The majority of it has been dissected and discussed in the papers."

I flexed my elbows, drawing myself up to the railing. "I was engaged. I was eighteen and thought my fiancé was wonderful, but on the day of the wedding my husband-to-be arrived at the church blotto. While the vicar was explaining to the guests that there would be a short delay, my fiancé found me in the little room at the back of the church. He was determined we should start the ceremony immediately, despite the fact he couldn't enunciate his words and was swaying like a sheet pinned on a laundry line. I told him we'd be laughingstocks if we went ahead while he was in his current state. That angered him. I had no idea he was an angry drunk. He pulled his arm back, fist clenched, but—I believe I mentioned that I know how to defend myself . . ."

Mr. Briarcliff said, "Yes, I remember."

"He was quite close to me. All I had to do was make one small movement."

"I don't suppose you . . . ?"

"Yes. Yes, I did. Megs, my governess, would have been so proud. She always said knowing how to deliver a well-placed kick is an essential skill every lady should know."

Mr. Briarcliff's soft laugh carried on the night air. "Indeed."

"So, with him in a heap on the floor, I fled, slamming the door to the little room behind me. As my fiancé was shouting and screaming—some words that should never be said in church, by the way—the vicar appeared and said, 'Oh dear, that door sticks. What a bother. We'll have to get some of the young men to apply their shoulders to it.'

"That was a bit funny. I can appreciate that now. At the time, I was frightfully upset. A stuck door was the least of my worries. I couldn't see the humor in the mild little vicar standing next to the heavy door, tutting. All I knew was that I wouldn't marry my fiancé. However, when I told my parents, they were insistent that we should go through with the ceremony. My father said not to be a ninny, that he'd sober up once he got some coffee into him. They were adamant. My father was never one to change his mind. I knew if he had to drag me down the aisle, he'd do it.

"It took a while for the men to get the door open. While my father was overseeing that, I slipped out a side door and hailed a taxi. I returned home, packed a bag, and fled—all the way to Switzerland. I've been on my own ever since. I'm the Jilter who left her groom at the altar, which was mortifying, but now I'm incredibly glad I'm not tied to him."

"You had a narrow escape. Well done."

I found myself blinking rapidly. "Oh." I didn't know

what to say. "No one ever says that. Of course, everyone knows he was drunk, but no one knows about the . . . other thing."

"You've been far too good to him. You should have shouted it from the rooftops."

"But I couldn't do that to my parents. They were so horribly embarrassed as it was. I couldn't make it worse." I let go of the railing and turned to him. "So you see, I won't stand for that sort of thing. There's no need to worry about me."

The rapid slap of approaching footsteps sounded as Hassan hurried up.

"Pardon me, Miss Windway, but I thought you'd want to know. Miss Honeyworth has summoned the doctor. She's not feeling well."

CHAPTER 29

Dear Amelia,

I've developed feelings for my best friend's kid sister, but I'm afraid it might jeopardize my friendship with her brother. Should I pursue this or let it go?

Dear Betwixt,

Before you proceed, consider: Is this a fleeting fancy or something worth risking a friendship for? If it's the latter, approach your friend first. After all, a good friendship, like a proper cup of tea, should be strong enough to withstand a little stirring.

*—Ask Amelia, The Illustrated Dispatch*

The next morning, I was pounding away on the typewriter in the captain's cabin when Mr. Briarcliff arrived. "Good morning, Miss Windway. How is Hildy?"

I yanked the page from the typewriter and rolled another into place. "She's put up a note in her window that says she's sleeping. Dr. Walsh checked on her last night and again this morning. She still has a fever and a sore throat. There's nothing to do now but wait and see if she breaks out in a rash."

This morning at breakfast, Dr. Walsh had announced the stewards would be going about their duties differently. They would leave food or other items like towels outside our cabin doors, and we'd retrieve them after the stewards left. Miss Fairweather had looked put out with the new way of doing things, but before she could protest, Dr. Walsh had clarified that the captain had given his full approval to the changes, and tables were already being positioned outside each cabin.

Mr. Briarcliff moved to the opposite side of the table but didn't take a seat. "I see. Does she need anything? Is there anything I can do?"

"I heaped magazines and books outside her door, and Hassan is seeing that she has plenty of liquids and plain food. In fact, she told me quite pointedly last night to leave her cabin." I knew she was trying to protect me from illness, but I hated the thought of her being alone when she wasn't feeling well. "So no, there's nothing we can do for Hildy, which is why I'm here typing."

I focused on my notebook, which I'd propped up against my coffee cup, and resumed typing.

"And doing so in a rather vicious manner, I see."

My fingers stilled. "What?"

"You're attacking those typewriter keys as if you're in a trench firing across no-man's-land."

"Better to take my worries out on the keyboard than on a person."

"Such as myself? Please don't glare at me. You were thinking it, even if you didn't say it. I'll leave you alone. Losing oneself in work is an excellent means of escaping daily life."

He sat down opposite me, opened his notebook, and began typing, which was exactly what I wanted. I was worried about Hildy, but I also didn't want to discuss my disclosures from the previous evening. In the bright morning light, I wished I'd kept quiet. Once a secret was revealed to one person, it was no longer a secret—or at least that had been my experience in the past. I tried to put my concerns about my secret and about Hildy out of my mind and concentrated on transferring my written notes to the type-written page. I finished the transcript of Mr. Listergraff's interview as well as Dr. Walsh's, then stretched, rotating my neck and shaking out my arms.

Mr. Briarcliff looked up from his typewriter. "Finished?"

"Far from it. Just taking a break."

"Then let's ring for tea. My index fingers could use a rest as well."

A little while later the steward knocked on the cabin door and called out that he was leaving the tea outside the door. Mr. Briarcliff retrieved it and set the tray on the table between us.

"I'll pour." I pulled the tray toward me. "Sugar?"

"No."

"I should have known you'd take your tea black."

I sat back with my cup, and we sipped in silence. After a bit, Mr. Briarcliff said, "Feeling better?"

I brushed my hand over the typewriter, sweeping away a bit of dust. "Yes. Sorry to be in such a black mood earlier."

"Think nothing of it. It's understandable."

I looked over the stack of typed pages. "I'm worried

about Hildy, but I'm also finding these statements frustrating."

"But you're a whiz of a typist."

"It's not the transcribing of them. It's the lack of information. I thought we'd uncover some detail that would show us how Mr. Shaw was poisoned. Even though I was in the saloon, my back was to him. I thought perhaps I'd missed the entrance of someone while I was absorbed in my reading, but apparently that didn't happen." I ran my hand across the open pages of my notebook. "If all the statements are to be believed, no one entered the saloon from the time Mr. Shaw sat down until the time he died."

Mr. Briarcliff finished the last of his tea in one gulp. "Which means the person who had the most close contact with him before he came into the saloon was Louisa."

"Yes, but Mr. Shaw worked there for quite a while, at least a half hour, maybe longer, before he went into distress and passed so suddenly. Dr. Walsh was quite clear that cyanide effects begin quickly."

"Dr. Walsh did qualify that statement." Mr. Briarcliff put his cup and saucer on the tray. "He said the size of the person and how the poison was administered could impact the onset of symptoms as well as if they'd eaten or not. It could possibly have taken up to a quarter of an hour for the onset of symptoms." He reached for his notebook. "Let's check the statements again."

For several moments, the only sound was the rustle of paper. I finished first and waited until Mr. Briarcliff looked up. "I see nothing that sheds any light on how Mr. Shaw was poisoned. Each of the ladies says they didn't see anyone else come into the saloon."

"And I can tell you that no one moved from our group."

Mr. Briarcliff picked up his pencil. "Which reminds me. Shall I take your statement now?"

"Yes, let's do that."

Mr. Briarcliff asked me all the questions we'd asked everyone else. When we finished, he said, "Well, no surprises there. Now it's my turn."

Because Mr. Briarcliff wasn't in the room when either man died, I didn't have many notes to take until I came to the question about whether he'd known the men prior to sailing. He gave a truncated version of his relationship with Mr. Fairweather and his actions in sending anonymous letters to him. I noted it all down, then looked up at him. "As with the others who have given us some rather sensitive information, shall we say I'll type this last bit up separately, and if needed, we'll attach it as an addendum?" He nodded his thanks, and I put down my pen and flexed my fingers. "There, that's done, but we're no closer to figuring out what happened."

"True. Your statement fits with what the other ladies who were in the saloon said." He tapped the written pages in his notebook. "No one moved from the group, and no one entered the saloon."

I pushed back my chair. "Even though Dr. Walsh checked Mr. Shaw's belongings, let's have a look ourselves. Perhaps he had some chewing gum or . . . I don't know . . . put his pen in his mouth."

Mr. Briarcliff removed the key from his waistcoat pocket and unlocked the cabinet. "We need to inventory everything that's here anyway."

"Yes. The police will need a list of his belongings."

Mr. Briarcliff began shifting the paper bags. The china cups rattled as he moved them aside. "I don't think we need to look at the teacups, but this might be helpful." He took out a bag labeled with the words *contents of Mr. Shaw's pockets*.

Paper rustled as Mr. Briarcliff unfolded the paper bag. "Mr. Shaw's other personal effects are still in his cabin. We can examine those tomorrow, but according to Dr. Walsh's limited window of time, surely it's what happened in the saloon that's important."

"I agree."

I reached for Mr. Shaw's case, which wasn't in a bag, then drew my hand back. "Fingerprints. Dr. Walsh was careful to not touch the cups when he collected them." I took my handkerchief from my pocket and shook it out. "I'll use this just in case."

"Good idea," he said.

Using the handkerchief to cover my hand, I set Mr. Shaw's case to one side as Mr. Briarcliff tipped the contents of the bag onto the table.

# CHAPTER 30

Two interesting facts came to light at the recent Egypt
Promotion Association's annual conference: 4,000 independent travelers will visit Egypt this season, a 50-percent
increase over last season, and it is estimated that next season
will see over 8,000 travel bookings from Americans alone.

*—The Nile*

The belongings that were in Mr. Shaw's pockets
tumbled onto the table as Mr. Briarcliff gently
shook the paper bag. He took his pencil from his pocket and
used it to nudge the items, spreading them apart.

"Nothing unusual here," I said, surveying a handkerchief, small comb, pocket watch, lighter, and two rubber
bands, along with a wallet and passport.

Mr. Briarcliff shook out his pocket square and covered his
hand with it before opening the passport, then he turned the
pages with the pencil's eraser. "I'll take these details down

so we'll have a record of them. It looks to be perfectly normal."

"Thank goodness. We don't need anything else to complicate this situation." Mr. Briarcliff sat down and copied the information while I used my handkerchief and pried open Mr. Shaw's wallet. "Only two five-pound notes in his wallet and a few business cards from companies in England. They're quite worn around the edges, so it's likely he had them for a long time. No familiar names among them."

Mr. Briarcliff nodded, head bent over his notebook. "I'll add those items to the list."

I turned to Mr. Shaw's case, which had a latch. It took a moment to unfasten the latch with the handkerchief covering my fingers. When it finally gave, I threw back the flap and caught a whiff of a floral fragrance. I bent closer to the case and sniffed.

Mr. Briarcliff looked up from his list. "What are you doing?"

"His case smells like flowers—a very feminine scent." I inhaled deeply. "I can't quite identify it. Not rose or gardenia . . . What do you think?" He dipped his head over it, then immediately turned away and sneezed into his handkerchief.

I said, "Hyacinth," and he nodded as he wiped his nose. "Definitely."

"You also sneezed when we were leaving the dining room this evening. You said something about the flowers, but there were no hyacinths in the arrangements. It was the scent Miss Fairweather wore. I noticed an aroma of hyacinth around her. Since you were on the other side of the table, you probably couldn't smell it until we followed her out."

"Yes, I should have thought of that. Mr. Martin is very particular that the Blue Lotus Line only uses flowers native to Egypt. But why does Mr. Shaw's case smell like hyacinths?"

"I have no idea." I was already removing a set of folders, using the handkerchief to handle them. I sniffed the folders and shook my head. I took out blank sheets of paper and a leather-bound ledger. "These just smell of paper and leather." I plucked out several envelopes, and the floral fragrance wafted out in a strong wave. I didn't even have to put them to my nose to sniff them. "The scent is coming from these."

"Are you sure?"

"Yes. Don't come any closer. It will—"

Mr. Briarcliff leaned over the envelopes, then straightened and stepped back as he took his pocket square and pressed it to his nose.

"—make you sneeze," I finished. There were three envelopes, all sealed and stamped. The addresses ranged from Cairo to London and were handwritten. "These will need to be posted." I pushed the envelopes to the far side of the table, away from Mr. Briarcliff, and emptied the rest of the contents of the case, which included pens, pencils, erasers, and unused carbon paper between the thick sheets of protective cardboard. I double-checked all the pockets. "Nothing else." I couldn't keep the frustration out of my voice. "No chewing gum and no teeth marks on any of the pens or pencils."

Mr. Briarcliff was still looking at the envelopes. "That's not the steamer's stationery. It's the wrong size."

I hadn't noticed it at first glance, but I realized he was correct. The three envelopes did look smaller than the envelopes in my cabin. "And they're white instead of ivory."

Mr. Briarcliff seemed to be transfixed by the envelopes.

He moved slowly closer, then draped his pocket square over one of the envelopes and picked it up.

"It'll make you sneeze again."

He held it out an arm's length, pinched between his fingertips, angling it so that he could examine the back and the front. "What if the poison was on the envelope?"

"You mean on the flap?"

"Yes, in the glue. Mr. Shaw would have licked the envelopes to seal them."

I dropped down into one of the chairs at the table. "Of course! It seems the envelopes are the only possibility."

Mr. Briarcliff carefully maneuvered all the envelopes into a pile, then used his pencil to slide them across the table and into the paper bag that had contained Mr. Shaw's belongings. "We must ask Dr. Walsh to test all of these."

Mr. Briarcliff wrote a note to Dr. Walsh, asking if he could check the envelopes. "I'll warn him to wear gloves as a precaution." He rang for a steward to deliver the paper bag and the message, then returned to his chair. "I emphasized that it was urgent. I hope he's able to do it soon."

I'd been lost in thought, but as he took a seat at the table, I stirred. "Why would someone go to all that trouble to poison Mr. Shaw? He didn't seem to have any enemies."

"Yes, he seemed to be quite innocuous." Mr. Briarcliff tapped the table with his knuckles absentmindedly. "Perhaps he knew something that threatened someone."

"He was Mr. Fairweather's secretary. I suppose it could have something to do with Mr. Fairweather."

Mr. Briarcliff voiced what I was thinking as he said, "And Mr. Fairweather is dead as well." We sat in silence for a moment, then Mr. Briarcliff pulled the purser's typewriter toward him. "Let's save our speculation until after we hear the results of Dr. Walsh's test. I'll keep typing, because in the time it takes me to type a single paragraph, you complete a page of text."

"I suppose that's the best thing to do. My governess Megs always said the surest way to make time pass quickly was to become immersed in a project." I rolled a fresh sheet of blank paper into the Remington Portable.

I hadn't noticed earlier because I was so focused on my own typing, but Mr. Briarcliff hadn't been falsely modest about his ability to touch type. He was painfully slow, but even though he typed at a snail's pace, he kept at it. For about three quarters of an hour, the cabin was filled with the staccato clacking of my typewriter keys and the counterpoint of Mr. Briarcliff's irregular clicks as he used two fingers.

A knock interrupted us, and he shoved back in his chair, massaging a shoulder. "Another break, thank goodness. I didn't realize typing was such exhausting work."

Dr. Walsh stood outside, several steps back from the threshold. I went and stood beside Mr. Briarcliff at the door, which left several feet of space between us and Dr. Walsh. "Shall I ring for some tea for you, Doctor? You look done in." And that was putting it mildly. His face was haggard, and his posture was bent. Dark circles shadowed his eyes, and his arms hung limply from his sagging shoulders.

"Thank you for the offer, but no. I can't linger. Another of the crew isn't feeling well, and I must look in on him."

He glanced up and down the deck, which was empty, then pointed to the paper bag, which was resting on the table outside the door. "Don't handle the envelopes. I pried up the flaps of all three and checked the glue. I had just enough chemicals to test each one. One envelope had cyanide in the glue, the other two did not. I wore gloves, as you suggested, Briarcliff, so any fingerprints on the paper have been preserved." He took a folded paper from his pocket and stretched out his arm to hand it across the empty space. "I wrote up the results and added my signature and date. I'm sure the officials in Luxor will want to conduct their own tests, but here's my statement about what I found. I'll keep the news about the envelopes to myself."

I leaned a shoulder against the doorframe, worry washing over me. "What grim news." We were all silent a moment, then Dr. Walsh said, "I must go."

"Any update on Hildy's condition?" I asked.

"No change at all. Don't worry too much about Miss Honeyworth. She's strong and has a good disposition. You'd be surprised how much of an advantage those two things go in fighting an infection. Briarcliff, you should know that it will become apparent today that the crew won't be able to function as usual with their reduced number. I hope I'm wrong, but they live in such close quarters that I'm worried more crew members may become ill. The good news is, so far the cases seem to be mild. Even Mr. Alexander appears to be through the worst of it. His fever broke within the last hour."

We hadn't told Dr. Walsh about our discovery that his patient was really Mr. Howard.

"It would be best if you kept him confined to his cabin," Mr. Briarcliff said.

Dr. Walsh was indeed tired because he missed the edgy undertone of Mr. Briarcliff's words and only said, "Of course. I'll see that he remains there for at least another full day. It's a sensible precaution."

"Good."

"Now, if there's nothing else . . ."

I held out a hand. "If you can spare just a few more moments, I have a few questions. Where would someone acquire cyanide?"

Dr. Walsh shrugged and moved a hand in a wide circle. "It's everywhere—pesticides, wallpaper, plants, even fruits, like peach and cherry pits."

"So it wouldn't be hard to come by?" I asked.

"Not at all."

Mr. Briarcliff asked, "And how would one add it to the envelopes?"

"That's easy as well. It dissolves in water, so once that's done, all one would need to do is brush the mixture over the glue on the envelope flap and let it dry. When Mr. Shaw licked the envelope, the poison absorbed through the membranes of his mouth quickly . . . and, well, you saw the result yourself, Miss Windway. The person who did this would have to be very careful, though. Cyanide is highly toxic. I'm glad of your caution to use gloves, Briarcliff, as it can absorb through the skin. Frightening to think someone among us is playing about with it. Now I really must attend to my patients." He pointed to the paper bag, which Mr. Briarcliff was holding away from his body, gripping it gingerly by the edge. "Lock that away."

"I'll do so immediately."

Once the bag was stowed in the locked cupboard, I said, "Someone prepared those envelopes. Which passenger is a poisoner?"

Mr. Briarcliff tucked the key to the cupboard in his waist-coat pocket and took a seat across from me. "Because of the hyacinth smell, you're thinking of Miss Fairweather, I suppose? I certainly am."

I nodded and sat down slowly at the table that was covered with our open notebooks and typed pages. "Do you think the envelopes originally belonged to her?"

He hunched over and placed an elbow on his knee, resting his chin on his fist. "That is the crux of the matter.

Who applied the cyanide, and how did those envelopes come to be in Mr. Shaw's case?"

"With their strong hyacinth aroma, it's logical to assume they were in Miss Fairweather's possession for quite some time. I know that Hildy's letters often smell of the gardenia scent she wears. I've noticed it when I post letters for her."

Mr. Briarcliff nodded but didn't reply.

"You don't agree?"

His hand dropped away from his chin. "That's possible, but isn't it also possible that someone applied a hyacinth scent to the envelopes to make it *seem* as if they came from Miss Fairweather?"

"Well, yes, that could have happened, but it's quite convoluted, isn't it? What you're saying is that in case the poison was discovered, the person who applied cyanide to the envelopes also added a flower scent, which would point to Miss Fairweather as the culprit."

Mr. Briarcliff pressed his hands to his knees and stood up with a sigh. "Yes, that would be quite devious."

"But applying poison to an envelope *is* devious." I scooted my chair forward, picked up a pen, and turned to a fresh page in my notebook. "Let's examine the most obvious person first—Miss Fairweather." I wrote her name down.

"I know why you've listed her first, but . . ." He grimaced. "It doesn't make sense. Why would she want to poison Mr. Shaw? She barely knew him."

"She could have lied. Perhaps they had some past association."

"Or he might have known some secret about her." Mr. Briarcliff paced to the corner of the room. "A few days ago, I would've said a woman like Miss Fairweather had nothing to keep quiet about, but after the revelations I've heard from the passengers on this cruise, I can't say that."

"Everyone has secrets. Mr. Shaw might have blackmailed her. Although I admit it is hard to picture lamblike Mr. Shaw having the gumption to threaten and blackmail."

Mr. Briarcliff rubbed his hand across the back of his neck as he walked around the table. "Let's go back to the envelope—that's the only solid thing we have."

I sketched an envelope in the margin. "Right. It wasn't the steamer's stationery. It was slightly smaller and a different color, white instead of ivory."

"But the differences were slight. One wouldn't be able to tell at first glance," Mr. Briarcliff added.

"It had a distinctive hyacinth aroma, and there were three envelopes all together, but only one had cyanide on the flap."

I tapped the pen, rapping the cap against the page as a wisp of memory floated like a tendril of fog blurring the outline of the landscape. "Someone said something about envelopes . . . What was it?" I murmured.

"That tapping sound is rather annoying."

"Oh!" I surged up and reached across the table. "May I see your notebook? I've just had a thought."

"Seeing as it's already in your hand, yes."

I flipped the pages, skimming for a name. "Here it is." I couldn't keep the excitement out of my voice, and Mr. Briarcliff stopped pacing. "This is from our chat with Miss Entwhistle. When Mr. Fairweather passed so suddenly, she went to check on Mr. Shaw because he was so pale. She was afraid he'd faint."

"Yes, I remember. She said he was rattling on."

"Right." I read the lines of Mr. Briarcliff's neat handwriting. "'Mr. Shaw said Mr. Fairweather was in a mood. He was annoyed because they'd run out of stationery and was impatient with how long Mr. Shaw was taking with the letters.

Mr. Fairweather took over writing one of the letters himself.'" I glanced up and caught his eye before reading the next part. "Miss Entwhistle said, 'I was quite surprised to hear Mr. Fairweather even fetched some envelopes from Louisa's portable writing desk and sealed up the letters while Mr. Shaw sorted the stamps. Mr. Shaw was rather perturbed about the stationery. Apparently, the steamer hadn't been resupplied with envelopes, and he hoped the ones he borrowed would be enough to last until Luxor, where he could get more.'"

He grasped the importance of the statement at once and leaned forward, palms flat on the table. "Then the envelopes he sealed up in the saloon before he died could have originally come from Louisa's writing desk."

"They must have. If he was out and couldn't find more in Mr. Shaw's desk, the logical thing to do would be to collect some from Louisa's portable writing desk."

Mr. Briarcliff spun away from the table while I copied down what Miss Entwhistle had said when she recounted Mr. Shaw's words. "So was Louisa the intended victim or the poisoner?"

I looked up from my notes. "She appeared to be fond of her husband, and her distress at his death seemed genuine. I suppose she could be putting up a front, though." Even I could hear the doubtful tone in my voice.

"She does stand to gain a substantial inheritance," Mr. Briarcliff said, but he also sounded far from convinced.

"If Louisa was the intended victim, and Miss Fairweather did it, there is a clear motive. The relationship between Louisa and her sister-in-law is strained. Remember Louisa even said her sister-in-law hated her." I doodled a bouquet of hyacinths.

Mr. Briarcliff said, "I'll grant you that I've learned

maiden ladies have hidden depths I'd never suspected, but . . . murder?"

"If we're considering Louisa, then we must also consider Miss Fairweather, no matter her age." I turned to a fresh page.

"New list?"

"Suspects," I said as I wrote the word across the top of the page, then put *Louisa* and *Miss Fairweather* underneath it. "Who else would have the ability to place the envelopes in Louisa's writing desk? Any of the crew, I assume, since doors are generally not locked."

"Mr. Fairweather was the exception to that practice. He said he was traveling with business paperwork that must be kept secure and always locked the cabin. His steward said he had to time his visits so that someone was there to let him in."

"But surely there's a passkey?"

"Yes, two, in fact. I have one and Hassan, whose reputation is impeccable, has the other."

"But if we're listing everyone . . ."

He waved a hand. "Yes, go ahead. Put my name and Hassan's, even though I know I didn't mess about with cyanide, and I'm sure Hassan didn't either."

"Miss Fairweather could have borrowed the key from her brother on some pretext or just slipped the envelopes into place when she visited the Fairweather cabin."

My head jerked up, and Mr. Briarcliff stopped pacing. "What is it?"

"What if more than one letter had poison on it?"

Mr. Briarcliff's brows came down in a frown. "But Dr. Walsh tested all three letters and only one had poison on it."

I slowly put the pen down, my thoughts racing. "What if

there was poison on a letter that had *already* gone out in the post?"

After a pause, Mr. Briarcliff drew in a deep breath and said, "You mean, you think Mr. Fairweather's death wasn't because of his heart."

"We just went over the statement that said Mr. Fairweather took the envelopes from Louisa's writing desk and sealed the letters shortly before he died in the saloon. What if there was cyanide on one of the envelopes Mr. Fairweather handled?"

# CHAPTER 31

Colonel W's new golf clubs, imported at great expense from St. Andrews, have yet to improve his game. Perhaps he should have invested in lessons instead? The 19th hole, at least, remains his forte.

*—About Town, The Nile*

"Oh my goodness." I fell back in my chair. "Dr. Walsh did say death from cyanide could take up to—what was it?—a quarter of an hour, I believe."

"Yes, that's right."

"So it could be possible. That would be two murders! It's exactly what Dr. Walsh suspected with Mr. Fairweather's death, but he couldn't find evidence to support his theory."

"And if it was cyanide," Mr. Briarcliff said, "then one of the murders was so subtle that it was mistaken for heart problems."

I bent my head and rubbed my temples. "How will we

ever figure this out? We have no way to link anyone directly to the envelopes—for either death. What about fingerprints? Could Dr. Walsh check the envelopes like he checked the coffee cups?"

"I can ask him, but I'm not sure it will help us."

I stared at him a moment, then realized what he meant. "Both Louisa and Miss Fairweather could explain away their fingerprints on the envelopes—Louisa because it's her cabin, and it would be reasonable for her to have handled them, and Miss Fairweather could say she was looking for something in the desk in their cabin."

Mr. Briarcliff had been pacing back and forth on the other side of the cabin, his preoccupied gaze at middle distance, but he suddenly stopped and turned toward me. "We have another problem. We only have Miss Entwhistle's statement that Mr. Fairweather took the envelopes from his wife's writing desk."

"That's right. No one else heard him say that." Frustration steamed through me, and I popped up from my chair. "We have nothing that definitely points to a single person as the culprit. We *must* figure this out. Otherwise, we'll have to reveal everyone's secrets to the officials when we arrive in Luxor, even Hildy's."

Mr. Briarcliff huffed out a little sigh. "That's true. I don't mind so much for myself. It will be embarrassing, and I will probably lose my position, but the possibility of breaking her contract seemed to distress Hildy."

"It did. And then besides those issues, a police investigation will cast a pall over everyone's reputations." I folded one arm across my waist, propped my elbow on it, and rested my chin on my hand. "No one commits a murder without leaving a trail. I'm convinced that there's got to be a way to figure it out. What have we missed?" I picked up the typed statements and began to read over them.

A tap sounded at the door. When Mr. Briarcliff opened it, Hassan stood outside. "The captain would like to speak to you before luncheon."

Mr. Briarcliff checked his watch. "Tell him I will be there shortly."

I looked at the time and began to tidy the table. "The morning has flown. It's almost time for luncheon."

Mr. Briarcliff stacked the notebooks and gathered up his typed pages. "Shall we meet back here in, say, an hour and a half?"

"Let's do that. I want to check on Hildy. Perhaps we'll see something we missed when we return."

"Tell her I send my best wishes for a quick recovery."

We left the typewriters in place but locked everything else in the cupboard, then went our separate ways.

The curtain at Hildy's window was drawn back, and she was reading in a nearby chair. She was in a dressing gown and had a shawl wrapped around her shoulders. I waved and pulled over one of the deck chairs near the window glass. "Can you hear me?"

"Yes, and before you ask, my health is unchanged, but I'm in good spirits." Her words were muted but audible, and even with the filter of the glass between us, I could hear the slight rasp as she spoke. She held up one of the books I had left earlier. "Thank you for this. It's helping me pass the time."

"I'm glad." She looked a little pale, but other than that, she looked like her normal self.

"Are you cold? Do you need anything else?"

"I'm fine, and Mr. Listergraff dropped by this morning to check on me, as did Louisa. I understand Miss Entwhistle has penciled me in for a session of chatting through the glass after luncheon."

"Mr. Briarcliff sends his wishes for a speedy recovery."

"How kind of him."

A steward arrived with a tray of food for her, and Hildy said, "You need to get along to the dining room. Luncheon will be served shortly."

"I'll stop by again this afternoon."

She waved me away. "No need to fuss over me. I'm doing fine," she said, and as I went away, she asked for another pot of tea and honey.

I took my usual seat in the dining room, but it felt strange with Hildy's empty chair across from me. I intended to invite Miss Entwhistle to sit with me, but I couldn't catch her eye. She'd brought a book with her and motioned to the steward that she'd take an unoccupied table.

Seffie must have decided to have a tray in her room because she wasn't in attendance. I hoped she wasn't feeling under the weather. Louisa arrived with Miss Fairweather. When they passed my table on the way to theirs, I noted that Louisa was again wearing her Chanel No. 5, and her copper curls were shiny and well-coiffed. I was glad she was taking care of herself. It was the most put-together she'd looked in a while. I stifled a cough as the cloud of Miss Fairweather's hyacinth scent enveloped me as she trailed behind Louisa. The two ladies didn't exchange a single word throughout the first course.

Mr. Listergraff arrived late, and I waved, motioning for him to join me if he'd like. As he took a seat, he said in a low voice, "Quiet as a grave in here today."

The only sounds were the clatter and clink of plates and cutlery. "I noticed too. And do you sense an atmosphere?"

"Definitely. There is a tension in the air."

He gave me a knowing look.

"Has something else happened?" I asked in a low voice.

Mr. Listergraff took a hurried sip of water. "A rumor has spread like wildfire through the passengers that Mr. Shaw was poisoned with cyanide."

"Where did you hear that?"

"My cabin attendant."

"I see." Someone must have overheard the conversation when Dr. Walsh delivered the news about his test of the envelopes.

"The subject is the main topic of conversation among the crew, and," Mr. Listergraff glanced around the dining room, "apparently the word has spread to the passengers. Everyone is keeping to themselves. No shuffleboard or chess today. I thought you should know."

"Did you hear any details?"

"As with most gossip, concrete details are sadly lacking. If you see Mr. Briarcliff, you'll let him know as well?"

At least the news that the cyanide was on the envelope hadn't gotten out yet. I was sure if that detail was known, it would be talked about. "Yes, of course."

"Thank you. And I won't put you in an awkward spot of asking if it's true or not, but I would advise you and Mr. Briarcliff to hurry along and rout out the truth since it seems we're traveling with a murderer. Now let's talk of less vexing topics. What is your opinion on moving pictures? Do you intend to add that to your presentations?"

We spent the rest of the meal discussing the challenges of working with cameras in the sandy atmosphere of the desert. Mr. Listergraff had filmed from his airplane. He'd shipped his camera ahead to Luxor and offered to let me borrow it in Luxor once we were off the S.S. *Cleopatra*.

I returned to the captain's cabin at the appointed time

and found Mr. Briarcliff already there. He looked up from the typed pages he was reading over. "How's Hildy?"

"She's no worse, which is good news."

"I'm glad to hear it. Hopefully, her case is mild, like Mr. Howard's."

"Have you heard?" I asked.

"That everyone knows Mr. Shaw was poisoned with cyanide? Yes. A distinct tension has settled over the steamer, especially among the crew. Every single one of them is frightened that they'll be blamed."

"But that doesn't make sense. Why would they poison someone on the steamer? You and the captain questioned them all and said they couldn't have done it."

"It's easiest to blame one of the crew."

It was a true statement—as I'd learned in Cairo when a death occurred at the pyramids. "But we won't do that."

"But they don't know that."

"Well, if the news is out, there's no way to keep it quiet."

"Right," Mr. Briarcliff said with a snap in his voice, which made me look at his face more carefully.

"Have you learned something?" I asked.

"No, I simply have an idea, but I must ruminate on it a bit before telling you about it."

"All right. I can understand that. A newly hatched idea is a delicate thing. Sometimes one must nurse it along until it matures a bit."

He chuckled. "Exactly."

I sat down, found the place I'd left off in the transcription, and put my fingers on the typewriter keys. "Perhaps something will come to light as we work through the rest of the interviews. I'm happy to take some of yours, if you'd like."

He ripped several pages out of the notebook and handed them over. "I'd be delighted."

We spent the rest of the afternoon typing and reading through the statements, but we weren't able to uncover any detail that pointed clearly to the culprit.

As we were clearing everything away, I said, "It's all quite frustrating. Louisa and Miss Fairweather are still the most likely candidates, but we discovered that Miss Entwhistle and Seffie also had reasons to dislike the Fairweather family. Miss Entwhistle's motive was strong, but Seffie's motive seemed to be a bit of a stretch. Would someone really kill over garden design?"

Mr. Briarcliff stacked our typed pages in the shelves. "Probably not, but Seffie's gardening certainly gives her knowledge about poisons as well as the means to do it."

I covered the Remington Portable with its case. "And, most frustrating of all, we know Mr. Shaw was murdered—Dr. Walsh's tests prove it—but no one seemed to have had any animus toward him." I snapped the lock down on the case. "In short, we have too many motives regarding Mr. Fairweather and no motives regarding Mr. Shaw."

Mr. Briarcliff closed the cabinet and locked it. "As well as a distinct lack of evidence to present to the officials in Luxor."

We stared glumly at each other for a moment, then I perked up. "Oh, your idea! Has it matured?"

"It's nearly there."

"We're almost out of time. We'll arrive at Luxor tomorrow."

"I'm sure we'll have our answer by then."

～

I THOUGHT about Mr. Briarcliff's enigmatic answer all through my solitary dinner, which was a very stilted meal, even quieter and more awkward than luncheon. The seating arrangement was the same as at luncheon, except that Seffie joined Mr. Listergraff and me. We spoke of the sites we'd seen in Cairo and the digs we hoped to see in Luxor once we were out of quarantine. As the tables were cleared after the final course, the head steward announced that the captain had requested the presence of all passengers who weren't ill in the saloon following dinner.

Before going to the saloon, I stopped by Hildy's cabin. She'd left a note wedged into the window frame that said she was sleeping. A chess game was set up on a table outside her door with a single empty chair positioned opposite the window. A game was clearly in progress, and I wondered if Mr. Listergraff had been her opponent.

I was the last to arrive in the saloon because of my detour, and I was surprised that the captain wasn't anywhere to be seen, but Mr. Briarcliff, who usually didn't join us after dinner, was leaning against the back of a chair, chatting with Mr. Listergraff.

As soon as Mr. Briarcliff caught sight of me, he picked up something from one of the tables and crossed the room, clearly intent on intercepting me before I could join Louisa and Seffie, who were seated in what I'd come to think of as their chairs in the center of the room. Miss Entwhistle sat alone at a table, sipping a cup of coffee.

Miss Fairweather was in the corner of the room, as far from the other women as she could possibly be, pacing back and forth, her arms crossed and her handbag on her wrist banging against her hip with every step. "When will the captain be here?" she asked Mr. Briarcliff. "The company is sadly lacking, and I'm ready to retire for the evening."

"The captain has asked me to make an announcement. Just give me a moment, Miss Fairweather."

She sent him a look that would have stopped most people in their tracks, but Mr. Briarcliff didn't seem to notice her displeasure and continued toward me. Miss Fairweather sighed loudly, then removed her fur throw and draped it over the back of a chair before she jerked up a discarded magazine and took a seat.

Mr. Briarcliff crossed the room to me. He removed a magazine that had been loosely folded length-wise from his inner jacket pocket. "Good news, Miss Windway. I found it, the third installment of *The Agony Column*."

I smoothed open *The Saturday Evening Post*. "However did you find it?"

"I sent a message to the other steamers around us and asked their crew managers to have a look for it. Turns out, there was a copy on one of the steamers going in the opposite direction. They sent it over with the supplies. We often transfer items among the various steamers that belong to the Blue Lotus Line."

I was so surprised that I was actually speechless for a moment. Mr. Briarcliff dipped his head. "I believe the words you're looking for are *thank you*."

"Such a thoughtful gesture, but then you had to go and ruin it."

He gave me a little flash of a grin. "I can't let things get too sentimental."

"I do thank you for it, though. I will quite enjoy reading the end of the story."

"My actions are not completely altruistic." He tapped the magazine. "It's a bribe."

"What for?"

"I hope that you'll play along."

"I don't understand."

He didn't answer me but turned away and addressed the room. "If I could have your attention for just a moment."

Mr. Listergraff, who was sitting at one of the tables arranging chess pieces, folded his hands. Miss Fairweather, who now had the magazine open on her lap, flipped it closed and tossed it aside. Louisa and Seffie swiveled so that they could look at Mr. Briarcliff. Miss Entwhistle, who was refilling her coffee cup, took a seat across from Louisa and Seffie.

"The captain has asked that I keep you informed about our current situation. The Blue Lotus Line appreciates your forbearance with the adjustments we've had to make. Fortunately, most of the crew members remain healthy, and I can report that Miss Windway says that Miss Honeyworth is in good spirits and her symptoms haven't worsened. Dr. Walsh is doing everything he can to see that everyone is cared for. We've been able to receive the supplies that we need from a passing steamer, and we've created a system that prevents any interaction between our crew members and those from other steamers, which we'll continue once we arrive in Luxor. Our supplies will be ferried out to us, left on the deck, and then the *Cleopatra*'s crew will retrieve them after the delivery crew has departed."

He clasped his hands together and took a few steps away from me. "Thank you all for participating in the interviews regarding the deaths of Mr. Shaw and Mr. Fairweather. On that front, Miss Windway and I have made progress."

Seffie twisted a little bit farther around and rested her elbow on the arm of the chair. "So you have news about poor Mr. Shaw?"

"We do. And I believe you are all aware of it, but I'll

make an official announcement now. Mr. Shaw was indeed poisoned with cyanide."

No one gasped in shock, confirming the news was indeed out.

"We have tracked down the source of the poison," Mr. Briarcliff continued. "It was on one of the envelopes Mr. Shaw handled here in the saloon." The pages of the magazine crinkled as my grip tightened. We hadn't discussed sharing that bit of information. What was Mr. Briarcliff doing? Why was he sharing the single detail that wasn't known? I reached out, intending to grip his arm, but he was already moving away from me.

He took a few steps toward Louisa and addressed her. "Unfortunately, there's more bad news. I'm sorry to inform you, Mrs. Fairweather, that Miss Windway and I suspect Mr. Fairweather's death may also be from cyanide."

I closed my eyes briefly. Infernal man! What in the world was he doing?

Louisa went pale. "But that can't be. He had heart problems—"

Miss Fairweather surged to her feet and launched herself at Louisa, yelling, "You hussy! How could you? I always knew you only wanted his money."

# CHAPTER 32

Dear Amelia,
I wish to end my courtship with a gentleman, but I'm at a loss for words. How does one break things off without causing a scene?

Dear Graceful Exit,
Ending a courtship requires the delicacy of a tea service and the firmness of a well-starched collar. Choose a private setting, be direct but kind, and remember: a clean break heals faster than a drawn-out farewell.

—*Ask Amelia, The Illustrated Dispatch*

*M*iss Fairweather shoved Seffie to the side, grabbed a fistful of Louisa's hair, and yanked her head back. Louisa let out a yelp and grabbed Miss Fairweather's wrist. She gave it a twist and deftly disengaged herself, then moved back several steps.

Mr. Briarcliff and Mr. Listergraff had both moved toward Miss Fairweather, but Seffie acted quickly, stepping between the two women and addressing Miss Fairweather in the soothing tones a nanny would use with a naughty child. "Now, now. That was inappropriate," she said as she gripped Miss Fairweather's upper arm and steered her to a chair several feet away from Louisa, who was breathing hard, her hair disarranged and hanging around her face. Seffie pushed Miss Fairweather down into the chair, then remained standing beside her with a firm hand on her shoulder so that she didn't pop up again. Seffie looked toward Mr. Briarcliff. "I assume you have more to tell us?"

Mr. Briarcliff straightened his lapels and gave Miss Fairweather a long look before replying. "Indeed, I do." He looked toward Louisa. "Mrs. Fairweather, are you up to hearing more, or would you prefer to retire to your room?"

Louisa reached out blindly, and her hand connected with a nearby chair arm. She slowly lowered herself onto the cushion. She tucked her hair behind her ears. "Please go on."

"We cannot reveal the culprit at the moment, but we should have a very good idea by tomorrow."

"What?" My voice was quite screechy, but my startled exclamation was lost among the sudden outburst from the other passengers.

Mr. Briarcliff, who was still only a short distance away from me, said in a quiet aside, "Please play along." Then he raised his voice. "If you'll give me your attention, I'll explain."

I leveled a scorching look at him, which he ignored. He took out his handkerchief and used it to remove a sealed envelope from the inner pocket of his suit jacket. He displayed it to the room, pivoting so that everyone could see it. The crumpled and creased envelope looked as if it had been discarded and stepped on a few times. "During our interviews, we learned that shortly before Mr. Fairweather died, he helped Mr. Shaw with some business correspondence. Mr. Fairweather addressed and sealed the envelopes himself. After we learned about those actions, I checked the postbox on board." He shook the envelope. "This envelope was wedged in the bottom. The edge of it had caught in a seam where two metal pieces of the postbox are joined. It wasn't removed with the rest of the post at our last stop. As you can see, there is no postmark."

Mr. Briarcliff returned the envelope to his pocket. "It will be turned over to the officials in Luxor tomorrow and analyzed."

Mr. Listergraff had returned to his seat by the chess game. "And if there is cyanide on the envelope?"

"Then Mr. Fairweather's death was undoubtedly murder. I've been careful not to leave my fingerprints on it. The police chaps are quite good at finding fingerprints now. Since only Mr. Fairweather and Mr. Shaw handled the envelopes, another set of fingerprints will be quite incriminating."

Mr. Listergraff tilted his head, his forehead wrinkling. He looked as if he was about to challenge that statement, but Mr. Briarcliff continued, "I imagine the authorities will instruct us to take everyone's fingerprints. They won't be able to come onto the steamer because of our quarantine, but gathering fingerprints will be something that can be carried out on their behalf. It's a simple process. I'm sorry for any inconvenience it will cause, and I'm truly sorry to cast a pall over this evening." Mr. Briarcliff tipped his head toward Louisa. "But the captain thought it best to keep everyone informed."

Louisa still looked quite shaken, and Seffie gave Miss

Fairweather a stern look before crossing over to Louisa to chafe her hands. "What a shock. Your fingers are ice cold. Would you like some brandy?"

Miss Fairweather stood up and rang for an attendant. "I certainly would."

I tucked the magazine under my arm. "Mr. Briarcliff, a moment of your time, please." I marched through the saloon's door, the tread of his footsteps sounding behind me as I crossed the promenade deck.

The night was cool and clear with the hint of a breeze. It would have been a lovely setting, but because of the anger fizzing through me, I barely noticed the surroundings. I kept my voice low. "What on earth are you doing? You didn't inform me you had found the envelope. I don't appreciate you keeping things from me, especially something of such importance."

He let out a relieved sigh. "Oh good. I'm glad my little ruse worked. I was afraid the envelope might not pass muster, but if you thought that it was real, that's quite a good sign."

"What!" I realized I'd practically shouted the word and dropped my voice to a whisper as I pointed to his chest. "You didn't find it in the postbox? You . . . *created* it? That's so . . . so . . . underhanded!"

"I realize you're upset—"

"Upset?"

"Angry."

I gave him a look.

"Furious, then." He touched his face. "Do I have burn marks? Your gaze is scorching."

"I can't believe you're joking at a time like this."

His manner shifted, and he sounded contrite. "I do apologize, but would you have gone along with it, if I'd told you?"

I hesitated.

"There. You see? You wouldn't have. If it works, then we've sussed out the culprit. You said yourself we weren't making any progress. My little performance was simply a spark to see if we can kindle a fire. Of course, the other possibility is that the spark flickers and goes out. However, if it works, then it may cause someone to take action and give themselves away. Did you have another way of breaking the deadlock we've reached in the investigation?"

I closed my eyes briefly and took a moment to calm myself. "Since you've gone so far down this path, we might as well see what happens."

Since Mr. Briarcliff had stirred everyone up, I wasn't about to retire to my cabin. I returned to the saloon, settled into a chair a little apart from everyone, and tried to read the magazine, but I couldn't immerse myself in the story. Mr. Briarcliff poured a cup of coffee and brought it to me, placing it on the table beside me, but he kept his distance, as if I were a dog that might bite him. "Cream, no sugar, correct?" I gave him a nod of acknowledgment. He turned to the room. "Can I pour a cup for anyone else?"

Mr. Listergraff said, "I'll take a cup, Rafe." Louisa, Seffie, and Miss Fairweather declined as they were sipping brandy, which must have arrived while Mr. Briarcliff and I were out of the room. Miss Entwhistle was immersed in her book and shook her head. Mr. Briarcliff poured coffee into two cups, handed one to Mr. Listergraff, and kept the other for himself.

I turned the pages of *The Saturday Evening Post*, scanning the advertisements. When I reached the end of it, I put it aside to read later when I could concentrate.

I picked up a discarded issue of *The Nile* and skimmed it,

keeping most of my attention on the occupants of the saloon. Given the strained dinner, I thought everyone would retire to their rooms immediately after Mr. Briarcliff's announcement, but no one hurried off, not even Miss Fairweather, who stayed planted in her seat, nursing her brandy. Mr. Listergraff invited Mr. Briarcliff to play chess, and they didn't speak as they concentrated on their game.

Miss Fairweather finally finished her brandy and put the glass down with a loud click. She hooked her handbag over her arm and marched across the saloon. Her path took her beside Louisa, and I tensed, but Miss Fairweather kept her chin in the air and didn't break her stride.

Once she was out of the room, Louisa sagged. Seffie persuaded her to retire, and the two women left, Louisa leaning on Seffie's much smaller frame. As the women passed the chess table, Louisa swayed, and both men stood. "Shall I escort you to your cabin, Mrs. Fairweather?" Mr. Briarcliff asked.

Louisa had braced a hand on the table for a moment, then pushed herself up and leaned into Seffie. "That's kind of you, Mr. Briarcliff, but I'm fine. My heel must have caught on the fringe of the rug. Sorry to disturb your game." Seffie put her arm firmly around Louisa, and they departed.

The click of the chess pieces on the board was the only sound. Miss Entwhistle turned a page and shifted closer to the lamp. A few moments later, Miss Fairweather stalked back into the saloon and jerked her fur wrap from the back of the chair.

As she marched back out, her handbag caught on the edge of the table where Mr. Briarcliff and Mr. Listergraff were playing, yanking her arm backward. She stumbled, and the contents of her handbag scattered over the rug. Mr. Briarcliff jumped up and helped her steady herself, but when she put her weight on her left foot, she bent forward in pain.

Mr. Briarcliff helped her take a seat in his chair. "Should I send for Dr. Walsh?"

She plopped down and moved her ankle in a circle, then flexed it back and forth. "No. I don't believe it's anything serious."

"Well, rest here a moment," Mr. Briarcliff said as he joined Mr. Listergraff in picking up the contents of Miss Fairweather's handbag. Mr. Listergraff gathered a handkerchief, an eyeglass case, and a comb while Mr. Briarcliff hunted for hairpins that had been flung all over the rug. He got to his feet. "I believe this is all of them."

"Thank you." She returned the items to her bag, then stood up and tested her weight on her ankle. "I must have just strained it. It feels fine now."

Mr. Briarcliff said, "I'll accompany you to your cabin."

"There's no need for that. I'm not infirm." The usual bite was back in her words, and I knew she wasn't seriously injured. "Please continue with your game."

As the men returned to their seats, Miss Entwhistle closed her novel. "Good night, all." The men again rose to their feet as she passed by them on her way out of the saloon. I was about to follow her, but the copy of *The Nile* was still open on my lap, and when I picked it up to put it away, a line in the *About Town* gossip column caught my eye.

*Mr. and Mrs. F depart on a Nile cruise soon, but whispers in high society indicate the former "hackette" intends to navigate the rocky shoals of divorce.*

I read the line twice. *Hackette* had to mean Mrs. Fairweather, referring to her prior life as a reporter. There weren't many reporters turned society ladies. Had Mrs. Fairweather considered divorce? The scandal sheets and gossip columns often printed "news" that wasn't anything more than fabrications, but if it were true, then she would have a motive to murder her husband. An inheritance would surely be much larger than a divorce settlement. And the death of Mr. Fairweather would mean she wouldn't have to deal with polite society's disapproval of a divorcée.

I went to the bookshelf, knelt down, and dug through the discarded newspapers and magazines. I found the other recent copies of *The Nile* and flipped through them, but the only other mention of Mr. and Mrs. F was a note on the arrival of the *rubber baron*, a play on words that was similar to *robber baron*.

I thought of keeping the news to myself—after the dirty trick Mr. Briarcliff had played on me, he deserved to be left out of the loop—but then I rocked back on my heels and got to my feet. Since the point in question was murder, I couldn't keep the news to myself in good conscience. However, when I looked around, Mr. Briarcliff's seat was empty.

Mr. Listergraff was replacing the chess pieces, positioning them so they'd be ready for another game. "Where's Mr. Briarcliff?"

"He went to bed. Could hardly keep his eyes open, poor lad. I told him he can't keep up this working all hours of the day and night."

I briefly considered finding Mr. Briarcliff's cabin and pounding on his door. It would serve him right after the stunt he'd pulled, but I discarded the idea. There was no need to share the news immediately. The tidbit about divorce didn't prove anything, only added another possible motive for Louisa, and a gossip column was hardly a reliable source.

Since I wouldn't be able to share my discovery until morning, I said, "Let me help you." I took the chess pieces that Mr. Briarcliff had captured and aligned the pawns on their squares. "Did you and Hildy perhaps start a game of chess this afternoon?" I picked up the bishop and knight and brushed the table clear of a few pieces of lint. I put the pieces in their places, then moved Mr. Briarcliff's empty coffee cup to the other side of the table to look for a missing pawn.

"Yes. She became tired, and I told her I'd leave the pieces on the board so we can continue tomorrow. It's fortunate that we have two chess sets. I imagine both will get a lot of use in the next few weeks. Miss Honeyworth is an excellent player, by the way."

"I bet she is. Goodness, where did all this lint come from?" I reached out to brush the specks away from the table's dark glossy surface, but then I realized it wasn't lint. The tiny specks were a fine powder. I rubbed my fingers together and felt a faint trace of roughness on my thumb where I'd gripped the saucer when I moved it. I tilted the coffee cup. Granular residue covered the inside of the china cup.

"Excuse me, Mr. Listergraff, but I must check on something." I dashed out of the saloon.

Any one of my many governesses would have had palpitations if they'd seen my lack of decorum as I galloped down the steps to the main deck, then raced along the corridor, checking each of the names on the little cards outside the doors, which were illuminated with tiny sconces interspersed between the cabins. When I came to Mr. Briarcliff's door, I hammered on it and called his name, but there was no answer.

I took half a step away, intending to search for Dr. Walsh, but then I turned back. Time was of the essence. I could spend quite a while chasing around the steamer looking for the doctor, and I wasn't even sure Mr. Briarcliff was in his cabin. I knocked again and shook the door handle. I was surprised when it turned at my touch, and the door swung open.

The cabin was dark, but the faint light coming in from the hallway was enough to show Mr. Briarcliff, still in his suit, lying motionless on the bed. I hurried across the room. I'd thrown open the door in such a hurry that it ricocheted against the wall and slammed closed, plunging the cabin into darkness. In the glimpse I'd caught before the door closed, I'd seen Mr. Briarcliff's hand trailing along the side of the bed, as if he'd barely made it there before collapsing.

The cabin was small, and a few steps through the blackness brought me to the bed. I grabbed Mr. Briarcliff's shoulders and shook him. "Wake up! You need to wake up!" Hands shot out and grabbed my wrists.

"Miss Windway, whatever are you doing?"

His deep voice wasn't slurred at all, and I sat back on my heels but didn't pull my wrists out of his grip. "You haven't been poisoned? There was a powdery substance on the table where you were sitting, and I was afraid that you'd ingested something . . . "

"Deadly? I assure you I was smart enough not to drink my coffee this evening."

I couldn't see his face in the darkness, but I could tell he was perfectly fine because of his usual acerbic tone. "But I saw you sipping it."

"I put it to my lips and *appeared* to drink it. There's a very conveniently placed potted plant near the table, where I deposited my coffee."

He moved his thumbs on my wrists, and I swallowed. My worry about him had completely pushed out of my mind the fact that we were inches apart in a dark room.

I pulled my elbows back, and he released his hold immediately. I made a move to stand but bumped into his legs, which were dangling off the side of the bed. I moved backward, and the bedding rustled as if he were scooting away. "So, you're lying here in the dark waiting for someone to attack you?" I asked.

"Exactly. That was the point of my little speech. I'm bait. I hope the culprit we're searching for will come after the envelope, which is here in my inner pocket." Fabric whispered, and there was a muted crinkle of paper. I imagined he was patting his chest where he'd stowed the envelope in his jacket. "But unless you leave, you've ruined my staging."

"Mr. Briarcliff, you are trying my patience. You're such a vexing man." I could tell from his voice that he was still lying on the bed, and I leaned over him. I was so angry I could only whisper. "Of all the idiotic ideas—"

A light tap sounded on the door.

Miss S caused quite a stir at yesterday's lawn tennis match, arriving in a shockingly short skirt that only grazed her knees. While some tsked, her improved mobility on the court was undeniable—as was her victory.

—*About Town, The Nile*

*I* froze, biting off the rest of my sentence. We waited in the silence, and after a few seconds there was another slightly louder tap on the door. A female voice that I wasn't able to identify whispered, "Mr. Briarcliff?"

Mr. Briarcliff reached out, and his hand bumped my arm, then he pushed me away as he breathed, "The wardrobe. Into the wardrobe. You've got to hide."

But I'd only had the brief glimpse of Mr. Briarcliff lying on the bed before the door closed. I had no idea where the wardrobe was.

Metal rattled, and I whispered back, "No time."

Light appeared around the edge of the door as it opened a sliver.

Mr. Briarcliff, his voice barely audible even to me, said, "Don't give me away."

There was nothing to do but scuttle backward as quickly and quietly as I could until my elbow connected with a sharp corner. I bit back a squawk of pain. I'd found the wardrobe.

Still bent double, I shifted to the side and melted into the gap between the wardrobe and the wall, heart thundering and feeling as winded as if I'd run several laps around the steamer.

The door opened wider, throwing an oblong shaft of light over Mr. Briarcliff's figure. "Mr. Briarcliff?" He was sprawled half on the bed, half off, with an arm and his feet trailing on the floor. His head wasn't even on the pillow. He didn't move, even when the sudden beam of torchlight danced across the room. He truly looked as if he'd just barely made it to the bed before passing out.

The woman closed the door and crossed to the bed, her shoes clicking rapidly across the uncarpeted wooden floor. She aimed the torch at Mr. Briarcliff's chest, flicked back the suit lapel, and extracted the envelope. I watched, trying not to move a muscle so I wouldn't give myself away through a tiny creak of a floorboard or whisper of fabric. I couldn't tell who the woman was. The light from the torch made her figure into a silhouette. Her build wasn't slight enough to be Seffie, but she was the only person I could rule out. Louisa, Miss Fairweather, and Miss Entwhistle had also passed by the men's table on their way out of the saloon. Any one of them could have dropped something into Mr. Briarcliff's coffee.

I tensed and tried to somehow make myself smaller, expecting her to swing around, splaying the light across the cabin as she retreated. But she straightened, tucked the letter into a pocket, then snapped the torch off, though she didn't move to the door. What was she doing?

I caught the floral fragrance as the mattress creaked, then almost simultaneously there was a thrashing about, and a sharp, startled scream. I inched out of my hiding place as something crashed to the floor. Sounds of a struggle, grunts and ripping fabric, sent me toward the door, where I traced my hand along the wall until I came to the light switch and pressed it.

For a moment, I thought I was seeing things. Downy white feathers were drifting lazily to the ground, and Miss Fairweather was hunched over as Mr. Briarcliff held one of her arms twisted behind her back.

She struggled, trying to free herself. "What are you doing? Unhand me this instant!"

"I think not, seeing as you tried to smother me."

Mr. Briarcliff pushed his hair off his forehead with his free hand. His shoulder seam was ripped, as was the seam of one of the bed pillows, which now lay on the floor like a deflated balloon. "Thank you for the light, Miss Windway—"

He broke off, turned his head away, and I yanked my clean handkerchief out of my pocket and handed it to him before he sneezed.

He sniffed. "Thank goodness I was able to fight that off until now. I would have been terribly disappointed in myself if I'd given the game away with a sneeze."

He was all smiles, which was rather startling because he was usually so stern-faced. The expression *a cool drink of water on a hot day* popped into my mind.

"Miss Windway?"

I snapped my wandering thoughts back to attention. "What?"

"I'm a bit incapacitated, perhaps you could—"

"Right." I sincerely hoped my cheeks didn't look as flushed as they felt. "Of course. I'll call for the captain, and then we're going to have a long chat about your reckless behavior, Mr. Briarcliff."

The famous lawn tennis champion, Mr. Augustus Ringwald, arrived in Cairo recently, and he has agreed to join a tournament next week at the Gezira Sporting Club.

*—Arrivals and Departures, The Nile*

*I* rang for a steward, and he arrived within moments. I sent him to fetch the captain. Mr. Briarcliff had released Miss Fairweather's arm, and she was massaging her shoulder while sending him murderous looks.

"Have a seat," he said, indicating the end of the bed.

"No, thank you. I'll be returning to my cabin."

I blocked her path. "But we have so much to discuss."

Mr. Briarcliff took a step forward, and Miss Fairweather hurriedly perched on the mattress. However, she turned her back to Mr. Briarcliff and addressed the wall opposite the door. "I have nothing to say to this cad. He accosted me."

There was no doubt in my mind that Miss Fairweather was the poisoner, but I was sure she'd deny everything and leverage her affluence in any way possible to save herself. It would be her word against mine and Mr. Briarcliff's, and she was more affluent than either of us.

"Fine. You can speak to me." There was no desk in the room, but a ladder-back chair stood in the corner. I dragged it over and took a seat directly in front of her. Could I salvage Mr. Briarcliff's rash act of setting himself up as bait? I had to try.

"I don't see why you're treating a lady like this." Her eyes welled with tears. "It was positively ghastly. He pounced on me. I had no choice but to defend myself."

Mr. Briarcliff looked disgusted and stepped forward.

I gave him a warning shake of the head. "*You* attacked *him*, Miss Fairweather. I was in the room. I heard the scuffle."

"It was dark as pitch in here. You couldn't see anything." She sniffed. "The man is a menace and should be locked up, attacking poor, defenseless ladies."

I bit back the comment that she gave poor, defenseless ladies a bad name. Instead, I asked, "Then what were you doing in his room?"

There was a tiny pause. "I sleepwalk."

"Fully clothed?"

Mr. Briarcliff, who had been looming over her shoulder, retreated and leaned against the wall, his arms crossed and a smile teasing at the corners of his mouth.

"I must have nodded off in my room." Miss Fairweather's head bobbed. "Yes, that's what happened. I remember sitting down in the armchair, feeling quite fatigued. I'm so fragile, you know. I tend to overdo. I nodded off—that's what happened."

"Then you left your room, wandered down the stairs to the main deck, and into this specific room? Handy of you to have remembered to pick up a torch in your sleepwalking state."

Her hand darted to her pocket, where the edge of the torch was visible. "Oh. How . . . strange. I don't know how that came to be there."

Movement beyond Miss Fairweather's shoulder caught my eye. I did my best to keep my attention focused on Miss Fairweather, but I was aware that the captain had opened the door. Mr. Briarcliff pushed off from the wall and put a finger to his lips. He motioned for the captain to come in, then silently closed the door. Captain Farouk stood to the side of the door beside Mr. Briarcliff.

"Miss Fairweather," I said, "let's end this charade. I don't for one minute believe you're a silly, helpless woman. You figured out how to poison two people with cyanide in a way that was so crafty it was almost overlooked. What I don't understand is why you killed your brother and Mr. Shaw."

She maintained eye contact with me, but the corners of her lips turned down, and her chin firmed as she gathered herself. "I don't know what you're talking about."

"There's no use in denying it. Your actions speak for themselves." I reached forward and plucked the envelope from her other pocket. "There's only one reason to retrieve this letter. You were worried you'd left your fingerprints on it."

"As I said, I don't know what you mean."

I continued as if she hadn't spoken. "It must have been stifling, living in the same home with your brother and his new, younger wife. After all, you'd run the house for years and acted as your brother's hostess for decades. How galling to have a new lady of the manor, especially someone as successful and beautiful as Mrs. Fairweather. Were you not aware that Mr. Fairweather had changed his will after he married and that you'd have to live at Nobilis Domus to receive your stipend?"

"I would never harm my brother. I don't know how you could even insinuate that." Her tones rang with genuine sincerity.

"Oh, then it was *Louisa* you hoped to do away with." Her eyes widened and her breathing quickened, her chest rising and falling. "It must have been difficult for you. It's understandable that you'd resent Louisa for taking your place. She is a beautiful, intelligent, and strong lady."

"She is *not* a lady."

I'd found her weak point, so I pressed ahead. "She's kind, intelligent, capable, and accomplished. Isn't that the very definition of a lady?"

"She's a grasping hussy. She has no idea how to run the estate. She didn't know the first thing about precedence. She constantly embarrassed my brother by fumbling the procession to the dining room. She didn't even reply to her letters. A true lady doesn't fall behind in her correspondence. If she were a genuine lady, she would have written to her family and friends as soon as we boarded the S.S. *Cleopatra* to let them know she'd departed on a Nile cruise and where to contact us once we reached Luxor. Did she do that? No. It's her fault my brother is dead. If she had performed her duties as expected, she would be dead, not my brother. I will never forgive her for that."

"You placed the envelopes with the poison in her writing desk, never thinking that your brother would use them."

"Foolish man." She swallowed and looked down at the floor. "He should have left work of that sort to Mr. Shaw. If he'd left well enough alone, everything could have gone back to the way it was before."

The captain stirred. "Mr. Briarcliff, I see your *fishing expedition*, as you called it, has been successful." He opened the door and motioned for the steward, who was waiting to follow him as he crossed the room to Miss Fairweather.

"Escort Miss Fairweather to the unoccupied cabin next door. Lock the door and remain on guard until we arrive at Luxor. She's not allowed to leave, and no one is allowed to enter."

# CHAPTER 35

Dear Amelia,
How does a lady know if a gentleman truly fancies her? I'm positively flummoxed by his mixed signals!

Dear Puzzled,
A gentleman's interest is often as clear as a London fog, my dear. Look for the little things: Does he seek your company, go out of his way to do favors for you, remember your favorite flowers, or laugh at your jokes—even the dreadful ones? If yes, then you may have caught his eye as surely as he's caught yours.

—*Ask Amelia, The Illustrated Dispatch*

"**G**ood shot, Miss Windway! You trounced me in this game." Miss Entwhistle used her makeshift shuffleboard cue to send the disks to the starting position.

Luxor was in sight, across the stretch of sparkling water that separated the steamer from the city. Moored a good distance from the city, the steamer hadn't moved since we'd arrived. There was constant traffic of other steamers, but there was no contact between us and the other vessels, except for the daily launch, which arrived ferrying a smaller boat loaded with supplies.

It had been several days since the tumult in Mr. Briarcliff's cabin. Miss Fairweather continued to be confined to the spare cabin. Once the quarantine was over, she'd be transferred to British authorities, who were currently putting together a case to charge her with the murders of her brother and Mr. Shaw.

The day we dropped anchor at Luxor, a launch had approached with a small, unoccupied boat trailing it. The bodies of the two men had been placed in the smaller boat and conveyed to Luxor, where they'd been buried immediately in the foreigner's cemetery. We'd held a short service for them before the boat arrived. Afterward, Louisa had stood at the railing, her eyes watery, watching the progress of the small boat across the water. "Ambrose would be appalled at this sort of send-off. He'd have wanted a funeral with a horse-drawn hearse and hundreds in attendance." She daubed at her eyes. "But we have to accept the situation. Quarantine bends for no man."

She'd spent the rest of the day in her cabin but had attended breakfast the next morning, looking pale and subdued. Since then, her manner was somber, but she'd participated in the schedule of activities that Miss Entwhistle had compiled for us. I was glad she wasn't keeping to herself and hoped her buoyant and keen manner would eventually return.

I helped Miss Entwhistle reset the shuffleboard game,

then held her cue as she took a pencil from her pocket and took down the clipboard from a hook on the railing. She made a hashmark under my name. "That's three games for each of us."

"Tomorrow's game will decide the winner."

Miss Entwhistle and I had taken to having a morning game of shuffleboard, which had grown into a round-robin tournament that involved all the passengers and even a few of the senior crew members. Miss Entwhistle had created brackets, and we were faithfully recording our scores after each game to see who would advance.

It appeared we'd come through the first surge of scarlet fever with only Mr. Howard, Hildy, and four crew members falling ill. All patients were improving, and no one else seemed to be feeling under the weather, which was an enormous relief. Hildy and Mr. Howard were out of isolation. When Mr. Howard joined us for dinner for the first time in several weeks, he tapped his glass after pudding, stood up, and cleared his throat. He announced that he'd been traveling under his first name instead of his true surname, Mr. Howard. Murmurs rippled around the room as he clenched his hands, waiting for the noise to die down. Although I was a few tables away from him, I could see the sheen of sweat at his temples. "It was for a job I'd taken on, but that's ended." He shot a shamefaced look at Hildy. "I never was an archaeologist as some of you may have suspected. I apologize for my deception."

He'd scurried from the dining room and retired immediately. I'd wondered if he'd spend the rest of our quarantine in his cabin, but the next morning he was breakfasting at Dr. and Mrs. Walsh's table. I suspected Dr. Walsh had sought him out and invited him to join them. After a day or so, it became clear that Mr. Howard wasn't divulging more details about his deception, and we settled back into a routine.

In our enforced state of suspended animation, we were doing our best to fill our days, but it felt as if we were walking in place. We'd discovered the value of planning activities and staggering events over the days. When each day stretched blankly ahead similar to the previous day, even a scheduled game of shuffleboard gave one something to look forward to.

I asked Miss Entwhistle, "Who's next on today's schedule?"

"Dr. and Mrs. Walsh, but they look quite busy at the moment. I'm sure they'll play when they're ready."

They were seated at the back of the promenade deck next to the wall. Seffie's chair was fully in the sun, the bright light beating down on her wide-brimmed hat. Dr. Walsh sat next to her in the shade, a stack of books open on his lap, his pipe in the corner of his mouth.

Miss Entwhistle rehung the clipboard. "It's good to see Dr. Walsh looking less haggard."

I propped up our shuffleboard cues by the clipboard. "It is. I was worried about him last week." Seffie told me that now that he had fewer patients, he'd actually been able to get a full night's sleep. I was sure the fact that Seffie remained healthy and hadn't come down with scarlet fever was a massive relief to him.

Dr. Walsh turned a page in the guidebook and asked Seffie, "What about Gebelein? Should we add that to our list? It's seventeen miles from Luxor by rail, and there's a ruin of a Middle Kingdom temple."

Seffie tilted her head. "Perhaps. Put it on our *Possible* list, but I'd like to visit Lady Granger. In her letter that arrived yesterday, she said their villa in Luxor has a Sinai Wild Rose in the garden. I'd like to see that."

Dr. Walsh took up his pen. "Well then, we'll add Lady Granger to our *Must* list."

I gave Dr. Walsh and Seffie a wave as Miss Entwhistle and I crossed the promenade deck. Miss Entwhistle headed for the saloon. "Off to work on the jigsaw puzzle again?" I asked.

"No, something different, an idea I had for a new game."

"A variation on shuffleboard?"

"No, it's a word puzzle. It's similar to a crossword, but with a single word instead of many."

"Interesting."

"I think five-letter words would be the perfect length—plenty of variety, but it wouldn't be too difficult to guess. I just have to work out the details of how to reveal correct and incorrect guesses when it comes to the individual letters."

"Well, good luck with it. We need more games. We're down to our last jigsaw, and it's almost finished."

We parted, and I went to check on Hildy. When I tapped on her cabin door, she called out for me to come in. She was seated at her dressing table, combing her hair. "Hello, Blix. How was shuffleboard?"

"I was victorious today."

"Oh, well done, you. I'm off to join Mr. Listergraff for a game of chess soon."

"You've been playing quite a lot of chess with Mr. Listergraff."

"One must pass the time."

"Yes, but it seems you've been in his company more and more since you've recovered."

"He *is* good company."

I tried to catch her gaze in the mirror, but she was busy

putting away her comb. She checked her watch as she picked up several thick envelopes and stood up. "Oh dear. I'll be late if I don't hurry. Could you drop these in the postbox for me?"

"I see what you're doing."

She opened a drawer and took out a clean handkerchief. "I have no idea what you're talking about."

"I'll drop these off, but I want to hear more about Mr. Listergraff soon."

She gave me a grin like a schoolgirl being let out of class early and said, "You're a dear," before hurrying out the door.

I followed her out and called, "Details," as I closed her cabin door behind me. "I want details."

She didn't turn around but waved a hand and continued on her way to the stern.

I dropped the letters in the postbox, then noticed that Louisa, who was seated at the table outside her cabin, was waving at me.

Mr. Howard had been at the table with her, but he was getting to his feet. He gave me a quick bow and scuttled away. Louisa capped her pen. "How are you today, Blix?"

"Still feeling fine, as far as my health goes, but decidedly fighting off itchy boredom."

"I understand completely." She picked up a leather briefcase. "We're all doing our best not to go a bit barmy."

"And Mr. Howard? How is he?"

She took up a stack of papers and tapped them on the table to align the pages. "Still quite repentant about hoodwinking us all. I offered him a job."

"A job?"

"A temporary job to begin with." She tucked the papers into the case along with her pen and motioned for me to have a seat. "I have some news to share. Perhaps it will chase off some of your boredom. I've decided to create a foundation."

I pulled out a chair. "I'd like to hear about it."

"I can't change the mistakes in the past, but I must do what I can to make amends for Ambrose's choices. Mr. Briarcliff told me what happened with the gas masks. He also told me you were in on the secret, so I thought you might be interested to hear my plans."

Mr. Briarcliff had taken my advice and spoken to Louisa? Staggering! "Yes, please tell me more about it."

"Mr. Briarcliff gave me information about the men he's concerned about. The foundation's first goal will be to help them, then we'll focus on helping the families of those who have already passed on."

"That's wonderful news."

She looked in the direction Mr. Howard had left. "I asked Mr. Howard to help with the correspondence. If he does well, I may make the position permanent."

"Really?" Hildy had received a letter of apology from Mr. Howard while she was confined to her cabin. She'd written back to him, accepting his apology, but he was still in my bad books because of his vindictive attitude toward her. However, I kept my expression neutral. Except for Mr. Briarcliff, no one else knew about his poison-pen letters or how he'd planned to reveal Hildy's secret.

Louisa said, "When I asked him if he was interested in taking on a bit of work for me, he confessed about his former job as a newspaper reporter." A wrinkle appeared between her brows. "I didn't quite understand, but he said after his experiences on this cruise, he didn't want to return to that type of work. Apparently, he was a newspaper reporter and came on the cruise, hoping for a scoop. For some reason that wasn't quite clear, that line of work no longer appeals." She waved her hand. "But those details don't matter at the moment. He's an excellent typist, and he's skilled in writing. I'll be able to put him to good use. It will be—"

Louisa focused on something over my shoulder for a moment, then picked up her case. "I'm meeting Seffie after her shuffleboard game. She has some ideas for bedding plants for a shady area in one of my gardens. Must be off."

"But I wanted to hear more about the foundation."

She glanced over my shoulder again. "I believe Mr. Briarcliff wants to speak with you. He's making his way down the deck with a very determined look on his face."

"How do you know he's not coming to talk to you?"

"There's really nothing left to discuss about the foundation, but I think there's quite a bit for you two to chat about. Don't pretend you don't know what I mean. Even I've noticed the vibrations in the air between you two when you're in the same room!" She left at a hurried clip.

I pushed back my chair and stood as Mr. Briarcliff stopped in front of me. "Good afternoon, Miss Windway."

"I take it this means you've finally decided to stop avoiding me."

He was usually so direct and forthright, but he looked away from me out to the shore. "I have to admit I wasn't looking forward to hearing your commentary on my actions."

"On your high-handed way of solving the case, you mean."

He cleared his throat. "I do apologize." Then his formal tone dropped away as he turned toward me and rested an arm on the railing. "I got the job done. I don't see why you had such a visceral reaction to it."

"It frightened me. It was reckless and ill advised."

"Would you have felt better if I'd taken you into my confidence?"

He looked genuinely puzzled, so instead of flaring up at him, I said, "Of course. I hate being kept in the dark. I don't like surprises. They remind me of my childhood, when my parents would suddenly announce over coffee and marmalade toast that they were leaving after breakfast for a year-long posting. My mother always said it was better that I didn't know ahead of time so I wouldn't be mopey and sad for days leading up to their departure. She said it was better to have a quick, painful break."

I stopped short, appalled that I'd shared those details of my childhood.

"I see. Then I'm sorry I sprang it on you like that."

I crossed my arms and leaned against the railing, hunching over so that I could look down into the gentle waves of the Nile. "Enough of that. I accept your apology, and I must thank you for finding the last installment of *The Agony Column*. It was quite entertaining. I gave the magazines to Hildy to read. I told her to pass them along to you when she's finished. You should definitely have a look at it as well. I think you'd enjoy it too. The main character is quite a rapscallion."

"With that endorsement, I must read it."

We were silent a moment, then Mr. Briarcliff asked, "How are you and Hildy holding up when it comes to quarantine?"

"We're a bit restless, of course. Thank goodness for Miss Entwhistle and her organizational skills. Tonight's entertainment will be another child's game. I think the only thing we haven't done is hunt the slipper."

"And sardines."

"That's hardly appropriate for people our age."

"Oh, I don't know. It could be quite entertaining."

He cut his gaze to me, and I had a brief flash of what playing sardines with Mr. Briarcliff would be like—cramming into a tiny space, pressed up against his chest . . .

I realized Mr. Briarcliff was speaking, and I drew my thoughts back to the conversation. What was wrong with me? Surely I wasn't attracted to this annoying man?

He was asking, ". . . will you do once we're allowed off of the steamer?"

"Hildy and I are planning our itinerary for Luxor. Mr. Listergraff has invited us to tour the site where he'll be working. That's at the top of Hildy's list."

"Has he? I've never known him to do that."

"Invite someone to a dig?"

"Invite a woman to a dig."

"Oh. I see. Since she was ill, they've become quite close. What about you, Mr. Briarcliff?"

"I was scheduled to take another steamer back to Cairo and evaluate the service on it, but because we're quarantined here, that plan's been scrapped. Perhaps I'll stay in Luxor for a while."

"I'd like that."

"You would?"

"I mean . . . you know all of the sites. I'm sure you could recommend . . . things. Outings and such."

"I am familiar with Luxor. I'd be happy to be your tour guide."

"Excellent."

"It's a plan, then." He pushed away from the railing. "And now I have something that may help with your ennui. If you'll follow me."

"Lead on. I'm interested in anything to break up the endless days." I noticed he was flexing his hands, closing them into fists, then splaying his fingers out as I followed him down the stairs to the main deck. For a moment, I thought he was taking me to the cabin where Miss Fairweather was isolated, but he continued on to the service area, which was past the smaller cabins.

He opened a door with a flourish, as if he were presenting a magic trick.

I was confused. "It's a . . . cupboard?" He looked a bit crestfallen, so I added, "It's a very nice cupboard."

"Let me demonstrate." He pulled the chain on the light in the ceiling, but instead of the normal light bulb, this one glowed red, casting a ruby tinge over everything in the room. "I believe this is what you need to develop your film."

I drew a quick breath. "A darkroom. How lovely!" I strode inside. The shelves had been cleared of whatever items they'd held for the steamer passengers. Now they were lined with shallow pans and bottles of chemicals.

"The pans and tongs are kitchen implements, but I believe they should work for you. For the chemicals, I did a bit of research, and I believe these are the right ones. If not, I'm sure I can locate what you need."

I quickly checked the bottles. "These should work fine. You did well."

He picked up a ball of string and stepped into the cupboard to point overhead. "There are nails so you can use the string to hang your photos to dry, and here are a few clips to hold them."

I spun around the small room, taking it all in, then I touched his shoulder. "Thank you so much. This is wonderful. It will keep me busy for hours."

"I'd like a few copies of some of the photos, if you have extra."

"I'll make you whatever copies you want." I'd been so

delighted, taking in all of the equipment and the setup, that I hadn't noticed how small the room was. Our shoulders were touching, and we were so close together that I could smell his fresh soap scent and the wool of his jacket.

We both fell silent. My heart began to beat in a fluttery, syncopated rhythm.

He stared at me for a moment, and his gaze dropped to my lips, then he cleared his throat and stepped back, bumping into one of the metal pans, which clanged and fell to the floor. We shuffled around, bumping into each other. He handed me the pan as he backed out the door. "I'll leave you to get set up, then." He turned and left. I leaned against the doorframe and watched his tall figure recede and then disappear as he sprinted up the stairs.

"I do believe he's smitten."

I jumped and found Hildy standing behind me, the copies of *The Saturday Evening Post* in her arms.

"I came to find Mr. Briarcliff to hand these off to him, as you suggested, but I'll have to give them to him another time."

"How long have you been there?"

"Long enough to know that our time in Luxor should be interesting indeed."

# THE STORY BEHIND THE STORY

Thank you for joining Blix on another adventure! I hope you enjoyed reading it as much as I did writing it. I find Egypt fascinating and loved delving into the history of Nile cruising and creating intriguing characters for the Blue Lotus passenger list.

I took some liberties and created the fictional Blue Lotus Line and the S.S. *Cleopatra*, which is smaller than most of the Nile steamers but the perfect size for this story.

Books always play a large part in my research process. I find travel guides from the time invaluable. They're worth a browse for the maps alone! Other resources I found helpful were Andrew Humphrey's *On the Nile in the Golden Age of Travel* as well as Alain Blottière's *Vintage Egypt*. I also ran across the vintage book *The Light Side of Egypt* by Lance Thackeray. Published in 1928, the title page includes this description: "containing twenty-four full-page illustrations in color," which gave me insight into the fashions and the activities of British tourists.

I found the details I needed to know about cyanide and possible uses in connection with envelopes at Dr. D. P. Lyle's blog, *Crime Writer's Fiction*. While researching cyanide, I learned about a toxicologist working at New York's Medical Examiner's Office, Alexander Gettler, who developed a way to test for cyanide in tissue. Gettler and the New York Medical Examiner, Charles Norris, worked together to change the way criminals were prosecuted, moving away from a corrupt system of favors and bribes to one that used forensic evidence to prove guilt or innocence. It's likely that a medical man like Dr. Walsh would have read about Gettler's test for cyanide in human tissue, which was used in a 1922 murder case in New York. You can find more details about that poisoning case in *The Poisoner's Handbook* by Deborah Blum.

For Louisa's backstory, I was able to explore the world of stunt-girl stunt reporters of the late 1800s, who exposed corruption and scams. If you want to know more about these early investigative reporters, check out *Sensational: The Hidden History of America's Girl Stunt Reporters* by Kim Todd.

*The Nile* newspaper is based on *The Sphinx*, a weekly illustrated newspaper that was published in Cairo for the English-speaking community. You can read issues of it at the American University in Cairo's website. The *About Town* and *Arrivals and Departures* epigraphs are fictional, but I tried to keep the same breezy, insider tone as the papers of the times. The news pieces, like the display of Nefertiti's bust and the Winter Olympics details, are from events of the time.

Did you catch the reference to Wordle in the last chapter when Miss Entwhistle shares her idea for a word game? Of course, Wordle's real creator developed a prototype of the game in 2013, so it's impossible that Miss Entwhistle could have created it, but word puzzles were all the rage in the 1920s. I can totally see Miss Entwhistle playing around with the idea of a five-letter word puzzle. People were keen on crosswords (both regular and cryptic), jigsaw puzzles, and board games. A different type of puzzle, the crime novel, also gained popularity during the decade.

I hope *Murder on the S.S. Cleopatra* gave you a good puzzle to solve. The *1920s Lady Traveler in Egypt* series is a trilogy, and there will be one more book in the series. Look for more adventures with Blix, Hildy, and Rafe in Luxor soon. Sign up here for updates about new releases, sales, my book recommendations, and giveaways.

# ABOUT THE AUTHOR

*USA Today* bestselling author Sara Rosett writes lighthearted mysteries for readers who enjoy atmospheric settings, fun characters, and puzzling whodunits. She loves reading Golden Age mysteries, watching Jane Austen adaptions, and travel.

She is the author of the High Society Lady Detective historical mystery series as well as three contemporary cozy series: the Murder on Location series, the On the Run series, and the Ellie Avery series. Sara is the creator of an online course, How to Outline A Cozy Mystery, and the author of *How to Write a Series*. Her nonfiction for readers includes *The Bookish Sleuth: Mystery Reader's Journal and Planner*.

*Publishers Weekly* called Sara's books "enchanting," "well-executed," and "sparkling." Sara loves to get new stamps in her passport and considers dark chocolate a daily requirement. Find out more at SaraRosett.com.

*Connect with Sara*
www.SaraRosett.com

*Menace at the Christmas Market (novella)*

*Death in an English Garden*

*Death at an English Wedding*

On the Run

*Elusive*

*Secretive*

*Deceptive*

*Suspicious*

*Devious*

*Treacherous*

*Duplicity*

Non-fiction

*The Bookish Sleuth: A Mystery Reader's Journal and Calendar*

*How to Write a Series*

*How to Outline a Cozy Mystery*